EX LIBRIS
VINTAGE **CLASSICS**

ERICH MARIA REMARQUE

Erich Maria Remarque was born in Osnabrück in 1898. Exiled from Nazi Germany, and deprived of his citizenship, he lived in America and Switzerland. The author of a dozen novels, Remarque died in 1970.

Brian Murdoch was born in 1944. He is Professor Emeritus of German at Stirling University.

ALSO BY ERICH MARIA REMARQUE

The Way Back

Three Comrades

The Spark of Life

A Time to Love and a Time to Die

ERICH MARIA REMARQUE

All Quiet on the Western Front

TRANSLATED FROM THE GERMAN BY
Brian Murdoch

AFTERWORD BY
Brian Murdoch

VINTAGE

042

Vintage
20 Vauxhall Bridge Road,
London SW1V 2SA

Vintage Classics is part of the Penguin Random House group of companies
whose addresses can be found at global.penguinrandomhouse.com.

First published under the title
Im Westen nichts Neues by Ullstein, Berlin, 1929
This edition first published in Great Britain by
Jonathan Cape Ltd, 1994
This edition reissued by Vintage in 2019
First Published by Vintage in 1996

www.vintage-books.co.uk

A CIP catalogue record for this book is available from the
British Library

ISBN 9780099532811

Printed and bound in Great Britain by Clays Ltd, Elcograf S.p.A.

Penguin Random House is committed to a sustainable future for our
business, our readers and our planet. This book is made from Forest
Stewardship Council® certified paper.

Translator's Note

This new translation has been made from the first edition of Erich Maria Remarque's *Im Westen nichts Neues,* published in Berlin by Ullstein under their Propyläen imprint early in 1929. The familiar English title of Remarque's novel, however, was provided by A. W. Wheen in 1929. Although it does not match the German exactly (there is a different kind of irony in the literal version, 'Nothing New on the Western Front'), Wheen's title has justly become part of the English language, and it is retained here with gratitude, and as a memorial to Remarque's first English translator.

This book is intended neither as an accusation nor as a confession, but simply as an attempt to give an account of a generation that was destroyed by the war – even those of it who survived the shelling.

I

We are in camp five miles behind the line. Yesterday our relief arrived; now our bellies are full of bully beef and beans, we've had enough to eat and we're well satisfied. We were even able to fill up a mess-tin for later, every one of us, and there are double rations of sausage and bread as well – that will keep us going. We haven't had a stroke of luck like this for ages; the cook-sergeant, the one with the ginger hair, is actually offering to dish out food, beckoning with his serving ladle to anyone who comes near him and giving him a massive helping. He's getting a bit worried because he can't see how he's going to empty his cooking pot. Tjaden and Müller have dug out a couple of washing bowls from somewhere and got him to fill them up to the brim as a reserve supply. Tjaden does things like that out of sheer greed; with Müller it's a precaution. Nobody knows where Tjaden puts it all. He's as thin as a rake and he always has been.

The most important thing, though, is that there are double rations of tobacco as well. Ten cigars, twenty cigarettes and two plugs of chewing tobacco for everyone, and that's a decent amount. I've swapped my chewing tobacco with Katczinsky for his cigarettes, and that gives me forty. You can last a day on that.

And on top of it all, we're not really entitled to this lot. The army is never *that* good to us. We've only got it because of a mistake.

Fourteen days ago we were sent up the line as relief troops. It was pretty quiet in our sector, and because of that the quartermaster drew the normal quantity of food for the day we were due back, and he catered for the full company of a hundred and fifty men. But then, on the very last day, we were taken by surprise by long-range shelling from the heavy artillery. The English guns kept on pounding our position, so we lost a lot of men, and only eighty of us came back.

It was night-time when we came in, and the first thing we did was get our heads down so that we could get a good night's sleep. Katczinsky is right when he says that the war wouldn't be nearly as bad if we could only get more sleep. But there is no chance of that at the front, and two weeks for every spell in the line is a long time.

It was already midday when the first of us crawled out of the huts. Within half an hour every man had his mess-tin in his hand and we were lining up by the cookhouse, where there was a smell of proper food cooked in good fat. Needless to say, the hungriest were at the front of the queue: little Albert Kropp, who is the cleverest of us, and was the first one to make it to acting lance-corporal. Then Müller – one of the five boys called that at our school – who still lugs his textbooks about with him and dreams about taking his school leaving diploma later under the special regulations. He even swots up physics formulae when there is a barrage going on. Then Leer, who has a beard, and is obsessed with the girls from the officers-only knocking-shops; he swears that they are obliged by army regulations to wear silk slips, and that they have to take a bath before entertaining any guest with the rank of captain or above. And fourthly me, Paul Bäumer. All four of us are nineteen years old, and all four of us went straight out of the same class at school into the war.

Close behind us are our friends. Tjaden, a skinny locksmith who is the same age as us and the biggest glutton in the company. He's thin when he sits down to eat and when he gets up again he's got a pot-belly; Haie Westhus, the same age, a peat-digger, who can quite easily hold an army-issue loaf in one great paw and ask, 'Guess what I've got in my hand?'; Detering, a farmer, who thinks about nothing but his bit of land and his wife; and finally Stanislaus Katczinsky, leader of our group, tough, crafty, shrewd, forty years old, with an earthy face, blue eyes, sloping shoulders and an amazing nose for trouble, good food and cushy jobs.

Our group was at the head of the grub queue. We were getting impatient, because the cook-sergeant didn't know what was going on and was still standing there waiting.

In the end Katczinsky shouted to him, 'Come on, mate, open up your soup kitchen! Anyone can see the beans are done!'

But he just shook his head dozily. 'You've all got to be here first.'

Tjaden grinned. 'We are all here.'

The cook-sergeant still didn't get it. 'That would suit you nicely, wouldn't it. Come on, where are the rest?'

'They won't be getting served by you today. It's either a field hospital or a mass grave for them.'

The cook was pretty shaken when he heard what had happened. He wasn't so sure of himself any more. 'But I cooked for a hundred and fifty men.'

Kropp elbowed him in the ribs. 'So for once we'll get enough to eat. Right, get on with it!'

Suddenly a light dawned in Tjaden's eyes. His pointed, mouse-like face positively glowed, his eyes narrowed with cunning, his cheeks twitched and he moved in closer. 'Bloody hell, then you must have drawn bread rations for a hundred and fifty men as well, right?'

The cook-sergeant nodded, confused and not thinking.

Tjaden grabbed him by the tunic. 'Sausage, too?'

Another nod from Ginger.

Tjaden's jaw was trembling. 'And tobacco?'

'Yes, the whole lot.'

Tjaden looked round, beaming all over his face. 'Christ Almighty, now that's what I call a bit of luck! Then all that stuff has to be for us! Everyone gets – hang on – right, exactly double of everything!'

When he heard that the ginger-headed cook-sergeant realized what was up, and told us that it wasn't on.

By now we were getting a bit restive, and pushed forward.

'Why isn't it on, carrot-top?' Katczinsky wanted to know.

'Eighty men can't have the rations for a hundred and fifty.'

'We'll soon show you,' growled Müller.

'I wouldn't mind about the meal, but I can only give out the other rations for eighty,' insisted Ginger.

Katczinsky was getting annoyed. 'Is it time they pensioned you off, or what? You didn't draw provisions for eighty men, you drew them for B Company, and that's that. So now you can issue them. We *are* B Company.'

We started to crowd him. He wasn't too popular – it was thanks to him that in the trenches we'd more than once got our food far too late, and cold into the bargain, just because he didn't dare bring his field kitchen close enough in when there was a little bit of shellfire; and that meant that our men had to make a far longer trip to fetch the food than those from other companies. On that score Bulcke, from A Company, was much better. It's true that he was as fat as a hamster in winter, but he used to carry the cooking-pots right to the front line himself if he had to.

We were just about in the right mood and there would certainly have been trouble if our company commander hadn't turned up. He asked what the argument was about, and for the moment all he said was, 'Yes, we had heavy losses yesterday –'

Then he looked into the cooking-pot. 'Those beans look good.'

Ginger nodded. 'Cooked in fat, with meat, too.'

Our lieutenant looked at us. He knew what we were thinking. He knew a lot of other things as well, because he had come to the company as an NCO and grown up with us. He took the lid off the pot again and had a sniff. 'Bring me a plateful as well. And give out all the rations. We can do with them.'

Ginger made a face. Tjaden danced around him.

'It's no skin off your nose! He acts as if the supplies depot was his own personal property. So get on with it now, you old skinflint, and make sure you don't get it wrong –'

'Go to hell,' spat Ginger. He was beaten – this was simply too much for him – everything was turned upside down. And as if he wanted to show that he just didn't care any more, he gave out half a pound of ersatz honey per head, off his own bat.

*

It really is a good day today. There is even mail, nearly everyone has a couple of letters and newspapers. So we wander out to the field behind the barracks. Kropp has the round lid of a big margarine tub under his arm.

On the right-hand edge of the field they have built a huge latrine block, a good solid building with a roof. But that is only for new recruits, who haven't yet learned to get the best they can out of everything. We want something a bit better. And scattered all around are small individual thunder-boxes with precisely the same function. They are square, clean, made of solid wood, closed in, and with a really comfortable seat. There are handles on the sides so that they can be carried about.

We pull three of them together in a circle and make ourselves comfortable. We shan't be getting up again for the next couple of hours.

I can still remember how embarrassed we were at the beginning, when we were recruits in the barracks and had to use the communal latrines. There are no doors, so that twenty men had to sit side by side as if they were on a train. That way they could all be seen at a glance – soldiers, of course, have to be under supervision at all times.

Since then we've learnt more than just how to cope with a bit of embarrassment. As time went by, our habits changed quite a bit.

Out here in the open air the whole business is a real pleasure. I can't understand why it was that we always used to skirt round these things so nervously – after all, it is just as natural as eating or drinking. And perhaps it wouldn't need to be mentioned at all if it didn't play such a significant part in our lives, and if it hadn't been new to us – the other men had long since got used to it.

A soldier is on much closer terms with his stomach and digestive system than anyone else is. Three-quarters of his vocabulary comes from this area and, whether he wants to express extreme delight or extreme indignation, he will use one of these pungent phrases to underline it. It is impossible to make a point as clearly and as succinctly in any other way. Our families and our teachers will be pretty surprised when we get home, but out here it's simply the language that everyone uses.

Being forced to do everything in public means that as far as we are concerned, the natural innocence of the business has returned. In fact it goes further than that. It has become so natural to us, that the convivial performance of this particular activity is as highly valued as, well, holding a cast-iron certainty of a hand when we are playing cards. It is not for nothing that the phrase 'latrine rumour' has come to mean all kinds of gossip; these places are the army equivalent of the street corner or a favourite bar.

Just at the moment we are happier than we would be in some luxuriously appointed lavatory, white tiles and all. The most a place like that could be is hygienic; out here, though, it is beautiful.

These are wonderfully mindless hours. The blue sky is above us. On the horizon we can see the yellow observation balloons with the sun shining on them, and white puffs of smoke from the tracer bullets. Sometimes you see a sudden sheaf of them going up, when they are chasing an airman.

The muted rumble of the front sounds like nothing more than very distant thunder. Even the bumble bees drown it out when they buzz past.

And all around us the fields are in flower. The grasses are waving, cabbage whites are fluttering about, swaying on the warm breezes of late summer, while we read our letters and newspapers, and smoke; we take our caps off and put them on the ground beside us, the wind plays with our hair and it plays with our words and with our thoughts.

The three thunder-boxes are standing amid glowing red poppies.

We put the lid of the margarine tub on our knees and that gives us a solid base to play cards. Kropp has brought a pack. After every few hands we have a round of 'lowest score wins'. You could sit like this for ever and ever.

There is the sound of an accordion coming from the huts. Every so often we put the cards down and look at one another. Then someone says, 'I tell you, lads . . .' or: 'It could easily have gone wrong that time . . .' and then we are silent for a moment. There is a strong feeling of restraint in us all, we are all aware of it and it doesn't have to be spelt out. It could easily have happened that we wouldn't be sitting on our boxes here today, it was all so damned close. And because of that, everything is new and full of life – the red poppies, the good food, the cigarettes and the summer breeze.

Kropp asks, 'Have any of you seen Kemmerich again?'

'He's over at St Joseph,' I say.

Müller reckons that he got one right through the thigh, a decent blighty wound.

We decide to go and see him that afternoon.

Kropp pulls out a letter. 'Kantorek sends his regards.'

We laugh. Müller tosses his cigarette away and says, 'I wish *he* was out here.'

*

Kantorek was our form-master at school, a short, strict man who wore a grey frock-coat and had a shrewish face. He was roughly the same size and shape as Corporal Himmelstoss, the 'terror of Klosterberg Barracks'. Incidentally, it's funny how often the miseries of this world are caused by short people – they are so much more quick-tempered and difficult to get on with than tall ones. I have always tried to avoid landing up in companies with commanders who are short – usually they are complete bastards.

Kantorek kept on lecturing at us in the PT lessons until the entire class marched under his leadership down to the local recruiting office and enlisted. I can still see him, his eyes shining at us through his spectacles and his voice trembling with emotion as he asked, 'You'll all go, won't you lads?'

Schoolmasters always seem to keep their sentiments handy in their waistcoat pockets; after all, they have to trot them out in lesson after lesson. But that never occurred to us for a moment at the time.

In fact, one of our class was reluctant, and didn't really want to go with us. That was Josef Behm, a tubby, cheerful chap. But in the end he let himself be persuaded, because he would have made things impossible for himself by not going. Maybe others felt the same way as he did; but it wasn't easy to stay out of it because at that time even our parents used the word 'coward' at the drop of a hat. People simply didn't have the slightest idea of what was coming. As a matter of fact it was the poorest and simplest people who were the most sensible; they saw the war as a disaster right from the start, whereas those who were better off were overjoyed about it, although they of all people should have been in a far better position to see the implications.

Katczinsky says it is all to do with education – it softens the brain. And if Kat says something, then he has given it some thought.

Oddly enough, Behm was one of the first to be killed. He was shot in the eye during an attack, and we left him for dead. We couldn't take him with us because we had to get back in a great rush ourselves. That afternoon we suddenly heard him shout out and saw him crawling around in no man's land. He had only been knocked unconscious. Because he couldn't see and was mad with pain he didn't take cover, so he was shot down from the other side before anyone could get out to fetch him.

That can't be linked directly with Kantorek, of course – where would we be if that counted as actual guilt? Anyway, there were thousands of Kantoreks, all of them convinced that they were acting for the best, in the way that was the most comfortable for themselves.

But as far as we are concerned, that is the very root of their moral bankruptcy.

They were supposed to be the ones who would help us

eighteen-year-olds to make the transition, who would guide us into adult life, into a world of work, of responsibilities, of civilized behaviour and progress – into the future. Quite often we ridiculed them and played tricks on them, but basically we believed in them. In our minds the idea of authority – which is what they represented – implied deeper insights and a more humane wisdom. But the first dead man that we saw shattered this conviction. We were forced to recognize that our generation was more honourable than theirs; they only had the advantage of us in phrase-making and in cleverness. Our first experience of heavy artillery fire showed us our mistake, and the view of life that their teaching had given us fell to pieces under that bombardment.

While they went on writing and making speeches, we saw field hospitals and men dying: while they preached the service of the state as the greatest thing, we already knew that the fear of death is even greater. This didn't make us into rebels or deserters, or turn us into cowards – and they were more than ready to use all of those words – because we loved our country just as much as they did, and so we went bravely into every attack. But now we were able to distinguish things clearly, all at once our eyes had been opened. And we saw that there was nothing left of their world. Suddenly we found ourselves horribly alone – and we had to come to terms with it alone as well.

★

Before we set off to see Kemmerich we pack his things up for him – he'll be glad of them on his way home.

The clearing station is very busy. It smells of carbolic, pus and sweat, just like it always does. You get used to a lot of things when you are in the barracks, but this can still really turn your stomach. We keep on asking people until we find out where Kemmerich is; he is in a long ward, and welcomes us weakly, with a look that is part pleasure and part helpless agitation. While he was unconscious, somebody stole his watch.

Müller shakes his head, 'I always said that you shouldn't take such a good watch with you, didn't I?'

Müller is a bit bossy and tactless. Otherwise he would have kept his mouth shut, because it is obvious to everyone that Kemmerich is never going to leave this room. It makes no difference whether he gets his watch back or not – the most it would mean is that we could send it back home for him.

'How's it going, then, Franz?' asks Kropp.

Kemmerich's head drops back. 'OK, I suppose. It's just that my damned foot hurts so much.'

We glance at his bed-cover. His leg is under a wire frame, which makes the coverlet bulge upwards. I kick Müller on the shin, because he would be quite capable of telling Kemmerich what the orderly told us before we came in; Kemmerich no longer *has* a foot. His leg has been amputated.

He looks terrible, yellow and pallid, and his face already has those weird lines that we are so familiar with because we have seen them a hundred times before. They aren't really lines at all, just signs. There is no longer any life pulsing under his skin – it has been forced out already to the very edges of his body, and death is working its way through him, moving outwards from the centre, it is already in his eyes. There in the bed is our pal Kemmerich, who was frying horse-meat with us not long ago, and squatting with us in a shell hole – it's still him, but it isn't really him any more; his image has faded, become blurred, like a photographic plate that's had too many copies made from it. Even his voice sounds like ashes.

I remember the day when we were drafted out. His mother, a pleasant, stout woman, saw him off at the station. She was crying all the time, and her face was puffy and swollen. This embarrassed Kemmerich, because she was the least composed of all of them, practically dissolving in fat and tears. What's more, she picked me out, and kept grabbing my arm and begging me to keep an eye on Franz when we got out here. As it happens, he did have a very young face, and his bones were so soft that after just a month of carrying a pack he got flat feet. But how can you keep an eye on someone on a battlefield?

'You'll be going home now,' says Kropp. 'You would have had to wait at least another three or four months before you got leave.'

Kemmerich nods. I can't look at his hands, they are like wax. The dirt of the trenches is underneath his fingernails, and it is bluey-grey, like poison. It occurs to me that those fingernails will go on getting longer and longer for a good while yet, like some ghastly underground growths, long after Kemmerich has stopped breathing. I can see them before my eyes, twisting like corkscrews and growing and growing, and with them the hair on his caved-in skull, like grass on good earth, just like grass – how can all that be?

Müller leans forward. 'We've brought your things, Franz.'

Kemmerich gestures with one hand. 'Put them under the bed.'

Müller does as he says. Kemmerich starts on about the watch again. How can we possibly calm him down without making him suspicious?

Müller bobs up again with a pair of airman's flying boots, best quality English ones made of soft yellow leather, the sort that come up to the knee, with lacing all the way to the top – something really worth having. The sight of them makes Müller excited, and he holds the soles against his own clumsy boots and says, 'Are you going to take these with you, Franz?'

All three of us are thinking the same thing: even if he did get better he would only be able to wear one of them, so they wouldn't be any use to him. But as things are it would be a pity to leave them here – the orderlies are bound to pinch them the moment he is dead.

Müller repeats, 'Why don't you leave them here?'

Kemmerich doesn't want to. They are his prize possession.

'We could do a swap,' suggests Müller, trying again, 'you can really do with boots like that out here.' But Kemmerich won't be persuaded.

I kick Müller, and reluctantly he puts the splendid boots back under the bed.

We chat for a bit longer, and then say goodbye. 'Chin up, Franz.'

I promise him that I will come back tomorrow. Müller says that he will as well. He is still thinking about the flying boots and he wants to keep an eye on things.

Kemmerich groans. He is feverish. We get hold of a medical orderly outside, and try and persuade him to give Kemmerich a shot of morphia.

He says no. 'If we wanted to give morphia to everyone we'd need buckets of the stuff –'

'Only give it to officers, then, do you?' snarls Kropp.

I step in quickly and the first thing I do is give the orderly a cigarette. He takes it. Then I ask him, 'Are you allowed to give shots at all?'

He is annoyed. 'If you think I can't, what are you asking me for – ?'

I press a few more cigarettes into his hand. 'Just as a favour –'

'Well, OK,' he says. Kropp goes in with him, because he doesn't trust him and wants to see him do it. We wait outside.

Müller starts on again about the flying boots. 'They would fit me perfectly. In these clodhoppers even my blisters get blisters. Do you think he'll last until we come off duty tomorrow? If he goes during the night we've seen the last of the boots –'

Albert comes back and says, 'Do you reckon –?'

'Had it,' says Müller, and that's that.

We walk back to camp. I'm thinking about the letter I shall have to write to Kemmerich's mother tomorrow. I'm shivering, I could do with a stiff drink. Müller is pulling up grass stems and he's chewing on one. Suddenly little Kropp tosses his cigarette away, stamps on it like a madman, stares round with an unfocused and disturbed look on his face and stammers, 'Shit! Shit! The whole damned thing is a load of shit!'

We walk on for a long time. Kropp calms down – we know what was wrong, it's just the strain of being at the front, we all get that way from time to time.

Müller asks him, 'What did Kantorek say in his letter?'

He laughs. 'He calls us "young men of iron".'

That makes the three of us laugh, though not because it is funny. Kropp curses. He is happy to be able to talk again –

And yes, that's it, that *is* what they think, those hundred thousand Kantoreks. Young men of iron. Young? None of us is more than twenty. But young? Young men? That was a long time ago. We are old now.

2

I find it strange to think that at home in a drawer there is the first part of a play I once started to write called 'Saul', and a stack of poems as well. I spent so many evenings on them – we all did things like that – but it has all become so unreal to me that I can't even imagine it any more.

When we came out here we were cut off, whether we liked it or not, from everything we had done up to that point. We often try to find a reason or an explanation for this, but we can never quite manage it. Things are particularly confused for us twenty-year-olds, for Kropp, Müller, Leer and me, the ones Kantorek called young men of iron. The older men still have firm ties to their earlier lives – they have property, wives, children, jobs and interests, and these bonds are all so strong that the war can't break them. But for us twenty-year-olds there are only our parents, and for some of us a girlfriend. That isn't much, because at our age parental influence is at its weakest, and girls haven't really taken over yet. Apart from that, we really didn't have much else; the occasional passion for something, a few hobbies, school; our lives didn't go much further than that as yet. And now nothing is left of it all.

Kantorek would say that we had been standing on the very threshold of life itself. It's pretty well true, too. We hadn't had a chance to put down any roots. The war swept us away. For the others, for the older men, the war is an interruption, and they can think beyond the end of it. But we were caught up by the war, and we can't see how things will turn out. All we know for the moment is that in some strange and melancholy way we have become hardened, although we don't often feel sad about it any more.

★

If Müller wants Kemmerich's flying boots, this doesn't make him any more unfeeling than somebody who would find such a wish too painful even to contemplate. It's just that he can keep things separate in his mind. If the boots were any use at all to Kemmerich, Müller would sooner walk barefoot over barbed-wire than give a single thought to getting them. But as it is, the boots are objects which now have nothing to do with Kemmerich's condition, whereas Müller can do with them. Kemmerich is going to die, whoever gets them. So why shouldn't Müller try and get hold of them – after all, he has more right to them than some orderly. Once Kemmerich is dead it will be too late. That's why Müller is keeping an eye on them now.

We have lost all our ability to see things in other ways, because they are artificial. For us, it is only the facts that count. And good boots are hard to come by.

★

We were not always like that. We went down to the local recruiting office, still a class of twenty young men, and then we marched off *en masse,* full of ourselves, to get a shave at the barber's – some of us for the first time – before we set foot on a parade-ground. We had no real plans for the future and only very few of us had thoughts of careers or jobs that were firm enough to be meaningful in practical terms. On the other hand, our heads were full of nebulous ideas which cast an idealized, almost romantic glow over life and even the war for us.

We had ten weeks of basic training, and that changed us more radically than ten years at school. We learnt that a polished tunic button is more important than a set of philosophy books. We came to realize – first with astonishment, then bitterness, and finally with indifference – that intellect apparently wasn't the most important thing, it was the kit-brush; not ideas, but the system; not freedom, but drill. We had joined up with enthusiasm and with good will; but they did everything to knock that out of us. After three weeks it no longer struck us as odd that an ex-postman with a couple of stripes should have more power over us than our parents ever had, or our teachers, or the whole course of civilization from Plato to Goethe. With our young, wide-open eyes we saw that the classical notion of patriotism we had heard from our teachers meant, in practical terms at that moment, surrendering our individual personalities more completely than we would ever have believed possible even in the most obsequious errand boy. Saluting, eyes front, marching, presenting arms, right and left about, snapping to attention, insults and a thousand varieties of bloody-mindedness – we had imagined that our task would be rather different from all this, but we discovered that we were being trained to be heroes the way they train circus horses, and we quickly got used to it. We even understood that some of these things were necessary, but that others, by the same token, were completely superfluous. Soldiers soon sort out which is which.

★

In threes and fours our class was scattered around the different squads as we were put in with fishermen from the Frisian Islands, farmers, labourers and artisans, and we soon got friendly with them. Kropp, Müller, Kemmerich and I were put into Number Nine Squad, the one commanded by Corporal Himmelstoss.

He was reckoned to be the stickiest bastard in the whole barracks, and he was proud of it. He was a short, stocky bloke with twelve years' service in the reserve, a gingery moustache with waxed ends, and in civilian life he was a postman. He took a particular dislike to Kropp, Tjaden, Westhus and me because he sensed our unspoken defiance.

One day I had to make his bed fourteen times. Every time he found some fault with it and pulled it apart. Over a period of twenty hours – with breaks, of course – I polished an ancient and rock-hard pair of boots until they were soft as butter and even Himmelstoss couldn't find anything to complain about. On his orders I scrubbed the floor of the corporals' mess with a toothbrush. Kropp and I once had a go at sweeping the parade-ground clear of snow with a dustpan and brush on his orders, and we would have carried on until we froze to death if a lieutenant hadn't turned up, sent us in, and given Himmelstoss a hell of a dressing-down. Unfortunately, this only turned Himmelstoss against us even more. Every Sunday for a month I was put on guard duty, and he made me room orderly for the same amount of time. I had to practise 'On your feet! Advance! Get down!' with full pack and rifle in a sodden ploughed field until I was nothing but a mass of mud myself and I collapsed, and then four hours later I had to present myself for inspection to Himmelstoss with all my gear spick and span, although my hands were raw and bleeding. Kropp, Westhus, Tjaden and I had to stand to attention without gloves in freezing weather, with our bare fingers on the barrels of our rifles, with Himmelstoss prowling around us waiting for the slightest movement so that he could fault us. I had to run eight times from the top floor of the barracks down to the parade-ground at two in the morning in my night things, because my underpants were protruding half an inch more than they should over the edge of the stool where we had to lay out our kit. Himmelstoss as duty corporal ran beside me and trod on my feet. At bayonet practice I was regularly paired with Himmelstoss, and I had to use a heavy iron weapon while he had a handy wooden one, so that it was easy for him to beat me black and blue around the arms. However, I once got so furious that I rushed blindly at him and gave him such a clout in the stomach that it knocked him flat. When he tried to put me on a charge the company commander just laughed and told him to be more careful; he knew Himmelstoss of old, and didn't seem to mind that he'd been caught out. I got to be first class at climbing on the assault course, and I was pretty nearly the best at physical jerks. We trembled just at the sound of his voice, but the runaway post-horse never broke us down.

One Sunday, when Kropp and I were detailed to lug the latrine buckets across the parade-ground on a pole between us, Himmelstoss happened to come along, all poshed up and ready to go out. He stopped in front of us and asked how we were enjoying ourselves, so we faked a stumble, regardless, and tipped a bucketful over his legs. He was furious, but we had reached breaking point.

'You'll get clink for that!' he shouted.

But Kropp had had enough. 'Not before there's been an inquiry, and that's where we'll spill the beans,' he said.

'Is that how you talk to an NCO?' roared Himmelstoss. 'Have you taken leave of your senses? Don't speak until you're spoken to! What did you say you'd do?'

'Spill the beans about Corporal Himmelstoss! Sir!' said Kropp, standing to attention.

Then Himmelstoss got the message, and cleared off without saying anything, although he did manage to snarl, 'I'll make you lot suffer for this,' before he disappeared – but it was the end of his power over us. During field practice he tried again with his 'Take cover! On the feet! Move, move!' We obeyed all his orders, of course, because orders are orders and have to be obeyed. But we followed them so slowly that it drove Himmelstoss to despair. Taking it at a nice comfortable pace, we went down on to our knees, then on to our elbows and so on, and meanwhile he had already shouted another enraged order. He was hoarse before we were even sweating.

From then on he left us in peace. He went on calling us miserable little swine, of course. But there was respect in his voice.

There were plenty of decent drill corporals around, men who were more reasonable; the decent ones were even in the majority. More than anything else every one of them wanted to hang on to his safe job here at home for as long as possible – and they could only do that by being tough with recruits.

In the process we probably picked up every little detail of parade-ground drill that there was, and often we were so angry that it brought us to screaming pitch. It made a good few of us ill, and one of us, Wolf, actually died of pneumonia. But we would have been ashamed of ourselves if we had thrown in the towel. We became tough, suspicious, hardhearted, vengeful and rough – and a good thing too, because they were just the qualities we needed. If they had sent us out into the trenches without this kind of training, then probably most of us would have gone mad. But this way we were prepared for what was waiting for us.

We didn't break; we adapted. The fact that we were only twenty helped us to do that, even though it made other things so difficult. But most important of all, we developed a firm, practical feeling of solidarity, which grew, on the battlefield, into the best thing that the war produced – comradeship in arms.

★

I'm sitting by Kemmerich's bed. He is failing more and more visibly. There's a lot of to-ing and fro-ing around us. A hospital train has come in, and they are sorting out any of the wounded that can be moved. A doctor goes past Kemmerich's bed and doesn't even look at him.

'Next time round, Franz,' I tell him.

He lifts himself up on one elbow, propped against the pillow. 'They've amputated my leg.'

So now he has realized after all. I nod and by way of a response I say, 'You want to be glad that you got away with that.'

He doesn't say anything.

I carry on talking. 'It could have been both your legs, Franz. Wegler lost his right arm. That's a lot worse. And it means you'll go home.'

He looks at me. 'Do you think so?'

'Of course I do.'

He says it again, 'Do you think so?'

'Of course you will, Franz. You just have to recover from the operation.'

He signals to me to come a bit closer. I lean over him and he whispers, 'I don't reckon I will.'

'Don't talk such rubbish, Franz, you'll see yourself that I'm right in a couple of days. It's not such a big thing, having a leg amputated. They patch up a lot of worse things here.'

He lifts his hand. 'Just have a look at my fingers.'

'That's all because of the operation. Just get a decent amount of grub into you, and you'll pick up again. Are they feeding you properly?'

He points to a dish, but it is still half full. I begin to get worked up. 'Franz, you've got to eat. Eating is the main thing. And the food's pretty good here.'

He shakes his head. After a while he says slowly, 'I used to want to be a forester.'

I try to reassure him. 'You still can be. They can make amazing artificial limbs these days – you hardly notice that they aren't real. They fix them on to the muscles. You can move the fingers on artificial hands and you can use them, you can even write. And besides, they are making improvements all the time.'

He lies there for a while without a word. Then he says, 'You can take my flying boots for Müller.'

I nod and try to think of something to say that will cheer him up. His lips are pallid, his mouth has got bigger and his teeth look very prominent, as if they were made of chalk. His flesh is melting away, his forehead is higher, his cheekbones more pronounced. The skeleton is working its way to the surface. His eyes are sinking already. In a few hours it will all be over.

He isn't the first one I have seen like this; but we grew up together, and that always makes it different. I've copied school exercises from him. In school he usually wore a brown jacket with a belt, with parts of the sleeves worn smooth. And he was the only one of us that could do a full arm-turn on the high bar. His hair flew into his face like silk when he did it. Kantorek was proud of him for being able to do it. But he couldn't stand cigarettes. His skin was very white, and there was something feminine about him.

I glance down at my own boots. They are big and heavy and my trousers are tucked into them; standing up, you look solid and strong in these wide-legged things. But when we undress for swimming we suddenly have thin legs and narrow shoulders. We aren't soldiers any more then, we are almost schoolboys again; nobody would believe that we could carry a full pack. It is really strange when we are naked; we are civilians again, and we almost feel like civilians.

Whenever we went swimming, Franz Kemmerich used to look as small and slim as a child. Now he is lying there – and for what reason? Everybody in the whole world ought to be made to walk past his bed and be told: 'This is Franz Kemmerich, he's nineteen and a half, and he doesn't want to die! Don't let him die!'

My thoughts run wild. This smell of carbolic and gangrene clogs the lungs, like thick, suffocating porridge.

It gets dark. Kemmerich's face gets paler, it stands out against his pillow and is so white that it looks luminous. He makes a small movement with his mouth. I get closer to him. He whispers, 'If you find my watch, send it home.'

I don't argue. There is no point any more. He is beyond convincing. I'm sick with helplessness. That forehead, sunk in at the temples, that mouth, which is all teeth now, that thin, sharp nose. And the fat, tearful woman at home that I shall have to write to – I wish I had that job behind me already.

Hospital orderlies move about with bottles and buckets. One comes up to us, glances at Kemmerich speculatively and goes away again. He is obviously waiting – probably he needs the bed.

I get close to Franz and start to talk, as if that could save him: 'Maybe you'll finish up in that convalescent home in Klosterberg, Franz, up where the big houses are. Then you'll be able to look out over the fields from your window, right across to the two trees on the horizon. It's the best time now, when the corn is ripening, and the fields look like mother-of-pearl when the evening sun is on them. And the row of poplars by the stream where we used to catch sticklebacks. You can get yourself an aquarium again and breed fish, and you can go out without having to ask permission and you can even play the piano again if you want to.'

I bend down over his face, which is now in shadow. He is still breathing, but faintly. His face is wet, he is crying. So much for my stupid chattering.

'Come on, Franz –' I put my arm around his shoulder and my face is close to his. 'Do you want to get some sleep now?'

He doesn't answer. The tears are running down his cheeks. I would like to wipe them away, but my handkerchief is too dirty.

An hour passes. I sit there, tense and watching his every movement, in case he might want to say something else. If only he would open his mouth wide and scream. But he just weeps, his head turned away. He doesn't talk about his mother or his brothers and sisters; he doesn't say anything. All that is probably already far behind him; now he is all alone with his life of nineteen short years, and he is crying because it is slipping away from him.

This is the hardest, the most desperately difficult leave-taking I have experienced, although it was bad with Tiedjen, too, who kept on shouting for his mother – Tiedjen was a great tough chap who held the doctor away from his bed with a bayonet, his eyes wide open with terror, until he collapsed.

Suddenly Kemmerich groans, and there is rattling in his throat.

I'm on my feet, rush outside and ask, 'Where's the doctor?' I see a white coat and grab hold of it. 'Please come quickly or Franz Kemmerich will die.'

He pulls away from me and says to a hospital orderly who is standing nearby, 'What's all this about?'

The orderly replies, 'Bed twenty-six, amputation at the upper thigh.'

'How should I know anything about it?' the doctor snaps, 'I've done five leg amputations today.' Then he pushes me out of the way, tells the orderly, 'Go and see to it,' and rushes off to the operating room.

I'm shaking with anger as I follow the orderly. The man looks round at me and says, 'One operation after the other since five o'clock this morning – crazy, I tell you; just today we've had another sixteen fatalities – your man will make seventeen. There's bound to be twenty at least –'

I feel faint; suddenly I can't go on. I don't even want to curse any more – it's pointless. I just want to throw myself down and never get up again.

We reach Kemmerich's bed. He is dead. His face is still wet with tears. His eyes are half open, and look as yellow as old-fashioned horn buttons.

The orderly nudges me. 'Taking his things with you?'

I nod.

'We've got to move him right away,' he continues. 'We need the bed. We've already got them lying on the ground out there.'

I take the things and undo Kemmerich's identity tag. The orderly asks for his pay book. It isn't there. I say that it is probably in the guard room, and leave. Behind me they are already bundling Franz on to a tarpaulin.

Once I get outside, the darkness and the wind are a salvation. I breathe as deeply as I can, and feel the air warmer and softer than ever before in my face. Images of girls, fields of flowers, of white clouds all pass rapidly through my mind. My feet move onwards in my boots, I am going faster, I'm running. Soldiers come towards me, their words excite me, even though I can't understand what they are saying. The whole earth is suffused with power and it is streaming into me, up through the soles of my feet. The night crackles with electricity, there is a dull thundering from the front line, like some concerto for kettle drums. My limbs are moving smoothly, there is strength in my joints as I pant with the effort. The night is alive, I am alive. What I feel is hunger, but a stronger hunger than just the desire to eat –

Müller is waiting for me in front of the huts. I give him the flying boots. We go in and he tries them on. They are a perfect fit –

He digs into his kit and gives me a decent chunk of salami. And there is hot tea with rum as well.

3

We are getting reinforcements. The gaps in the ranks are filled, and the empty straw palliasses in the huts are soon occupied. Some of them are old hands, but twenty-five young replacement troops straight from the recruiting depots have been assigned to our company as well. They are almost a year younger than we are. Kropp nudges me. 'Have you seen the kids?'

I nod. We strut about, get ourselves shaved on the parade-ground, put our hands in our pockets, look at the new recruits and feel as if we have been in the army for a thousand years.

Katczinsky joins us. We wander through the stables and come across the recruits, who are just being given their gasmasks and some coffee. Kat asks one of the youngest of them, 'I bet you lot haven't had any decent grub for a good long time, eh?'

The recruit pulls a face. 'Bread made out of turnips for breakfast, turnips for lunch and turnip cutlets with turnip salad in the evening.'

Katczinsky gives an appreciative whistle. 'Bread made from turnips? You were lucky – they're already making it out of sawdust. But what about beans? Do you fancy some?'

The young soldier colours up. 'You don't have to take the mickey.'

All Katczinsky says is, 'Bring your mess-tin.'

Curious, we follow him. He leads us to a big container next to his palliasse. Sure enough, it is half full of beans with bully beef. Katczinsky stands in front of it like a general and says, 'Eyes bright and fingers light! That's the army motto!'

We are amazed. 'Bloody hell, Kat,' I ask, 'how did you come by that?'

'Old Ginger was glad to get it off his hands. I gave him three pieces of parachute silk for it. Well, beans taste just as good cold.'

With a generous flourish he gives the young soldier a portion and tells him, 'Next time you turn up here with your mess-tin, you'll have a cigar or some chewing tobacco in the other hand. Got it?'

Then he turns to us. 'You lot get yours for nothing, of course.'

★

We could not do without Katczinsky; he has a sixth sense. There are men like him everywhere, but you can't tell who they are just by looking. Every company has one or two of them. Katczinsky is the sharpest I know. I think he's a shoemaker by trade, but that's got nothing to do with it – he's a master of everything. It's good to be a friend of his. Kropp and I both are, and Haie Westhus half belongs to the group as well, but he is really only an instrument, working on Kat's orders whenever something's going on that needs a strong right arm, then he's a good man to have around.

For example, we turn up one night in some completely unknown place, a miserable dump where you can see at a glance that it has been stripped of everything that wasn't screwed down. We're quartered in a small, dark, factory building that has only just been fitted up for use. It has beds in it, or rather, bedsteads, a couple of planks with wire-mesh between them.

Wire-mesh is hard. We haven't got a blanket to cover it with, we need ours to put over us. Tarpaulin is too thin.

Kat sizes it up and says to Haie Westhus, 'Come on.' Off they go into this completely unknown place. Half an hour later they are back with their arms full of straw. Kat has found some stables and that's where the straw comes from. We could sleep warmly now, if only we weren't so damned hungry.

Kat asks a gunner who has already been in the area for a while, 'Is there a canteen anywhere round here?'

He laughs. 'Not a chance. There's nothing. You won't find a crust of bread round here.'

'Aren't there any locals left, then?'

He spits. 'Oh yes, there are one or two. But they just hang around every field kitchen they see and scrounge what they can.'

That's pretty bad. In that case we'll just have to tighten our belts and wait until tomorrow when the rations come up.

Then I see Kat putting his cap on. 'Where are you off to, Kat?'

'Just for a sniff around.' He slopes out.

The gunner grins sarcastically. 'Sniff away. Mind you don't strain yourself picking things up.'

We lie down, disappointed, and wonder whether to break into our iron rations or not. But we don't want to risk being left without. So we try to get a bit of shut-eye instead.

Kropp breaks a cigarette in two and gives me half. Tjaden describes his local speciality, broad beans cooked with bacon. He is scathing about people who try to cook it without the right chopped herbs. But the main thing is that the ingredients all have to be cooked together – the potatoes, beans and bacon must not, for God's sake, be cooked separately. Somebody grumbles that he will chop Tjaden into the right herbs if he doesn't shut up at once. And then it is quiet in the big room. Only a couple of candles flicker in the necks of empty bottles, and the gunner spits from time to time.

We are already dozing a bit when the door opens and Kat appears. I think I am dreaming: he is carrying two loaves under his arm, and a blood-stained sandbag full of horsemeat in his hand.

The gunner's pipe drops out of his mouth. He feels the bread. 'Straight up, it's real bread, and still warm.'

Kat doesn't say another thing. He has the bread and that is it; nothing else is of any importance. I'm quite sure that if he were dropped in the desert he would get a meal of dates, roast meat and wine together within the hour.

He gives Haie the brief command, 'Chop some wood.'

From under his coat he brings out a frying-pan, then he takes a handful of salt and a chunk of fat from a pocket – he has thought of everything. Haie gets a fire going on the floor. Its crackling can be heard all through the empty factory. We scramble out of bed.

The gunner isn't sure what to do. He wonders whether or not to congratulate Kat, so that maybe he will get a share too. But Katczinsky doesn't even notice him – he might as well be invisible. So he wanders off, swearing.

Kat has the knack of cooking horsemeat so that it is really tender. You mustn't put it straight into the pan or it will be too tough. It has to be parboiled in a little water beforehand. We sit around in a circle with our knives, and fill our bellies.

That's Kat. If there were some place where something edible could be found only in one particular hour in the year, then he would turn up precisely during that hour as if led there by some kind of inspiration. He'd put on his cap, go out, make a bee-line for it, and find it.

He can find anything – camp stoves and firewood when it is cold, hay and straw, tables, chairs – but above all he can find food. No one understands how he does it, and it's as if he conjures it out of thin air. His masterpiece was four cans of lobster. Mind you, we would really have preferred dripping instead.

★

We've sprawled out on the sunny side of the camp. It smells of tar, summertime and sweaty feet.

Kat is sitting next to me, because he enjoys a chat. We had an hour of saluting practice this afternoon because Tjaden gave a major a sloppy salute. Kat can't get over this. 'Watch out, lads,' he says, 'we'll lose the war because we are too good at saluting.'

Kropp pads across to us barefoot, with his trousers rolled up. He has washed his socks and lays them out on the grass to dry. Kat gazes at the sky, lets off a really loud one, and says dreamily by way of commentary, 'Every little bean, my boys, makes you make a little noise.'

He and Kropp start to argue. At the same time they manage to bet a bottle of beer on the outcome of a dogfight that is going on between a couple of planes above us.

Kat will not budge from a point of view that he, old soldier that he is, sums up with a little rhyme: 'Equal rations, equal pay, war's forgotten in a day –'

Kropp, on the other hand, is more philosophical. He reckons that all declarations of war ought to be made into a kind of festival, with entrance tickets and music, like they have at bullfights. Then the ministers and generals of the two countries would have to come into the ring, wearing boxing shorts, and armed with rubber truncheons, and have a go at each other. Whoever is left on his feet, his country is declared the winner. That would be simpler and fairer than things are out here, where the wrong people are fighting each other.

The idea appeals to us. Then the conversation moves on to drill.

An image comes into my head. Bright midday sunshine on the parade-ground at Klosterberg barracks. The heat is hanging there and the place is quiet. The barracks seem dead. Everything is asleep. All you can hear is the drummers practising – they have set things up somewhere and are practising without much skill, monotonously, mindlessly. What a trio: midday heat, the parade-ground and drummers practising.

The barrack windows are empty and dark. Battledress trousers are hanging out of a few of them, drying. You look enviously across at the barracks, where the rooms are cool –

Oh, you dark and musty platoon huts, with your iron bedsteads, chequered bedding and the tall lockers with those stools in front of them! Even you can turn into objects of longing; seen from out here, you can even take on some of the wonderful aura of home, you great rooms, so full of the smells of stale food, sleep, smoke and clothes!

Katczinsky describes them in glowing colours and with great

fervour. What would we not give to be able to go back to those rooms. We don't dare to think any further than that –

You rifle drills, first thing in the morning! 'How do you break down a standard-issue rifle?' You PT sessions in the afternoon! 'Fall out anyone who can play the piano! Right turn! Report to the kitchens for spud bashing!'

We wallow in our memories. Then Kropp laughs suddenly and says, 'Change at Löhne!'

That was Corporal Himmelstoss's favourite game. Löhne is a station where you have to change trains, and so that anyone going on leave did not get lost when he got there, Himmelstoss used to practise changing platforms with us in the barracks. We were supposed to learn that you reach the connecting train in Löhne by way of an underpass. Our beds represented the underpass and everyone had to stand to attention on the left-hand side. Then came the order 'Change at Löhne!' and everyone had to scramble as quickly as possible under the bed and out the other side. We practised that for hours on end . . .

Meanwhile the German plane has been shot down. It plummets, with a trail of smoke behind it like a comet. Kropp has lost a bottle of beer on it, and pays up with ill grace.

'I'm sure Himmelstoss is quite a quiet chap as a postman,' I say, once Kropp has got over his disappointment. 'So how come he is such a bastard as a drill corporal?'

The question gets Kropp going again. 'It isn't just Himmelstoss, there are loads of them. As soon as they get a couple of stripes or a pip or two they turn into entirely different people and start behaving as if they chew iron bars for breakfast.'

'So it's the uniform that does that?' I ask.

'More or less,' says Kat, and settles himself down to develop the point. 'But the real reasons are a bit different. Look, if you train a dog so that it only eats potatoes, and then after a while you offer it a chunk of meat, it'll still grab it because it's in its nature. And if you offer a man a bit of power, the same thing happens; he'll grab it. It's instinctive, because when it comes down to it, a man is basically a beast, and it's only later that a bit of decency gets smeared on top, the way you can spread dripping on your bread. The main thing about the army is that there is always somebody with the power to give orders to the rest. The bad thing is that they've all got far too much power: a corporal can harass a private, a lieutenant can harass an NCO or a captain can harass a lieutenant so badly that it can drive him mad. And because every one of them knows it, they all get used to the idea. Just take the simplest example: we're on our way back from the parade-ground and we're dog tired. Then comes the order to sing. Well, the singing isn't too lively because we're all happy if we can still carry our rifles without dropping them. And the next thing we know, the company is about-turned and we have an hour's punishment drill. On the march back we get the order to sing again, and this time we sing. What's the point of the whole thing? The man in command has got his way, because he's got the power to do so. Nobody's going to blame him – quite the reverse – he gets a reputation for being strict. And that's just a trivial thing – there are plenty of other ways for them to mess you about. So I ask you: whatever a man is in civilian life, what sort of job could he possibly find where he could get away with that sort of behaviour without getting a punch on the nose for it? The only place he can do it is in the army. See what I mean – it always goes to their heads. And the less they had to say for themselves in civvy street, the more it goes to their heads now.'

'They do say that discipline is necessary . . .' Kropp puts in casually.

'They can always come up with reasons,' growls Kat. 'And that might be true. But you mustn't mess people about. And you just try and explain it to a locksmith, or a stable lad, or a labourer, try and explain it to the poor bloody infantry – they're the majority out here, after all. All *they* see is that they get messed about, and then they get sent up the line, and they know perfectly well what's necessary and what isn't. I tell you, it's amazing that the ordinary soldier sticks it here at the front at all. It's amazing.'

Everyone agrees, because we all know that it is not till you are actually in the trenches that parade-ground drill disappears, and that it starts up again before you've gone back a mile behind the lines, no matter how big a piece of nonsense it might be, like saluting or formation marching. Because there is one unbreakable rule: a soldier has to be fully occupied all the time.

But now Tjaden turns up, red in the face. He is so worked up that he is stuttering, but he still gets the words out, grinning all over his face: 'Himmelstoss is on his way here. He's been sent to the front.'

*

Tjaden really detests Himmelstoss, because Himmelstoss decided to teach him a lesson in his own special way back in the barracks. Tjaden wets the bed – when he is asleep at night it just happens. Himmelstoss insisted that it was pure laziness, and wouldn't be persuaded otherwise, so he came up with a method of curing Tjaden that was really typical of the man.

He hunted out another bed-wetter from one of the other barracks, a man called Kindervater, and put him in with Tjaden. The barracks where we did our training had the usual arrangement of bunks, one bed above the other, with the bottom part of each bed made of wire-mesh. Himmelstoss arranged things so that the pair of them were together, one on the top and the other on the bottom bunk. The one underneath, of course, had a really raw deal. To compensate, they had to change places for the next night, so that the one from the bottom bunk got the top bunk, and could get his revenge. That was Himmelstoss's idea of self-help.

It was mean-minded, but logically it was sound. Unfortunately it didn't work, because the basic premisses were wrong: it wasn't laziness that made either of the two men do it. Anyone could see that by looking at their sickly complexions. The whole business ended with them taking it in turns to sleep on the floor. The one doing that could easily have caught his death of cold –

Meanwhile Haie has come and sat down beside us. He gives me

a glance with his eyes twinkling, and rubs his great paws thoughtfully. He and I shared the best day of our army career. It was the night before we had to go off to the front. We had been assigned to one of the newly formed regiments, but before that we had been ordered back to the garrison for kitting out, not to the recruiting depot though, but one of the other barracks. The morning after that we would be leaving very early. That evening we set out to get even with Himmelstoss. We had sworn weeks before that we would. Kropp had even gone so far as to declare that after the war he would try for an administrative job in the postal service, so that later on, when Himmelstoss was a postman again, he could get to be his boss. He painted a rosy picture of how he would clobber him. That was the real reason that Himmelstoss never managed to grind us down: we always counted on the fact that we'd get him sometime, by the end of the war at the latest.

Meanwhile we wanted to give him a damned good hiding. What could they do to us if he didn't recognize us and if we were off early next morning anyway?

We knew what bar he spent his evenings in. To get from the bar back to the barracks he had to go down a dark lane without any buildings. We lay in wait for him there, hiding behind a pile of rocks. I had a quilt-cover with me. We were trembling with anticipation, wondering if he would be on his own. At last we heard his footsteps – that was a sound we knew very well indeed, we'd heard him often enough in the mornings, when the door would fly open and he would bellow, 'Out of bed!'

'On his own?' whispered Kropp.

'On his own.' Tjaden and I crept round the pile of rocks.

We could already see the light reflected off his belt-buckle. Himmelstoss seemed to be a bit tipsy and he was singing. He went past without noticing a thing.

We got a firm grip on the quilt-cover, moved forward quietly, slipped it over his head from behind and pulled it downwards, so that he stood there as if in a white sack, unable to move his arms. The singing died away.

The next moment Haie Westhus was there. He pushed us aside with his arms spread out, just so that he could have the first go. With great delight he took up a stance, raised his arm like a railway signal, his hand as big as a shovel, and gave the white sack a wallop that would have felled an ox.

Himmelstoss lost his balance, rolled half-a-dozen yards and started to yell. We'd thought of that as well, and brought a pillow with us. Haie squatted down, put the pillow on his knee, grabbed at where he guessed Himmelstoss's head to be and shoved it into the pillow. The noise was stifled right away. Haie let him take a breath from time to time, and what came from his throat then was a wonderful, high-pitched shriek that soon got cut off.

Now Tjaden unbuttoned Himmelstoss's braces and pulled his trousers down. Meanwhile, he held a cane carpet-beater between his teeth. Then he stood up and moved into action.

It was a wonderful sight: Himmelstoss on the ground, Haie bending over him, holding the man's head on his knees, with a fiendish grin on his face, his mouth wide open with delight, and then the twitching striped underpants, and the knock-kneed pair of legs which, trousers around the ankles, were performing spectacular movements with every blow that fell; and Tjaden, who showed no signs of tiring, standing over him like a woodcutter. In the end we literally had to pull him away, so that we could have our turns.

At last Haie pulled Himmelstoss to his feet again, and gave a private performance as the final act. He drew his right arm so far back before clouting him that it looked as if he was trying to pluck stars out of the night sky. Himmelstoss went down. Haie picked him up again, lined him up and gave him a second magnificently aimed wallop with his left hand. Himmelstoss howled, and fled on all fours. His striped postman's backside shone in the moonlight.

We made ourselves scarce as fast as we could.

Haie looked around, and said with an air of grim satisfaction, though a bit oddly, 'Revenge is as good as a feast.'

In fact Himmelstoss should have been pleased: his principle, that we should train each other, had borne fruit – when we used it on him. We had been dutiful pupils, quick to pick up his methods.

He never found out whom he had to thank for the whole thing. Anyway, he got a quilt-cover out of it; when we went back half an hour later to look for it again it was nowhere to be found.

That night was the reason that on the following morning we were able to set off in a reasonably cheerful state of mind. And because of that, some old goat was so moved that he referred to us as 'young heroes'.

4

We've been ordered up the line on wiring duty. The trucks turn up for us as soon as it starts to get dark. We scramble aboard. It is a warm evening, the twilight is like a blanket wrapped around us, and we feel comforted by this protection. It brings us closer together; even Tjaden, who is usually a bit stingy, gives me a cigarette and lights it for me.

We stand next to one another, packed tightly, and no one can sit down. We aren't used to sitting down anyway. At last Müller is in a good mood again; he is wearing his new boots.

The engines rev up, the trucks rattle and clatter. The road surfaces are worn out and full of holes. No lights are allowed, and so we run into the holes and all but get thrown out of the truck. That possibility doesn't bother us much. What would it matter – a broken arm is better than a hole through the belly, and plenty of us would actually welcome a chance like that to get sent home.

Alongside us, long columns of munition trucks are moving up. They are in a hurry and keep on overtaking us. We shout out jokes to the men and they answer us.

We make out a wall, which belongs to a house set a little way back from the road. Suddenly I prick up my ears. Can it be true? Then I hear it again, perfectly clearly. Geese! A glance towards Katczinsky; a glance back from him; we understand each other.

'Kat, I think I can hear a candidate for the cooking-pot –'

He nods. 'We'll do it when we get back. I know my way around here.'

Of course Kat knows his way around. I bet he knows every drumstick on every goose for miles.

The trucks reach the firing area. The gun emplacements are camouflaged with greenery against air reconnaissance, and it all looks like a military version of that Jewish festival where they build little huts outdoors. These leafy bowers would look peaceful and cheerful if they didn't have guns inside them.

The air is getting hazy with smoke from the guns and fog. The cordite tastes bitter on the tongue. The thunder of the artillery fire makes our truck shake, the echo rolls on after the firing and everything shudders. Our faces change imperceptibly. We don't have to go into the trenches, just on wiring duty, but you can read it on every face: this is the front, we're within reach of the front.

It isn't fear, not yet. Anyone who has been at the front as often as we have gets thick-skinned about it. Only the young recruits are jumpy. Kat gives them a lesson. 'That was a twelve-inch. You can hear that from the report – you'll hear the burst in a minute.'

But the dull thud of the shell-bursts can't be heard at this distance. Everything is swallowed up in the rumble of the front. Kat listens carefully. 'There'll be a show tonight.'

We all listen. The front is restless. 'Tommy's already firing,' says Kropp.

You can hear the guns clearly. It is the British batteries, to the right of our sector. They are starting an hour early. Ours never start until ten on the dot.

'What's up with them?' calls out Müller. 'Are their watches fast or something?'

'There'll be a show, I tell you. I can feel it in my bones.' Kat shrugs his shoulders.

Three guns thunder out just beside us. The gunflash shoots away diagonally into the mist, the artillery roars and rumbles. We shiver, happy that we'll be back in camp by tomorrow morning.

Our faces are no more flushed and no paler than they usually are; they are neither more alert nor more relaxed, and yet they *are* different. We feel as if something inside us, in our blood, has been switched on. That's not just a phrase – it is a fact. It is the front, the awareness of the front, that has made that electrical contact. The moment we hear the whistle of the first shells, or when the air is torn by artillery fire, a tense expectancy suddenly gets into our veins, our hands and our eyes, a readiness, a heightened wakefulness, a strange suppleness of the senses. All at once the body is completely ready.

It often seems to me as if it is the disturbed and vibrating air that suddenly comes over us with silent force; or as if the front itself is sending out its own electricity to put those unconscious nerve endings on to the alert.

It is the same every time. When we set out we are just soldiers – we might be grumbling or we might be cheerful; and then we get to the first gun emplacements, and every single word that we utter takes on a new sound.

If Kat stands in front of the huts and says 'There's going to be a show' then that is his own opinion, nothing else. But if he says it out here, then the same words are as sharp as a bayonet on a moonlit night, cutting straight through the normal workings of the brain, more immediate, and speaking directly to that unknown element that has grown inside us with a dark significance – 'There's going to be a show'. Perhaps it is our innermost and most secret life that gives a shudder, and then prepares to defend itself.

★

For me, the front is as sinister as a whirlpool. Even when you are a long way away from its centre, out in calm waters, you can still feel its suction pulling you towards it, slowly, inexorably, meeting little resistance.

But the power to defend ourselves flows back into us out of the earth and out of the air – and most of all it flows out of the earth. The earth is more important to the soldier than to anybody else. When he presses himself to the earth, long and violently, when he urges himself deep into it with his face and with his limbs, under fire and with the fear of death upon him, then the earth is his only friend, his brother, his mother, he groans out his terror and screams into its silence and safety, the earth absorbs it all and gives him another ten seconds of life, ten seconds to run, then takes hold of him again – sometimes for ever.

Earth – earth – earth – !

Earth, with your ridges and holes and hollows into which a man can throw himself, where a man can hide! Earth – in the agony of terror, the explosion of annihilation, in the death-roar of the shell-bursts you gave us that massive resurgence of reconquered life. The madness, the tempest of an existence that had practically been torn to shreds flowed back from you into our hands, and so we burrowed deep into you for safety, and in the speechless fear and relief of having survived the moment, our mouths bit deeply into you!

With the first rumble of shellfire, one part of our being hurls itself back a thousand years. An animal instinct awakens in us, and it directs and protects us. It is not conscious, it is far quicker, far more accurate and far more reliable than conscious thought. You can't explain it. You are moving up, not thinking of anything, then suddenly you are in a hollow in the ground with shrapnel flying over your head; but you can't remember having heard the shell coming or having thought about taking cover. If you had relied on thought, you would have been so many pieces of meat by now. It was something else, some prescient, unconscious awareness inside us, that threw us down and saved us without our realizing. But for this, there would long since have been not a single man left alive between Flanders and the Vosges.

We set out as soldiers, and we might be grumbling or we might be cheerful – we reach the zone where the front line begins, and we have turned into human animals.

★

We move into a rather scrappy wood. We pass the field kitchens. Just beyond the wood we climb down from the trucks and they go back. They will be picking us up again before first light tomorrow.

Mist and smoke from the artillery is chest-high over the meadows. The moon is shining on it. Troops are moving on the roadway. The steel helmets give a dull reflection in the moonlight. Heads and rifles stick out from the white mists, nodding heads and swaying rifle barrels.

Further on, the mist clears. The heads turn into whole figures – tunics, trousers and boots come out of the mist as if from a pool of milk. They form into a column. The column marches, straight ahead, the figures become a wedge, and you can no longer make out individual men, just this dark wedge, pushing forwards, made even more strange by the heads and rifles bobbing along on the misty lake. A column – not men.

Light artillery and munition wagons move in from a side road. The backs of the horses shine in the moonlight and their movements are good to see – they toss their heads and their eyes flash. The guns and the wagons glide past against an indistinct background like a lunar landscape, while the steel-helmeted cavalrymen look like knights in armour from a bygone age – somehow it is moving and beautiful.

We make for the equipment dump. Some of our men load the angled, sharpened iron uprights on to their shoulders, the rest stick straight iron bars through rolls of barbed-wire and carry them away. They are awkward and heavy loads.

The terrain gets more pitted. Reports come back to us from up ahead: 'Watch where you're going, there's a deep shell hole on the left' – 'Mind the trench' –

We keep our eyes wide open, and test the ground with our feet and with the bars before we put all our weight down. The column stops suddenly; you bang your face into the barbed-wire roll that the man in front is carrying, and you swear.

A couple of shot-up trucks are in the way. A new order comes: 'Pipes and cigarettes out!' We are close to the frontline trenches.

In the meantime it has gone completely dark. We skirt around a little copse and our sector is there before us.

There is an indistinct reddish glow from one end of the horizon to the other. It changes constantly, punctuated by flashes from the gun batteries. Verey lights go up high above it, silver and red balls which burst with a shower of white, red and green stars. French rockets shoot up, the ones with silk parachutes that open in the air and let them drift down really slowly. They light up everything as clear as day, and their brightness even reaches across to us, so that we can see our shadows stark against the ground. The lights hang in the sky for minutes at a time before they burn out. New ones shoot up at once, everywhere, and there are still the green, red and blue stars.

'Going to be a bad do,' says Kat.

The thunder of the guns gets stronger until it becomes a single dull roar, and then it breaks down again into individual bursts. The dry voiced machine-guns rattle. Above our heads the air is full of invisible menace, howling, whistling and hissing. This is from the smaller guns; but every so often comes the deep sound of the big crump shells, the really heavy stuff, moving through the dark and landing far behind us. They make a bellowing, throaty, distant noise, like a rutting stag, and they go far above the howl and the whistle of the small shells.

Searchlights begin to sweep the black sky. They skim across it like huge blackboard pointers, tapering down at the bottom. One of them pauses, shaking a little. At once another is beside it, they cross and there is a black, winged insect trapped and trying to escape: an airman. He wavers, is dazzled and falls.

★

We ram the iron posts in firmly at set intervals. There are always two men holding the roll while the others pay out the barbed-wire. It is that horrible wire with a lot of long spikes, close together. I am out of practice at paying it out, and rip my hand open.

After a few hours we have finished. But there is still some time before the trucks are due. Most of us lie down and sleep. I try to as well, but it is too cold. You can tell that we are not far from the sea, because you are always waking up from the cold.

At one point I do fall into a deep sleep. When I wake up suddenly with a jolt, I have no idea where I am. I see the stars and I see the rockets, and just for a moment I imagine that I have fallen asleep in the garden at home, during a fireworks party of some sort. I don't know whether it is morning or evening, and I lie there in the pale cradle of dawn waiting for the gentle words which must surely come, gentle and comforting – am I crying? I put my hand to my face; it is baffling, am I a child? Smooth skin – it only lasts for a second and then I recognize the silhouette of Katczinsky. He is sitting there quite calmly, old soldier that he is, smoking his pipe – one of those with a lid over the bowl, of course. When he sees that I am awake he says, 'That made you jump. It was only a detonator, it whizzed off into the bushes over there.'

I sit up; I feel terribly alone. It is good that Kat is there. He looks thoughtfully at the front and says, 'Lovely fireworks. If only they weren't so dangerous.'

A shell lands behind us. A couple of the new recruits jump up in fright. A few minutes later another shell comes over, closer than before. Kat knocks out his pipe. 'Here we go.'

It has started. We crawl away as fast as we can. The next shell lands amongst us.

Some of the men scream. Green rockets go up over the horizon. Dirt flies up. Shrapnel buzzes. You can hear it landing when the noise of the blast has long gone.

Close by us there is a recruit, a blond lad, and he is terrified. He has pressed his face into his hands. His helmet has rolled off. I reach for it and try to put it on to his head. He looks up, pushes the helmet away and huddles in under my arm like a child, his head against my chest. His narrow shoulders are shaking, shoulders just like Kemmerich had.

I let him stay there. But to get some use out of his helmet I shove it over his backside, not as some kind of a joke, but deliberately, because it's the most exposed area. Even though the flesh is solid, a wound there can be bloody painful, and besides, you have to lie on your stomach for months in a military hospital, and afterwards you are pretty certain to have a limp.

There's been a direct hit somewhere not far off. Between the impacts you can hear screaming.

At last it calms down. The shellfire has swept over us and moved on to the back line of reserve trenches. We risk a look out. Red rockets are shimmering in the sky. Probably there will be an attack.

It stays quiet where we are. I sit up and shake the recruit by the shoulder. 'It's all over, old son. We got through again.'

He looks around in bewilderment. 'You'll get used to it,' I tell him.

He notices his helmet and puts it on his head. Slowly he comes to himself. Then suddenly he blushes scarlet and his face has a look of embarrassment. Cautiously he puts his hand to his rear end and gives me an agonized look. I understand at once: the barrage scared the shit out of him. That wasn't the precise reason that I put his helmet where I did – but all the same I comfort him. 'No shame in that, plenty of soldiers before you have filled their pants when they came under fire for the first time. Go behind that bush, chuck your underpants away, and that's that –'

*

He clears off. It gets quieter, but the screaming doesn't stop. 'What's up, Albert?' I ask.

'A couple of the columns over there got direct hits.'

The screaming goes on and on. It can't be men, they couldn't scream that horribly.

'Wounded horses,' says Kat.

I have never heard a horse scream and I can hardly believe it. There is a whole world of pain in that sound, creation itself under torture, a wild and horrifying agony. We go pale. Detering sits up. 'Bastards, bastards! For Christ's sake shoot them!'

He is a farmer and used to handling horses. It really gets to him.

And as if on purpose the firing dies away almost completely. The screams of the animals become that much clearer. You can't tell where it is coming from any more in that quiet, silver landscape, it is invisible, ghostly, it is everywhere, between the earth and the heavens, and it swells out immeasurably. Detering is going crazy and roars out, 'Shoot them, for Christ's sake, shoot them!'

'They've got to get the wounded men out first,' says Kat.

We stand up and try to see where they are. If we can actually see the animals, it will be easier to cope with. Meyer has some field glasses with him. We can make out a dark group of orderlies with stretchers, and then some bigger things, black mounds that are moving. Those are the wounded horses. But not all of them. Some gallop off a little way, collapse, and then run on again. The belly of one of the horses has been ripped open and its guts are trailing out. It gets its feet caught up in them and falls, but it gets to its feet again.

Detering raises his rifle and takes aim. Kat knocks the barrel upwards. 'Are you crazy?'

Detering shudders and throws his gun on to the ground.

We sit down and press our hands over our ears. But the terrible crying and groaning and howling still gets through, it penetrates everything.

We can all stand a lot, but this brings us out in a cold sweat. You want to get up and run away, anywhere just so as not to hear that screaming any more. And it isn't men, just horses.

Some more stretchers are moved away from the dark mass. Then a few shots ring out. The big shapes twitch a little and then become less prominent. At last! But it isn't over yet. No one can catch the wounded animals who have bolted in terror, their wide-open mouths filled with all that pain. One of the figures goes down on one knee, a shot – one horse collapses – and then there is another. The last horse supports itself on its forelegs, and moves in a circle like a carousel, turning around in a sitting position with its forelegs stiff – probably its back is broken. The soldier runs across and shoots it down. Slowly, humbly, it sinks to the ground.

We take our hands away from our ears. The screaming has

stopped. Just a long-drawn-out, dying sigh is still there in the air. Then, just like before, there are only the rockets, the singing of the shells, and the stars – and it feels almost eerie.

Detering walks about cursing. 'What have they done to deserve that, that's what I want to know?' And later on he comes back to it again. His voice is agitated and he sounds as if he is making a speech when he says, 'I tell you this: it is the most despicable thing of all to drag animals into a war.'

★

We go back. It's time to head for the trucks. The sky has become just a trace lighter. Three a.m. The wind is fresh and cool and at that livid hour our faces look grey.

We move slowly forwards in Indian file through the trenches and shell holes and at last we reach the foggy area once again. Katczinsky is uneasy, and that is a bad sign.

'What's the matter, Kat?' asks Kropp.

'I just wish we were home.' Home – he means back in camp.

'Won't be long now, Kat.'

He is nervous. 'I don't know, I don't know . . .'

We get to the communication trenches and then back to the meadows. The little wood is in front of us; we know every inch of ground here. We can already see the graves of the rifle brigade, with the mounds of earth still piled up, and the black crosses.

At that very moment we hear a whistling noise behind us, it gets louder, there is a crash and then a roar. We've ducked down – a hundred yards in front of us a wall of flame shoots up.

The next moment part of the wood is lifted up above the tree tops when the second shell hits, three or four trees go up with it and are smashed into pieces in the process. The follow-up shells are already hissing down with a sound like a safety valve – heavy fire –

'Take cover!' somebody shouts, 'Take cover!'

The meadows are flat, the wood is too far away and too dangerous; the only cover is the military cemetery and the grave mounds. We stumble into the darkness, and soon every man has flattened himself behind one of the mounds.

Not a moment too soon. The dark turns into madness. It rocks and rages. Dark things, darker than the night itself, rush upon us in great waves, over us and onwards. The flashes of the explosions light up the cemetery.

There is no way out. In the light of one of the shell-bursts I risk a glance out on to the meadows. They are like a storm-tossed sea, with the flames from the impacts spurting up like fountains. No one could possibly get across that.

The wood disappears, splintered, shattered, smashed. We have to stay in the cemetery.

The earth explodes in front of us. Great clumps of it come raining down on top of us. I feel a jolt. My sleeve has been ripped by some shrapnel. I clench my fist. No pain. But that is no comfort, wounds never start to hurt until afterwards. I run my hand over the arm. It is scratched but still in one piece. Then I get a knock on the head and everything blurs. But as quick as a flash comes the thought: you mustn't faint! I sink down into the black mud but get up again immediately. A piece of shrapnel hit my helmet, but it came from so far off that it didn't cut through the steel. I wipe the dirt out of my eyes. A hole has been blown in the ground right in front of me, I can just about make it out. Shells don't often land in the same place twice and I want to get into that hole. Without stopping I wriggle across towards it as fast as I can, flat as an eel on the ground – there is a whistling noise again, I curl up quickly and grab for some cover, feel something to my left and press against it, it gives, I groan, and the earth is torn up again, the blast thunders in my ears, I crawl under whatever it was that gave way when I touched it, pull it over me – it is wood, cloth, cover, cover, pretty poor cover against falling shrapnel.

I open my eyes; my fingers are gripped tight on a sleeve, an arm. A wounded soldier? I shout out to him – no answer – must be dead. My hand gropes on and finds more shattered wood – then I remember that we've taken cover in a cemetery.

But the shelling is stronger than anything else. It wipes out all other considerations and I just crawl deeper and deeper beneath the coffin so that it will protect me, even if Death himself is already in it.

The shell hole is gaping in front of me. I fix my eyes on it, grasping at it almost physically, I have to get to it in one jump.

Then I feel a blow in the face, and a hand grabs me by the shoulder – has the dead man come back to life? The hand shakes me, I turn my head, and in a flash of light that lasts only a second I find myself looking into Katczinsky's face. His mouth is wide open and he is bellowing, but I can't hear anything; he shakes me and comes closer; the noise ebbs for a moment and I can make out his voice: 'Gas – gaaas – gaaaaas – pass it on!'

I pull out my gas-mask case . . . Someone is lying a little way away from me. All I can think of is that I've got to tell him: 'Gaaas . . . gaaaas.'

I shout, crawl across to him, hit at him with the gas-mask case but he doesn't notice – I do it again, and then again – he only ducks – it is one of the new recruits – I look despairingly at Kat, who has his mask on already – I tear mine out of the case, my helmet is knocked aside as I get the mask over my face, I reach the man and his gas-mask case is by my hand, so I get hold of the mask and shove it over his head – he grabs it, I let go, and with a sudden jolt I am lying in the shell hole.

The dull thud of the gas shells is mixed in with the sharp noise of the high explosives. In between the explosions a bell rings the warning, gongs and metal rattles spread the word – Gas – gas – gaas –

There is a noise as someone drops behind me, once, twice. I wipe the window of my gas-mask clear of condensation. It is Kat, Kropp and somebody else. There are four of us lying here, tensed and waiting, breathing as shallowly as we can.

The first few minutes with the mask tell you whether you will live or die. Is it airtight? I know the terrible sights from the field hospital, soldiers who have been gassed, choking for days on end as they spew up their burned-out lungs, bit by bit.

I breathe carefully, with my mouth pressed against the mouthpiece. By now the gas is snaking over the ground and sinking into all the hollows. It insinuates itself into our shell hole wriggling its way in like a broad, soft jellyfish. I give Kat a nudge: it is better to crawl out and lie up on top rather than here, where the gas concentrates itself the most. But we can't. A second hail of shellfire starts. It's as if it is not the guns that are roaring; it's as if the very earth is raging.

There is a crash as something black flies over and on to us. It strikes the ground right beside us: a coffin that has been blown through the air.

I see Kat move, and crawl across to him. The coffin has crashed down on to the outstretched arm of the fourth man in our shell hole. He tries to tear off his gas-mask with his other hand. Kropp gets to him just in time, twists that arm hard behind his back and holds it there.

Kat and I set about freeing the wounded arm. The coffin lid is loose and damaged, and we easily manage to wrench it free; we throw out the corpse, which flops down, and then we try to loosen the rest of the coffin.

Luckily, the man passes out, and Albert is able to help us. Now we don't have to be so careful, and we work like mad until the coffin gives way with a sighing noise to the spades which we shove in underneath it.

It is lighter now. Kat takes a piece of the coffin lid and puts it under the shattered arm, and we wrap the bandages from all our field dressing packs around it. There isn't anything else we can do at the moment.

My head is throbbing and buzzing in the gas-mask, it is nearly bursting. Your lungs get strained, they only have stagnant, overheated, used-up air to breathe, the veins on your temples bulge and you think you are going to suffocate –

A grey light trickles into our shell hole. Wind sweeps the cemetery. I haul myself up to the edge of the hole. Lying in front of me in the dirty light of dawn is a leg that has been torn off, with the boot on it still completely undamaged – I see it all perfectly clearly in a moment. But now, a few yards away, somebody is standing up; I clean the goggles, and because I am agitated they mist over again at once, but I stare across – the man over there isn't wearing his gas-mask any more.

I wait for a few seconds longer – but he doesn't collapse, he looks around cautiously and takes a few steps – the wind has dispersed the gas, the air is clear – and gasping for breath I rip my mask away from my face too, and my knees give way. The air pours into me like cold water, my eyes feel as if they could burst from my head, the wave sweeps over me and plunges me into darkness.

★

The shelling has stopped. I turn back to the crater and wave to the others. They scramble up and tear off their masks. We pick up the wounded man, one of us holds the arm with the splint on it. And in a group we stumble away as quickly as possible.

The cemetery has been blown to pieces. Coffins and corpses are scattered all around. They have been killed for a second time; but every corpse that was shattered saved the life of one of us.

The fence has been wrecked, the rails of the field railway on the other side have been ripped out and bent upwards, so that they point to the sky. Someone is lying on the ground in front of us. We stop. Kropp goes on alone with the wounded man.

The man on the ground is a recruit. He has blood smeared all over one hip; he is so exhausted that I reach for my flask, which has tea with rum in it. Kat holds back my hand and bends over him. 'Where did you cop it, mate?'

He moves his eyes, too weak to answer.

Carefully we cut away his trousers. He moans. 'It's OK, OK, it'll soon be better . . .'

If he's been hit in the stomach then he mustn't drink anything. He has thrown up, and that is a good sign. We expose the hip area.

It is just a pulp of torn flesh and splintered bone. The joint has been hit. This lad will never walk again.

I wet my fingers and run them across his forehead, then give him a drink. Some life comes into his eyes. It's only now that we realize that his right arm is bleeding as well.

Kat spreads out two field dressings as wide as he can, so that they cover the wound. I look around for some cloth, so that I can tie it up loosely. We haven't got anything, so I cut more of the wounded man's trousers away so that I can use a piece of his underpants as a bandage. But he isn't wearing any. I look at him more closely. It's the blond lad from earlier on.

Meanwhile Kat has fetched a couple more field dressings from the pockets of dead soldiers, and we place them carefully on the wound. The lad is looking at us with a fixed gaze.

'We'll go and get a stretcher now.'

But he opens his mouth and whispers, 'Stay here –'

Kat says, 'We'll be back in a minute. We're going to get a stretcher for you.'

It is impossible to say whether he understands or not; he whimpers like a child behind us as we go: 'Stay here –'

Kat looks all round and then whispers, 'Wouldn't it be best just to take a revolver and put him out of his misery?'

The lad is not likely to survive being moved, and at the very most he'll last a couple of days. But everything he's been through so far will be nothing compared to those few days until he dies. At the moment he is still in shock and can't feel anything. Within an hour he'll be a screaming mass of unbearable agonies, and the few days he still has left to live will just be an incessant raging torture. And what difference does it make to anyone whether he has to suffer them or not?

I nod. 'You're right, Kat. The best thing would be a bullet.'

'Give me a gun,' he says, and stops walking. I can see that he is set on it. We look around – but we're not alone any more. A small group is gathering near us, and heads are appearing out of the shell holes and trenches.

We bring a stretcher.

Kat shakes his head. 'Such young lads –' He says it again: 'Such young, innocent lads –'

*

Our losses are not as bad as might have been expected: five dead and eight wounded. It was only a short barrage. Two of our dead are lying in one of the re-opened graves; all we have to do is fill it in.

We go back. We trot along silently, in line one behind the other. The wounded are taken to the dressing station. The morning is overcast, the orderlies scurry about with tags and numbers, the wounded whimper. It starts to rain.

Within an hour we reach our truck and climb aboard. There is more room on it now than there was before.

The rain gets heavier. We open up tarpaulins and put them over our heads. The drops drum down on top of them. Streams of rain pour off the sides. The trucks splash through the holes in the road and we rock backwards and forwards, half asleep.

Two men at the front of the truck have long forked poles with them. They watch out for the telephone wires that hang down so low across the roadway that they could take your head off. The two men make sure they get them with their forked sticks and lift them over our heads. We hear them shouting, 'Mind the wires!' and still half asleep we bob down and then straighten up again.

The trucks roll monotonously onwards, the shouts are monotonous, the falling rain is monotonous. It falls on our heads and on the heads of the dead men up at the front of the truck, on the body of the little recruit with a wound that is far too big for his hip, it's falling on Kemmerich's grave, and it's falling in our hearts.

From somewhere we hear the sound of a shell-burst. We snap

to, our eyes wide open, our hands ready again to heave our bodies over the side of the truck into the ditch by the roadside.

But we don't hear any more. Just the monotonous shouts of 'Mind the wires!' – we bob down – we're half asleep again.

5

It's a nuisance trying to kill every single louse when you've got hundreds of them. The beasts are hard, and it gets to be a bore when you are forever pinching them between your nails. So Tjaden has rigged up a boot-polish lid hanging on a piece of wire over a burning candle-end. You just have to toss the lice into this little frying-pan – there is a sharp crack, and that's it.

We're sitting around, shirts on our knees, stripped to the waist in the warm air, our fingers working on the lice. Haie has a particularly splendid species of louse: they have a red cross on their heads. Because of that he maintains that he brought them back from the military hospital in Tourhout, where he claims they were the personal property of a senior staff surgeon. He also wants to use the grease that is very slowly accumulating in the tin lid to polish his boots, and roars with laughter for a good half-hour at his own joke.

But today nobody takes much notice. We have something else far too important on our minds.

The rumour turned out to be true. Himmelstoss is here. He turned up yesterday, and we have already heard his familiar tones. Apparently he was a little bit too vigorous with a couple of recruits on the training field. He didn't know that one of them was the son of the chairman of the district council. That did for him.

He is in for a surprise. For hours Tjaden has been running through the things he wants to say to him. Haie keeps looking speculatively at his gigantic paws and winking at me. Beating up Himmelstoss was the high point of his existence; he told me that he still dreams about it.

★

Kropp and Müller are having a discussion. Kropp has managed to nab a mess-tin full of lentils for himself, probably from the sappers' kitchens. Müller gives it a greedy look, but gets a grip on himself and asks, 'Albert, what would you do if all of a sudden it was peacetime?'

'There's no such thing as peacetime,' replies Albert curtly.

Müller persists. 'Yes, but *if* . . . what would you do?'

'I'd bugger off out of it,' grumbles Kropp.

''Course. And then what?'

'Get blind drunk,' says Albert.

'Don't talk rubbish, I'm being serious –'

'Me too,' says Albert, 'what else would there be to do?'

The idea interests Kat. He claims a portion of Kropp's lentils, gets his whack, then he ponders for a long while and offers the view 'Well, you *could* get drunk, of course, but otherwise it would be off to the nearest train – and home to mother. Bloody hell, Albert, peacetime . . .'

He grubs around in his oilskin wallet for a photograph and passes it around proudly. 'My missus.' Then he stows it away and curses: 'Lousy bloody war . . .'

'It's all right for you,' I say, 'you've got your wife and your lad.'

He nods. 'That's true, and I have to make sure they've got enough to eat.'

We all laugh. 'There won't be any problem there, Kat, you'd just requisition something.'

Müller is hungry and says he still isn't satisfied with the answers. He shakes Haie Westhus out of his daydreams of beating up Himmelstoss. 'Haie, what would you do if the war ended?'

'What he ought to do is kick your arse from here to kingdom come for talking about that sort of thing here,' I put in. 'Where did you get the idea anyway?'

'Where do the flies go in winter?' is Müller's brief answer before he turns to Haie Westhus again.

Haie is suddenly finding it all a bit difficult. He puts his freckled head in his hands: 'You mean, when there isn't any more war?'

'Dead right. You've got it in one.'

'Then there'd be women around again, wouldn't there?' Haie licks his lips.

'That as well.'

'Christ almighty,' says Haie, and his expression softens, 'the first thing I'd do is pick myself up some strapping great bint, know what I mean, some big, bouncy kitchen wench with plenty to get your hands round, then straight into bed and no messing! Think about it! Proper feather-beds with sprung mattresses. I tell you, lads, I wouldn't put my trousers back on for a week!'

Silence all round. The image is just too fantastic. It sends tremors right across the skin. Eventually Müller gets a grip and asks, 'And what about after that?'

A pause. Then Haie goes on, a little hesitantly, 'If I was an NCO I'd stay in the army and sign on as a regular.'

'Haie, you're barmy,' I say.

But he answers me amiably with another question. 'Have you ever tried peat-digging? Have a go sometime.' With that he pulls his spoon out of the top of his high boot and digs into Albert's mess-tin.

'It can't be worse than digging trenches in France,' I reply.

Haie chews and grins. 'Lasts longer, though. And you can't skive off.'

'Come on, Haie, it must be better at home.'

'Sometimes, sometimes,' he says, and sinks into a kind of reverie, sitting there with his mouth open.

You can read in his face what he is thinking. A run-down shack on the moors, hard work on the hot heathlands from early in the morning until late at night, lousy pay, the dirty clothes a labourer wears –

'In the peacetime army you don't have to worry about anything,' he tells us. 'You get your grub every day, and if you don't you kick up a fuss, you've got your bed, clean sheets every week just like a toff, you do your bit of duty when you're an NCO, you get all your gear – and in the evening you're a free man and you can go for a drink.'

Haie is extraordinarily proud of his idea. He falls in love with it. 'And when you've served your twelve years they give you your discharge settlement, and you get to be a country copper. Then you're just out and about all day.'

This future brings him out in a sweat. 'Just think about how they treat you then! A brandy here, a beer there – everyone wants to be on good terms with the local copper.'

'You'll never make it to NCO,' throws in Kat.

Haie gives him a hurt look, and shuts up. In his mind he's probably already enjoying the clear autumn evenings, the Sundays on the heath, the village church bells, afternoons and evenings with the girls, the buckwheat pancakes with bacon, the hours of aimless conversation in the bar –

He can't cope with so much imagining all at once; so he just snarls angrily, 'You and your bloody stupid questions.'

He slips his shirt down over his head and does up his battledress tunic.

'What would you do, Tjaden?' Kropp calls across to him.

Tjaden has only one thing in mind. 'Make sure that Himmelstoss doesn't get away.'

Probably what he would like best is to keep him in a cage and set about him with a cudgel every morning. He urges Kropp with great enthusiasm, 'If I were you I'd make sure I got to be a lieutenant. Then you could make him run like his arse was on fire.'

'What about you, Detering?' Müller continues. He's a proper schoolmaster with these questions round the class.

Detering is the silent type. But this time he does have an answer. He stares up at the sky and utters a single sentence. 'I'd just get home in time for the harvest.'

With that he gets up and walks away.

He is worried. His wife has to look after his smallholding. Besides that, two of his horses have been taken from him. Every day he looks in the local papers that are sent to him to see whether the rain has started yet in his little corner of Oldenburg. If it has, they won't be able to get the hay in.

Just at this moment, Himmelstoss appears. He comes straight for our group. Tjaden's face goes blotchy. He stretches out in the grass and shuts his eyes because he is so worked up.

Himmelstoss wavers and slows down. Then he marches towards us. Nobody makes any move to stand up. Kropp looks at him with interest.

He stands right in front of us and waits. When nobody says a word, he comes out with a 'Well?'

A few moments pass; Himmelstoss clearly has no idea how he should behave. What he would most like to do is bawl us out good and proper; but for all that, he does seem to have learnt already that the front is no parade-ground. He tries again, and instead of addressing us all he picks on one of us, in the hope of getting an answer more easily. Kropp is nearest to him, and so he gets the honour. 'Well, well, you here too?'

But Albert is no friend of his. He gives the sharp retort, 'I reckon I've been here a bit longer than you have.'

The gingery moustache twitches. 'I suppose you lot don't remember me, then?'

Tjaden opens his eyes. 'Oh yes, we do.'

Himmelstoss turns to him. 'Tjaden, isn't it?'

Tjaden lifts his head. 'And do you know what you are, chum?'

Himmelstoss is taken aback. 'What do you mean, "chum"? I don't think we've ever drunk ourselves into the gutter together.'

He has absolutely no idea of how to cope with the situation. He wasn't expecting this open aggression. But for the moment he is cautious. Someone has clearly fed him that nonsense about NCOs getting shot in the back.

Tjaden has been made so angry by the crack about the gutter that he becomes positively sharp. 'No, you were in the gutter all by yourself, pal.'

By now Himmelstoss is seething with rage as well, but Tjaden rushes to get in before him. He has to say his piece. 'You want to know what you are, chum? You're a shit, that's what you are! I've wanted to tell you that for a long time.'

The satisfaction that comes from months of waiting is shining in his piggy eyes when he comes out with the word 'shit'.

Himmelstoss lets fly too. 'What do you mean, you miserable little sod, you filthy bloody peasant? Stand up and stand to attention when a superior officer is speaking to you.'

Tjaden gives a gracious wave of his hand. 'You may stand easy, Himmelstoss. Dismiss!'

Himmelstoss turns into a raging mass of drill regulations. The Kaiser himself couldn't be more insulted. 'Tjaden!' he screams. 'This is an order! Stand up!'

'Anything else you'd like?' asks Tjaden.

'Are you going to carry out my order or not?'

Tjaden gives an unworried and conclusive reply, quoting (although he doesn't know he's doing so) one of Goethe's best-known lines, the one about kissing a specific part of his anatomy. At the same time he sticks his backside up in the air.

Himmelstoss storms away. 'You'll be court martialled for this!'

We watch him disappear in the direction of the orderly room.

Haie and Tjaden collapse in a great peat-diggers' roar. Haie laughs so much that he puts his lower jaw out of joint, and suddenly stands there helplessly with his mouth open. Albert has to punch it, to get him back to normal.

Kat is worried. 'If he reports you, there'll be trouble.'

'Do you think he will?' asks Tjaden.

'Bound to,' I say.

'You'll get five days' close arrest at the very least,' says Kat.

That doesn't bother Tjaden. 'Five days in clink means five days rest.'

'And what if they take you away and put you in jug?' asks the indefatigable Müller.

'Then the war is over for me until I get out.'

Tjaden is a happy-go-lucky type. He never worries. He clears off with Haie and Leer, so that when the balloon goes up they won't be able to find him for a bit.

★

Meanwhile, Müller still hasn't finished. He comes back to Kropp again. 'Albert, if you really got to go home, what would you do?'

Kropp is full up now, and this makes him more expansive. 'How many of our class at school would there be now?'

We reckon it up: out of twenty, seven are dead, four are wounded and one's in an asylum. We could only get twelve together at the most.

'Three of them are second lieutenants,' says Müller. 'Do you think they'd let Kantorek bawl them out nowadays?'

We don't think they would. We wouldn't let Kantorek bawl us out any more, either.

'Come on, outline the tripartite plot of Schiller's *William Tell,'* Kropp reminds us suddenly, and roars with laughter.

'What were the principal aims of the Göttingen poetic movement in the eighteenth century?' demands Müller with a sudden severity.

'How many children did Charles the Bold have?' I put in calmly.

'You'll never get on in life, Bäumer,' says Müller.

'When was the battle of Zama?' Kropp wants to know.

'You are completely lacking in moral fibre and high seriousness, Kropp. Sit down. C-minus –' I throw in.

'What did Lycurgus consider to be the principal responsibilities of the State?' hisses Müller, pretending to fiddle around with a pince-nez.

'Is it "We Germans fear God and no one else in the world . . ." or "We comma Germans comma –"?' I offer as food for thought.

Müller twitters back, 'What is the population of Melbourne?'

'How on earth are you going to get on in life if you don't know that?' I ask Albert indignantly.

But he trumps this with, 'What do you understand by cohesion?'

We don't remember much about all that stuff any more. It was no use to us anyway. Nobody taught us at school how to light a cigarette in a rainstorm, or how it is still possible to make a fire even with soaking wet wood – or that the best place to stick a bayonet is into the belly, because it can't get jammed in there, the way it can in the ribs.

Müller thinks for a bit, and then says, 'It's no good; we'll still have to go back to school.'

I think that's quite out of the question. 'Perhaps we could just sit the exams under the special regulations.'

'You still need some preparation. And even if you pass, what happens then? Being a student isn't much better. If you haven't got much money, you have to study really hard.'

'It *is* a bit better, but it's still rubbish, all the stuff they fill your head with.'

Kropp sums it up for us when he says, 'How can you take all that lot seriously when you've been out here?'

'But you have to have some kind of job,' puts in Müller, as if he were Kantorek himself.

Albert is cleaning his nails with the point of a knife. We are amazed by this genteel behaviour, but it is only because he is thinking. He puts the knife aside and says, 'That's the problem. Kat and Detering and Haie will go back to their old jobs because they had them already. So will Himmelstoss. We never had one. And how is this lot –' he gestures over towards the front – 'supposed to prepare us for anything?'

'What you need is a private income and then you could go away and live on your own in the middle of some forest –' I say, but at once I feel silly for coming up with such a daft idea.

'What will become of us if and when we *do* get back?' wonders Müller, and even he is anxious.

Kropp shrugs. 'I don't know. Let's just get there first and then see what happens.'

None of us really has any ideas. 'What could we possibly do?' I ask.

'There isn't anything I fancy doing,' Kropp answers wearily. 'One day you'll be dead anyway, and what have you got then? In any case, I don't think we'll ever get home.'

'If I think about it, Albert,' I say after a little while, rolling over on to my back, 'when I hear the word "peace", and if peace really came, what comes into my head is that I'd like to do something, well, unimaginable. Something – you know what I mean – that would make it all worthwhile, being out here under fire and all the rest. But I just can't picture what it could be. The only possibilities there are – all this business with a job, studying, earning money and so on – they all make me sick, because they were always there and they put me off. I can't think of anything, Albert, I can't think of anything.'

All at once everything seems to me to be pointless and desperate.

Kropp takes it further along the same line. 'It will be just as difficult for all of us. I wonder whether the people back at home don't worry about it themselves occasionally? Two years of rifle fire and hand-grenades – you can't just take it all off like a pair of socks afterwards –'

We all agree that it is the same for everyone; not only for us here, but for everyone who is in the same boat, some to a greater, others to a lesser extent. It is the common fate of our generation.

Albert puts it into words. 'The war has ruined us for everything.'

He is right. We're no longer young men. We've lost any desire to conquer the world. We are refugees. We are fleeing from ourselves. From our lives. We were eighteen years old, and we had just begun to love the world and to love being in it; but we had to shoot at it. The first shell to land went straight for our hearts. We've been cut off from real action, from getting on, from progress. We don't believe in those things any more; we believe in the war.

⋆

There is a buzz of activity in the orderly room. Himmelstoss seems to have stirred them up. At the head of the little column trots the fat sergeant major. It's funny how regular CSMs are nearly always fat.

Next in line comes Himmelstoss, hungry for revenge. His boots are gleaming in the sun.

We stand up. The sergeant major puffs, 'Where's Tjaden?'

None of us knows, of course. Himmelstoss glares angrily at us. 'Of course you know, you lot. You just don't want to tell us. Come on, out with it.'

The CSM looks all round him, but Tjaden is nowhere to be seen. He tries a different tack. 'Tjaden is to present himself at the orderly room in ten minutes.'

With that he clears off, with Himmelstoss in his wake.

'I've got a feeling that a roll of barbed-wire is going to fall on to Himmelstoss's legs when we're on wiring fatigues again,' reckons Kropp.

'We'll get a good bit of fun out of him yet,' laughs Müller.

That's the extent of our ambition now: taking a postman down a peg or two . . .

I go off to the hut to warn Tjaden, so that he can disappear.

We shift along a bit, then lie down again to play cards. Because that is what we are good at: playing cards, swearing and making war. Not much for twenty years – too much for twenty years.

Half an hour later Himmelstoss is back. Nobody takes any notice of him. He asks where Tjaden is. We shrug our shoulders. 'You lot were supposed to look for him.'

'What do you mean "you lot"?' asks Kropp.

'Well, you lot here –'

'I should like to request, Corporal Himmelstoss, that you address us in an appropriate military fashion,' says Kropp, sounding like a colonel.

Himmelstoss is thunderstruck. 'Who's addressing you any other way?'

'You, Corporal Himmelstoss, sir.'

'Me?'

'Yes.'

It is getting to him. He looks suspiciously at Kropp because he hasn't any idea of what he is talking about. At all events, he loses confidence and backs down. 'Didn't you lot find him?'

Kropp lies back in the grass and says, 'Have you ever been out here before, Corporal Himmelstoss, sir?'

'That is quite irrelevant, Private Kropp,' says Himmelstoss, 'and I demand an answer.'

'Right,' says Kropp and gets up. 'Have a look over there, Corporal, sir, where the little white clouds are. That's the flak going for the aircraft. That's where we were yesterday. Five dead, eight wounded. And that was actually an easy one. So the next time we go up the line, Corporal, sir, the platoons will all parade in front of you before they die, click their heels and request in proper military fashion "Permission to fall out, sir! Permission to fall down dead, sir!" People like you are all we need out here, Corporal, sir.'

He sits down again and Himmelstoss shoots off like a rocket.

'Three days CB,' reckons Kat.

'Next time *I'll* let him have it,' I tell Albert.

That is the end of the matter for now. Instead, there is a hearing during the evening roll call. Our lieutenant, Bertinck, is sitting in the orderly room and he has us brought in one after the other.

I have to appear as a witness, and I explain why Tjaden blew up. The story about wetting the bed makes an impression. Himmelstoss is fetched in and I repeat my statement.

'Is that true?' Bertinck asks Himmelstoss.

He fidgets a bit and eventually has to admit that it is, once Kropp has told the same story.

'Why did none of you report this at the time?' asks Bertinck.

We say nothing. He must know himself how much effect a complaint about something as trivial as that would have had in the army. Can you make complaints in the army at all? Anyway, he gets the point, gives Himmelstoss a dressing-down and makes it clear to him that the front is no parade-ground. Then it is Tjaden's turn for a stronger version – he gets a full-blown sermon and three days' open arrest. Bertinck has a twinkle in his eye when he sentences Kropp to one day. 'Has to be done,' he tells him with a tone of regret. He's a decent chap.

Open arrest is quite pleasant. The jail was once a chicken-run; both of them can have visitors and we agree at once to go and see them. Close arrest would have meant a cellar somewhere. They used to lash you to a tree, but that isn't allowed any more. Sometimes we get treated quite like human beings.

When Tjaden and Kropp have been behind the chicken-wire for an hour we go and visit them. Tjaden crows with delight when he sees us. Then we play cards well into the night. Tjaden wins, of course, the lucky bastard.

*

When roll call is over Kat says to me, 'How do you fancy roast goose?'

'Not a bad idea,' I reply.

We climb on to a munitions convoy. The ride costs us two cigarettes. Kat has taken careful note of the place. The shed belongs to the headquarters of some regiment. I decide that I will fetch the goose, and I get instructions on how to do it. The shed is behind the wall, and only barred with a wooden peg.

Kat cradles his hands for me, I put my foot in and scramble up over the wall. Meanwhile Kat keeps a look-out.

I wait for a few moments to let my eyes get used to the dark, then pick out where the shed is. I creep towards it very quietly, grope for the peg, take it out and open the door.

I can make out two white shapes. Two geese. That's a nuisance; if you grab one, the other one will make a racket. So it'll have to be both of them – it should work, if I'm quick.

I make a jump for them. I get one of them straight away, then a couple of seconds later the other one. I bang their heads against the wall like a madman, trying to stun them. But I obviously don't use enough force. The beasts hiss and beat out all round them with their wings and their feet. I fight on grimly, but my God, geese are strong! They tug at me and I stumble this way and that. In the dark these white things have become terrifying, my arms have sprouted wings and I'm almost afraid that I'll take off into the skies, just as if I had a couple of observation balloons in my hands.

And then the noise starts; one of them has got some air into his throat and sounds off like an alarm clock. Before I can do anything about it I hear noises coming towards me from outside, something shoves me and I'm lying on the ground listening to angry growling. A dog. I look to one side, and he makes for my throat. I lie still at once and pull my chin down into my collar.

It's a bull mastiff. After an eternity it draws its head back and sits down beside me. But whenever I try to move, it growls. I think for a moment. The only thing I can do is try and get hold of my service revolver. At all events I have to get out of here before anyone comes. Inch by inch I move my hand along.

I feel as if this is all going on for hours. Every time I make a slight movement there is a threatening growl; I lie still and try again. The minute I get hold of my gun, my hand starts to tremble. I press down against the ground and think it out: pull the gun out, shoot before he can get at me, and get the hell out as quickly as possible.

I take a deep breath and calm myself. Then I hold my breath, jerk up the revolver, there is a shot and the mastiff lurches aside, howling, I make it to the door of the shed and tumble over one of the geese, which was flapping out of the way.

I make a grab while I'm still running, hurl it with a great swing over the wall and start to scramble up myself. I'm not quite over the wall when the mastiff, which has come to itself again, is there and jumping up at me. I drop down quickly. Ten paces away from me stands Kat with the goose in his arms. As soon as he sees me, we run for it.

At last we can get our breath back. The goose is dead, Kat saw to that in a moment. We want to roast it straight away, before anyone realizes what has happened. I fetch pots and some wood from the huts, and we crawl into a small, deserted shed that we know about and which is useful for things like this. We put up a thick covering to block the only window hole. There is a makeshift cooker there – an iron plate lying across some bricks. We light a fire.

Kat plucks and draws the goose. We put the feathers carefully to one side. We want to use them to stuff two small pillows, with the motto 'Sweet Dreams Though the Guns Are Booming' on them.

The barrage from the front can be heard as a dull humming all around our hideout. Firelight flickers on our faces, shadows dance on the walls. Airmen drop bombs. At one point we hear muffled screaming. One of the huts must have been hit.

Aircraft roar. The *ratatat* of the machine-guns gets louder. But our light can't be seen from anywhere outside.

And so we sit facing one another, Kat and I, two soldiers in shabby battledress, roasting a goose in the middle of the night. We don't talk much, but we have a greater and more gentle consideration for each other than I should think even lovers do. We are two human beings, two tiny sparks of life; outside there is just the night, and all around us, death. We are sitting right at the edge of all that, in danger but secure, goose fat runs over our fingers, our hearts are close to one another, and time and place merge into one – the brightnesses and shadows of our emotions come and go in the flickering light of a gentle fire. What does he know about me? What do I know about him? Before the war we wouldn't have had a single thought in common – and now here we are, sitting with a goose roasting in front of us, aware of our existence and so close to each other that we can't even talk about it.

It takes a long time to roast a goose, even when it is young, and there is plenty of fat. And so we take turns. One does the basting, while the other gets a bit of sleep. Gradually there is a wonderful smell all around us.

The noises from outside all merge into one another, become a dream which disappears from the waking memory. Half asleep, I watch Kat as he lifts and lowers the basting spoon. I love him; his shoulders, his angular, slightly stooped frame – and then I see woods and stars behind him, and a kindly voice says words to me that bring me peace, me, an ordinary soldier with his big boots and his webbing, and his pack, who is making his tiny way under the sky's great vault along the road that lies before him, who forgets things quickly and who isn't even depressed much any more, but who just goes onwards under the great night sky.

A little soldier and a kindly voice, and if anyone were to caress him, he probably wouldn't understand the gesture any more, that soldier with the big boots and a heart that has been buried alive, a soldier who marches because he is wearing marching boots and who has forgotten everything except marching. Aren't those things flowers, over there on the horizon, in a landscape that is so calm and quiet that the soldier could weep? Are those not images that he has not exactly lost, because he never had them to lose, confusing images, but nevertheless of things that can no longer be his? Are those not his twenty years of life?

Is my face wet, and where am I? Kat is standing in front of me, his gigantic distorted shadow falls across me like home. He says something softly, smiles and goes back to the fire.

Then he says, 'It's ready.'

'OK, Kat.'

I shake myself. The golden-brown roast is glowing in the middle of the room. We get out our folding forks and pocket-knives and carve ourselves off a leg each. We eat it with army-issue bread that we dip into the gravy.. We eat slowly and enjoy it to the full.

'Like it, Kat?'

'Great. How about you?'

'Great, Kat.'

We are brothers, pressing one another to take the best pieces. When we have finished I smoke a cigarette and Kat has a cigar. There is a lot left over.

'Kat, how about us taking a bit over to Kropp and Tjaden?'

'Right,' he says. We cut off a chunk and wrap it up carefully in newspaper. We were planning to take the rest back to our billets, but Kat laughs and just says, 'Tjaden.'

I agree that we'll have to take it all. So we make our way to the hen-run prison to wake up the pair of them. Before we go we pack away the feathers.

Kropp and Tjaden think we are a mirage. Then they get stuck in. Tjaden is gnawing away, holding a wing with both hands as if he were playing a mouth organ. He slurps the gravy out of the pot and smacks his lips. 'I'll never forget you for this.'

We walk back to the huts. There is the great sky again, and the stars, and the first streaks of dawn, and I am walking beneath that sky, a soldier with big boots and a full belly, a little soldier in the early morning – and beside me walks Kat, angular and slightly stooping, my pal.

The silhouettes of the huts loom over us in the dawn light like a black and welcome sleep.

6

There are rumours of an offensive. We go up the line two days earlier than usual. On the way we pass a school that has been shelled to bits. Stacked up two deep all along its front is a wall of brand-new, untreated, whitewood coffins. They still smell of resin, pine, the forest. There are at least a hundred of them.

'That's a fine preparation for an offensive,' says Müller in surprise.

'Those are for us,' growls Detering.

'Don't talk rubbish,' Kat snaps back at him.

'You'll be lucky to get a coffin at all,' grins Tjaden, 'they'll just use a tarpaulin to wrap up that target-practice dummy you call a body, you wait and see.'

Other men make jokes as well, uncomfortable jokes, but what else can we do? Obviously the coffins really *are* for us, of course. Arrangements are always efficient where that sort of thing is concerned.

Up ahead of us there is a rumbling noise all around. On the first night we try and get our bearings. Because it is still relatively quiet we can hear the transports on the move behind the enemy lines, rolling forwards, without a break, well beyond dawn. Kat says that they are not going back, just bringing in troops. Troops, munitions and guns.

The British artillery has been strengthened – that much we can hear immediately. Over to the right of the farm, there are at least four extra batteries of eight-inch guns, and they've put in trench mortars behind the poplar stump. As well as all that they've got a lot of those little French bastards with instantaneous fuses.

Morale is low. Two hours after we reach our dugouts, our own artillery drops some shells on to our trenches. That's the third time this month. If they were just making mistakes with the gun-laying, nobody would say anything; but it's because the gun barrels are worn out; sometimes the shots are so unpredictable that they scatter shrapnel right into our sector. Tonight two of our men are wounded that way.

★

The front is a cage, and you have to wait nervously in it for whatever happens to you. Here we lie under a criss-cross of shell trajectories, and we live in the tension of uncertainty. Chance is hovering over us. If there is a shot, all I can do is duck; I don't know for sure and I can't influence where it is going to come down.

It's this awareness of chance that makes us so indifferent. A few months ago I was playing cards in a dugout; after a bit I got up and went out to go and talk to some men I knew in another dugout. When I got back, there was nothing left of the first one, a direct hit from a heavy shell had flattened it. I went back to the other dugout and got there just in time to help dig the men out. While I was away it had been buried.

It is simply a matter of chance whether I am hit or whether I go on living. I can be squashed flat in a bomb-proof dugout, and I can survive ten hours in the open under heavy barrage without a scratch. Every soldier owes the fact that he is still alive to a thousand lucky chances and nothing else. And every soldier believes in and trusts to chance.

★

We have to watch out for our bread. There are many more rats lately, ever since the trenches stopped being properly maintained.

Detering reckons that this is the clearest sign that we are in for it.

The rats here are especially repulsive, because they are so huge. They are the sort they call corpse-rats. They have horrible, evil-looking, naked faces and the sight of their long, bare tails can make you feel sick.

They seem to be really hungry. They have had a go at practically everybody's bread. Kropp has wrapped his in tarpaulin and put it under his head, but he can't sleep because they run across his face to try and get at it. Detering tried to outwit them; he fixed a thin wire to the ceiling and hooked the bundle with his bread on to it. During the night he puts on his flashlight and sees the wire swinging backwards and forwards. Riding on his bread there is a great fat rat.

In the end we decide that something has to be done. Carefully we cut off the pieces of bread that have been gnawed by the rats; we can't throw the bread away, of course, or we would have nothing to eat tomorrow.

We put the bits we have cut off all together in the middle of the floor. Everyone grabs a spade and gets ready to hit out. Detering, Kropp and Kat have their flashlights ready.

After a few minutes we hear the first scuffles and scurrying. It gets louder, now it is the sound of lots of little feet. Then the lamps come on and we all lay into the dark mass, which breaks up. The results are good. We shovel what is left of the rats over the edge of the trench and lie in wait again.

It works a few more times. By then the beasts have realized, or they have smelt the blood. No more come. All the same, they have taken what is left of the scraps of bread by the morning.

In one of the adjacent sectors the rats attacked two big cats and a dog, bit them to death and ate them.

★

The next day we are issued with Edam cheese. Every man gets almost a quarter of a cheese. This is fine in one way, because Edam tastes good – but bad in another, because for us these thick red balls of cheese have always been a sure sign that we are in for a hell of a battering. Our suspicions grow when we are given an issue of liquor. We drink it, but it doesn't make us feel any better.

During the day we have competitions about who can shoot the most rats, and we lounge around. Supplies of cartridges and of hand-grenades are increased. We check the bayonets ourselves. The reason for this is that you sometimes find bayonets that are saw-toothed along the blunt edge. Anybody caught by the enemy with one of those out there has had it. In the sector next to ours some men from our side were found afterwards with their noses sawn off by these bayonets, and their eyes poked out. Then their mouths had been stuffed with sawdust so that they suffocated.

A few recruits have weapons like that; we get rid of them and get them different ones.

In any case, the bayonet isn't as important as it used to be. It's more usual now to go into the attack with hand-grenades and your entrenching tool. The sharpened spade is a lighter and more versatile weapon – not only can you get a man under the chin, but more to the point you can strike a blow with a lot more force behind it; that's especially true if you can bring it down diagonally between the neck and the shoulder, because then you can split down as far as the chest. When you put a bayonet in, it can stick, and you have to give the other man a hefty kick in the guts to get it out, and in the meantime you might easily have copped it yourself. Besides, quite often it snaps off.

At night gas gets blown across at us. We are expecting the attack and lie with our gas-masks handy, ready to tear them out as soon as we see the first shadow of a cloud.

The grey light of morning comes, but nothing happens. There is just that continuous and nerve-wracking rolling on the other side, trains, more trains, trucks and more trucks – what is all the concentration for? Our own artillery keeps on sending shells across, but it doesn't stop, it doesn't stop . . .

Our faces are tired and we stare past one another. 'It'll be just like it was on the Somme, it finished up with seven days and nights unbroken shelling,' says Kat gloomily. He isn't making jokes any more, and that's bad. Kat is an old sweat and he can sense these things. Only Tjaden is happy about the extra rations and the rum; he even reckons that we might make it back without being fired on, that maybe nothing will happen.

It almost looks as if it could be like that. One day goes past after another. At night I sit in a forward sap on sentry duty, listening. Rockets and Verey lights go up and come down over my head. I am watchful and tense, my heart is pounding. Time and again I look at the luminous dial of my watch; the hands don't seem to want to move. Sleep is heavy on my eyelids, I wriggle my toes in my boots to stay awake. Nothing happens, and then my relief comes up – there was nothing but that constant rolling over there. Gradually we calm down, and play cards all the time. Maybe we'll be lucky, after all.

During the day the sky is full of observation balloons. Word gets around that they are going to bring in tanks over on the other side when they attack, and fighter aircraft. We are less interested in that news, though, than what we hear about the new flame-throwers.

In the middle of the night we wake up. The ground is rumbling, there is a heavy bombardment going on above us. We huddle into the corners. We can pick out shells of pretty well every calibre.

We all grab hold of our kit, and keep on checking that it is there. The dugout shakes, and the night is all roars and flashes. We look at each other in the moments of light, and shake our heads, our faces pale and our lips pressed tight.

We can all feel it when the heavy shelling rips away the parapet and churns into the bulkheads, shattering the topmost blocks of concrete. We hear the duller, angrier impact when a shell hits our trench, like the blow from the claws of some snarling beast of prey. By morning a few of the recruits are already green and throwing up. They haven't had enough experience of it all yet.

Slowly an unpleasant grey light trickles into our posts and makes the flashes of the impacts look paler. It is morning. Now we can hear trench mortars exploding, in amongst the shellfire. They cause the worst devastation possible. Wherever one of those lands, all you get is a mass grave.

The reliefs go out and the observers stumble in, trembling and covered with dirt. One lies down in a corner without saying anything and starts to eat, the other, one of the older reservists, just sobs; he has been thrown over the parapet twice by the blast without suffering anything more than shell shock.

The recruits are looking at him. That sort of thing is contagious, and we have to keep an eye on it; already a few lips are starting to quiver. It's a good thing that it is daylight; perhaps the attack will come this morning.

The shelling doesn't die down. It is behind us as well. All around, as far as you can see, fountains of mud and iron are shooting up. They are raking a very broad belt indeed.

The attack doesn't come, but the bombardment goes on. Gradually we become deaf. Hardly anyone speaks any more. It's impossible to understand one another anyway.

Our trench has been shelled nearly to pieces. In several places there is less than a couple of feet of wall left standing, and it is full of holes, craters and piles of earth. A shell bursts just in front of our post. Immediately everything goes dark. We have been buried and have to dig ourselves out. After an hour the entrance is clear again, and we are a bit calmer because we have had something to occupy us.

Our company commander climbs in and reports that two of the dugouts are gone. The recruits calm down when they see him. He tells us that they are going to try to get food up to us tonight.

That sounds comforting. No one had given it any thought except Tjaden. Food is something else that might bring the outside world a bit closer – if food is going to be brought in, then it can't be as bad as all that, reckon the recruits. We don't contradict them, although we know that food is just as important as ammunition, and it is only for that reason that it has to be brought in.

But the attempt to fetch it fails. A second party sets out, but turns back as well. The last group contains Kat, but even he has to return empty-handed. No one can get through, a dog's tail wouldn't be thin enough to slip through that kind of fire.

We tighten our belts and chew each mouthful three times as long as usual. But it still isn't enough; we are bloody hungry. I save myself a crust of bread; I eat the soft part and leave the crust in my pack; every so often I nibble at it.

*

The night is unbearable. We can't sleep, we just stare in front of us and doze. Tjaden is sorry that we wasted the scraps of bread that had been gnawed on by the rats. He says we should have gone ahead and kept it, and that we would all eat it now. Water is short as well, but we are not quite so badly off on that score.

Towards morning, while it is still dark, there is a sudden commotion. A mob of fleeing rats storms into the dugout and they run up the walls. Our flashlights show up the chaos. Everyone screams and curses and starts hitting out. It is the working off of all the anger and frustration of all those long hours. Faces are distorted, arms flail, the rats squeak and it is hard for us to stop – we were almost on the point of setting about each other.

The sudden exertion has exhausted us. We lie down and wait again. It is a miracle that our dugout hasn't had any casualties. It is one of the few deep dugouts still intact.

An NCO climbs down to us; he has some bread with him. Three men did manage to get through last night and fetch some provisions. They reported that the shellfire was constant and just as heavy all the way back to our gun emplacements. They say it is a mystery where the other side is getting so much artillery.

We have to wait, wait. Around midday something happens that I have been expecting to happen. One of the recruits cracks. I have been watching him for a long time, seeing the way he has been constantly grinding his teeth and clenching and unclenching his fists. We are all too familiar with those hunted, wild eyes. In the last few hours he seems to have quietened down, but it isn't real. He has collapsed in on himself like a tree that is rotten inside.

Now he gets up and creeps quietly through the dugout, then rushes for the door. I turn over on to my side and ask, 'Where are you off to?'

'I won't be a minute,' he says, and tries to get past me.

'Hang on for a while, the shelling is already dying down a bit.'

He listens and his eyes clear for a moment. Then they take on that dull shine again, just like a rabid dog, and he pushes me aside without saying anything.

'Just a minute, chum!' I shout. Kat sees what is going on. As the recruit pushes me, Kat grabs him and we hold on to him tightly.

Straight away he begins to rave. 'Let go of me, let me out, I have to get out of here!'

He won't listen, and flails out, spitting out words that are gurgling nonsense. It's claustrophobia from being in the dugout, he feels that he is suffocating and has one basic urge: to get outside. If we let him go he'd run off somewhere and not take cover. He isn't the first.

Because he is raging and his eyes are rolling, there is nothing for it but to hit him, so that he comes to himself. We do so quickly and without mercy and manage to get him sitting quietly again for the time being. The others turn pale when they see all this; let's hope it scares them off doing the same. This concentrated artillery fire is too much for the poor lads; they've come straight from the recruiting depot into a bombardment that would give grey hairs even to one of the old hands.

The stifling air in the dugout gets on our nerves even more after this incident. It's as if we were sitting in our own grave, just waiting for someone to bury us.

Suddenly there is a terrible noise and flash of light, and every joint in the dugout creaks under the impact of a direct hit – luckily not a heavy one, and one that the concrete blocks could withstand. There is a fearsome metallic rattling, the walls shake, rifles, steel helmets, earth, mud and dust fly around. Sulphurous fumes penetrate the walls. If we had been in one of the light shelters that they are building these days, instead of our solid dugout, we'd all be dead by now.

But even so the effect it has is bad enough. The recruit who had the fit earlier is raving again, and two more have joined in. One breaks away and runs for it. We have trouble holding the other two. I rush out after the one who ran away and I wonder if I should shoot him in the leg; then there is a whistling noise, I throw myself flat, and when I get up there are fragments of hot shrapnel, scraps of flesh and torn pieces of uniform spattered on the walls of the trench. I scramble back inside.

The first recruit seems to have gone completely crazy. If we let go of him he butts his head against the wall like a goat. Tonight we shall have to try to get him back into the rear zone. For the moment we tie him up securely, but in such a way that we can release him if there is an attack.

Kat suggests a game of cards; what else can we do, perhaps it will make things easier? But it is no good, we are listening to every impact that sounds close, we lose count and we lead the wrong suits. We have to give up. It's as if we were sitting inside a massive echoing metal boiler that is being pounded on every side.

Another night. The tension has worn us out. It is a deadly tension that feels as if a jagged knife blade is being scraped along the spine. Our legs won't function, our hands are trembling and our bodies are like thin membranes stretched over barely repressed madness, holding in what would otherwise be an unrestrained outburst of endless screams. We have no flesh, no muscles now, we cannot even look at one another for fear of seeing the unimaginable. And so we press our lips together tightly – it has to stop, it has to stop – perhaps we'll get through it all.

★

Suddenly there are no more close explosions. The shelling goes on, but it has drawn back a little, our trench is clear. We grab hold of our hand-grenades, heave them out in front of the dugout and then leap out. The constant artillery fire has stopped, but in its place there is heavy defensive fire from behind us. It is the attack.

Nobody would believe that there could still be human beings in this churned-up wilderness; but everywhere steel helmets are appearing from the trenches, and fifty yards from us a machine-gun has already been set up and starts to bark away.

The wire entanglements have been torn to bits. Even so, the wire is still holding up in places. We can see the attackers coming. Our big guns fire, machine-guns rattle, rifles crack. They are working their way across and on to us. Haie and Kropp start on the grenades. They throw them as fast as they can, and the grenades are handed to them ready primed. Haie throws them sixty yards, Kropp fifty – this has been tested and it is important. The men from the other side can't do much until they are within thirty yards of us.

We recognize the distorted faces and the flattened helmets – it's the French. They reach what is left of our wire and already they've clearly had losses. A whole line of them is wiped out by the machine-gun near us; but then it starts to jam, and they move in closer.

I see one of them run into a knife-rest, his face lifted upwards. His body slumps, and his hands stay caught, raised up as if he is praying. Then the body falls away completely and only the shot-off hands and the stumps of the arms are left hanging in the wire.

In the seconds when we turn to go back, three faces come up from the ground in front of us. Beneath one of the helmets there is a dark moustache and two eyes which are fixed on me. I raise my arm, but I can't throw a grenade towards those strange eyes, and for one crazy moment the whole battle rages round me and round those two eyes like a circus, then the head looks up, there is a hand, a movement, and my grenade flies across and into them.

We run back, pull the wooden wire-cradles into the trench and toss primed grenades behind us, to ensure fire cover to the rear. The machine-guns are firing from the next post.

We have turned into dangerous animals. We are not fighting, we are defending ourselves from annihilation. We are not hurling our grenades against human beings – what do we know about all that in the heat of the moment? – the hands and the helmets that are after us belong to Death himself, and for the first time in three days we are able to look Death in the eyes, for the first time in three days we can defend ourselves against it, we are maddened with fury, not lying there waiting impotently for the executioner any more, we can destroy and we can kill to save ourselves, to save ourselves and to take revenge.

We squat down behind every corner, behind every wire-cradle, and throw exploding bundles at the feet of those coming at us before we get away. The blast of our hand-grenades strikes hard against our legs and arms as we run, stooping like cats, swept by the wave that carries us onwards, the wave that makes us cruel, makes us into highwaymen, into murderers, I suppose into devils, this wave which multiplies our strength in fear and fury and the urge to live, which seeks and fights for a way out for us. If your own father came across with those from the other side you wouldn't hesitate to hurl a hand-grenade straight at him!

We've given up the front-line trenches. Are they still trenches at all? They have been shot to pieces, destroyed – there are just odd sections of trench, craters linked to one another by shallow communication alleys, groups of shell holes, nothing else. But the numbers of losses from the other side are increasing. They didn't reckon on so much resistance.

★

It is getting on for midday. The sun burns down and sweat stings our eyes, and when we wipe it away on our sleeves there is often blood there, too. We make it back to the first of our better maintained trenches. It is manned and ready to withstand the counter-attack, and the men take us in. Our artillery gets going at full blast and makes an attack impossible.

The lines of men following us have to stop. They can't move forwards. Their attack is cut to pieces by our artillery. We lie in wait. The shellfire lifts a hundred yards and we go over the top again. Right next to me a lance-corporal gets his head blown off. He runs on for a few paces more with blood shooting up out of his neck like a fountain.

It doesn't come to hand-to-hand fighting. The others are forced back. We get back to our original bits of trench and then go on beyond them.

God, this turning! You get to the protection of the reserve trenches and you just want to crawl into them and disappear; but you have to turn around and go back into the terror. If we hadn't turned into automata at this moment we would have just lain down, exhausted, stripped of any will to go on. But we are dragged along forwards again with everyone else, unwilling but crazed, wild and raging, we want to kill, because now the others are our deadly enemies, their grenades and rifles are aimed at us, and if we don't destroy them they will destroy us.

The brown earth, the torn and mangled brown earth, shimmering greasily under the sun's rays, becomes a backdrop for our dulled and ever-moving automatic actions, our harsh breathing is the rasping of the clockwork, our lips are dry and our heads feel worse than after a night's hard drinking – and so we stumble onwards, while into our bullet-ridden, shot-through souls the image of the brown earth insinuates itself painfully, the brown earth with the greasy sun and the dead or twitching soldiers, who lie there as if that were perfectly normal, and who grab at our legs and scream as we try to jump over them.

We have lost all feelings for others, we barely recognize each other when somebody else comes into our line of vision, agitated as we are. We are dead men with no feelings, who are able by some trick, some dangerous magic, to keep on running and keep on killing.

A young Frenchman falls behind, we catch up with him, he raises his hands and he still has a revolver in one of them – we don't know if he wants to shoot or to surrender. A blow with an entrenching tool splits his face in two. A second Frenchman sees this and tries to get away, and a bayonet hisses into his back. He leaps in the air and then stumbles away, his arms outstretched and his mouth wide open in a scream, the bayonet swaying in his back. A third throws down his rifle and cowers with his hands over his eyes. He stays behind with a few other prisoners-of-war, to help carry off the wounded.

Suddenly in our pursuit we reach the enemy lines.

We are so close behind our fleeing opponents that we get there at almost the same time as they do. Because of that, we don't have too many casualties. A machine-gun barks out, but is silenced with a hand-grenade. All the same, those few seconds were enough for five of our men to get stomach wounds. With the butt of his rifle, Kat smashes to pulp the face of one of the machine-gunners, who hasn't been wounded. We bayonet the others before they can get their grenades out. Then we gulp down thirstily the water they have been using to cool their gun.

All around there is the clicking of wire-cutters, planks are manhandled across the entanglements and we jump through the narrow gaps into the trenches. Haie hits a massive Frenchman in the throat with his spade and throws the first hand-grenade; for a second or so we duck down behind a parapet, and then the straight section of trench in front of us is empty. The next throw whistles over the corner of the trench and gives us clear passage, and as we go past we toss explosives into the dugouts; the earth shakes, creaking, smoking and groaning, we stumble on over slippery fragments of flesh, over soft bodies; I fall into a belly that has been ripped open, and on the body is a new, clean, French officer's cap.

The fighting stops. We lose our contact with the enemy. Since we can't hold out here for a long time, we are brought back to our original position under covering fire from our artillery. We hardly know what we are doing as we dive into the nearest dugout to grab what we can of any provisions that we happen to see before we get away, especially tins of corned beef.

We get back in one piece. For the moment there are no more attacks from over there. We lie on the ground for more than an hour, getting our breath and resting, before anyone says anything. We are so completely done in that we don't even think of the tinned beef, even though we are ravenously hungry. Only gradually do we turn into something like human beings again.

The corned beef that they get on the other side is famous all along the front. Occasionally it serves as the main reason for a surprise raid from our side, because our provisions are generally bad; we are always hungry.

We've got hold of five tins altogether. Those people over there get looked after well, it's the lap of luxury compared to us lot here in hungry corner, with our turnip jam – on the other side the beef is just sitting around, all you need to do is take it. Haie has also snaffled a thin loaf of French white bread and tucked it in his belt like a spade. There's a bit of blood on one end of it, but that can be cut off.

It's lucky that we've got some decent food to eat now; we'll still need all our strength. Having a full belly is just as important as a good dugout; that's why we are so keen to get hold of food, because it can save our lives.

Tjaden has even managed to get hold of a couple of water bottles full of cognac. We pass them round.

★

The evening benediction starts. Night falls, and mist rises out of the shell holes. It looks as if the craters are full of ghostly secrets. The white vapour creeps around fearfully before it dares to float up over the edge and away. Then long streaks drift from one shell hole to the next.

It's cold. I'm on look-out, staring into the darkness. I feel limp and drained, just like I always do after an attack, and so I find it hard to be alone with my own thoughts. They are not really thoughts; they are memories that come to torment me in my weakness and put me into a strange mood.

Up go the Verey lights – and I see a picture of a summer evening, and I'm in the cloistered courtyard of the cathedral looking at the tall rose trees that grow in the middle of the little garden there, where the deans of the chapter are buried. All around are stone carvings for the different stations of the cross. There is nobody there; this flower-filled square is caught up in a profound silence, the sun shines warm on the thick grey stones, I place my hand on one and feel the warmth. Above the right-hand end of the cloister's slate roof the green spire of the cathedral rises up into the pale blue wash of the evening sky. Between the slender sunlit columns of the cloisters themselves is that cool darkness that only churches have, and I am standing there and thinking that by the time I am twenty I shall have learnt the secret of the confusion that women cause in men's minds.

The picture is astonishingly close, it touches me before it dissolves under the flash of the next Verey light.

I grip my rifle and hold it properly upright. The barrel is wet, and I put my hand round it and wipe off the dampness with my fingers.

Between the meadows behind our home town there was a row of old poplar trees that rose up by the side of a stream. You could see them from a long way off, and although they were actually only along one side, the place was still known as the poplar avenue. Even when we were children it was a favourite place and those poplars had an inexplicable attraction for us, so that we used to spend whole days there listening to their gentle rustling. We used to sit beneath them on the banks of the stream and dangle our feet in the bright, fast-moving eddies. The clean scent of the water and the song of the wind in the poplars captured our imagination. We really loved them, and picturing those days still makes my heart race, before the image vanishes again.

It is a strange thing that all the memories have these two qualities. They are always full of quietness, that is the most striking thing about them; and even when things weren't like that in reality, they still seem to have that quality. They are soundless apparitions, which speak to me by looks and gestures, wordless and silent – and their silence is precisely what disturbs me, forces me to hold on to my sleeve or my rifle so that I don't abandon myself to this seductive dissolution, in which my body would like to disperse itself and flow away towards the silent powers that lie behind all things.

The pictures are so silent because that is something which is quite incomprehensible to us. There is no silence at the front and the spell of the front is so strong that we are never away from it. Even in the depots way behind the lines, or in the rest areas, the buzz and the muted thundering of the shellfire is always in our ears. We are never so far away that we can't hear it any more. But in the last few days it has been unbearable.

The quietness is the reason why all these images awaken in us not so much desire as sadness – a vast and inexplicable melancholy. The scenes existed once – but they will never return. They are gone, they are another world, a world that is in the past for us. When we were doing our basic training, those scenes called up in us a wild and rebellious longing, they were still a part of us then, we belonged to them and they to us, even if we had been taken away from them. They rose up out of the soldiers' songs that we sang, when we marched off to the heath for exercises on the long, long trail a-winding between the red rays of dawn and the black silhouettes of the forest, they were still a strong memory then, a memory that was inside us and came from within us.

But here in the trenches we have lost that memory. It no longer rises up from inside us – we are dead and the memory is far off on some distant horizon, an apparition, a puzzling reflection come to haunt us, something we are afraid of and which we love without hope. It is strong, and our desire is strong; but it is unattainable, and we know it. It is just as impossible as the chance of becoming a general.

And even if someone were to give us it back, that landscape of our youth, we wouldn't have much idea of how to handle it. The tender, secret forces that bound it to us cannot come back to life. We should be in the landscape, wandering around; we should remember, and love it, and be moved by the sight of it. But it would be just the same as when we see a photograph of one of our friends who has been killed, and we stop to think about it. The features are his, the face is his, and the days we spent with him take on a deceptive life in our memories; but it isn't really him.

Nowadays we would no longer have any real links with the way we used to be. It wasn't the awareness of how beautiful it was that meant so much to us, or of how good the atmosphere was, but the feeling of community, the way we all felt a kinship with the objects and events of our existence. That's what set us apart and made our parents' world a little difficult for us to understand; because somehow we were always gently bound up with that world, submissive to it all, and the smallest thing led us onwards along the path of eternity. Perhaps it was just the privilege of our youth – we were not yet able to see any restrictions, and we could not admit to ourselves that things would ever come to an end; expectation was in our blood, and this meant that we were at one with our lives as the days went by.

Now we would wander around like strangers in those landscapes of our youth. We have been consumed in the fires of reality, we perceive differences only in the way tradesmen do, and we see necessities like butchers. We are free of care no longer – we are terrifyingly indifferent. We might be present in that world, but would we be alive in it?

We are like children who have been abandoned and we are as experienced as old men, we are coarse, unhappy and superficial – I think that we are lost.

*

My hands get cold and my flesh shivers; even though it is a warm night. Only the mist is chilly, that ghastly mist that creeps across the dead men in front of us and sucks out their last, concealed scraps of life. By tomorrow they will be green and pallid and their blood will be thickened and black.

The Verey lights are still shooting upwards and throwing their merciless glare over the stony landscape, which is full of craters and a shining coldness, like some dead moon. The blood beneath my skin brings fear and disquiet into my thoughts. They become weak, they tremble, they need warmth and life. They cannot survive without comfort and illusion, they become confused in the face of naked despair.

I hear mess-tins rattling, and at once I have a fierce desire for hot food, which will do me good and calm me down. With some difficulty I force myself to wait until I am relieved.

Then I go into the dugout and get hold of a mug of barley broth. The pearl barley has been cooked in fat and tastes good, and I eat it slowly. But I keep to myself, even though the others are in better spirits now that the shelling has died down.

⋆

The days roll by and every hour is incomprehensible and matter of fact at the same time. Attacks alternate with counter-attacks and slowly the dead pile up between the trenches in no man's land. We can usually get out and fetch back any wounded men that aren't too far away. Some have to lie there for a long time, though, and we listen to them dying.

We search for one of them for two whole days, in vain. He must be lying face downwards, and can't turn over. It's the only explanation for why we can't find him; because only when someone is screaming with his mouth close to the ground does it make it hard to gauge the direction.

He'll have one of the worst sort of wounds, one of those that are not so bad as to weaken the body quickly and let you just drift off in a half-numbed state, but not so light that you can bear the pain with any reasonable expectation of getting over it. Kat reckons that either his pelvis has been shattered, or he has been hit in the spine. He says that his chest can't have been hit, or he wouldn't have so much strength to scream, but if he had some other kind of wound you would be able to see him moving.

Gradually he gets hoarser. His voice sounds so weird that it could come from anywhere. Three times during the first night groups of our men go out there. But every time they think they have the right direction and are crawling towards him, the next time they hear his voice it is coming from somewhere else. We search in vain until it starts to get light. During the daytime we scan the area with field glasses; not a trace. By the second day the man is quieter, and you can tell that his throat and lips are parched.

Our company commander has promised priority leave and three extra days to anyone who finds him. That is a huge incentive, but even without it we would do all we could anyway; the shouting is so awful. Kat and Kropp even make another sortie during the afternoon. In the process Kropp gets an earlobe shot off. But it is no use, and they come back without him.

And on top of it all you can hear quite clearly what he is shouting. At first he just screamed for help all the time – then in the second night he must have become feverish, because he is talking to his wife and children, and we can pick out the name Elise. Today he is just crying. Towards evening the voice dies away to just a croak. But he groans softly all through the night. We can hear him so clearly because the wind is blowing towards our trench. In the morning, when we think he must have gone to his rest long since, we hear a gurgling rattle once again.

The days are hot and the dead lie unburied. We can't fetch them all, and we don't know where to put them. The shells bury them for us. Quite often their bellies swell up like balloons. They hiss, belch and move because of the gases which are rumbling about inside them.

The sky is blue and cloudless. In the evenings it becomes oppressive, and the heat rises out of the ground. When the wind is in our direction it brings the smell of blood, heavy, and with a repulsive sweetness, a waft of death breathing out of the shell holes, a smell that seems to be composed of a mixture of chloroform and decomposition, and which makes us feel faint, or makes us vomit.

*

The nights turn quiet, and the hunt for copper driving bands from shells, or for the silk parachutes from French rocket flares starts up. Nobody really knows why the driving bands are so eagerly sought after. The men who collect them simply declare that they are valuable. There are people who hump so many of these away with them that they are bent and staggering under their weight when we withdraw.

Haie at least gives a reason for collecting them: he wants to send them to his girlfriend as a substitute for garters. When they hear this, there is naturally a great outburst of merriment among the other lads from his part of the world; they slap their thighs – 'That's a good 'un, bloody hell, old Haie, he's a sharp one and no mistake!' Of all of them, Tjaden is the one who just can't stop laughing; he's got the biggest of the driving bands and is forever sticking his leg through it to show how much room there is to spare. 'Christ, Haie, she must have a pair of thighs, thighs!'

And mentally he moves up a bit – 'and a bum, too, she must have a bum like – like an elephant's.'

He can't get over it. 'I wouldn't mind a bit of slap and tickle with her, not half I wouldn't –'

Haie beams to hear his girlfriend getting all this acclaim, and says in a self-satisfied and succinct manner, 'Oh aye, she's a big lass.'

The silk parachutes are of greater practical value. Three or four will make up a blouse, depending on bust size. Kropp and I use them for handkerchiefs. The others send them home. If their womenfolk could see the risks that the men sometimes take fetching these flimsy rags it would really give them a shock.

Kat catches Tjaden trying to hammer the driving band off a dud shell, calm as you please. With anyone else, the thing would have exploded, but Tjaden is lucky – he always is.

For the whole morning two butterflies have been playing around our trench. They are brimstones, and their yellow wings have orange spots on them. I wonder what could have brought them here? There are no plants or flowers for miles. They settle on the teeth of a skull. The birds are just as carefree as the butterflies, because they have long since got used to the war. Every morning larks rise between the two front-line trenches. A year ago we watched them nesting, and they even brought up a brood of young ones.

For the time being our trenches are free of rats. They have moved up ahead, and we know why. They are getting fat; whenever we see one, we shoot it. At night we hear once again the rolling noises from over there. During the day we just get ordinary shellfire, so we have a chance to sort out our trenches. There is also a certain amount of entertainment – the airmen see to that. Every day the audience can watch any number of dogfights.

We don't mind the fighter planes, but we hate the reconnaissance aircraft like the plague; they are the ones that direct the artillery fire towards us. A few moments after they appear there is a hail of shrapnel and shells. Because of that we lose eleven men in a single day, five stretcher-bearers amongst them. Two are so smashed up that Tjaden reckons you could scrape them off the trench wall with a spoon and bury them in a mess-tin. Another one has his legs and the lower part of his body torn off. He's dead, leaning with his chest against the trench wall, his face is bright yellow and there is a cigarette glowing between his bearded lips. It carries on glowing until it burns down to his lips, then goes out with a hiss.

For the moment we place the dead into a huge shell hole. They are three deep so far.

*

Suddenly the shelling starts to thunder again. Soon we are sitting there, tense and rigid once more in that helpless waiting.

Attack, counter-attack, charge, counter-strike – they are all just words, but what is contained in them. We lose a lot of men, mainly recruits. Fresh troops are being sent into our sector again. They are from one of the newly raised regiments, almost exclusively young men from the latest age group to be drafted. They've had hardly any training, nothing more than a bit of theory, before they were sent up the line. For example, they know what a hand-grenade is, but they have no idea about taking cover, and above all else they can't spot things. A ridge has to be two feet high before they can make it out.

Even though we desperately need reinforcements, the new recruits almost make more trouble for us than they are worth. In this sector, where we are under heavy attack, they are helpless and go down like flies. Modern trench warfare demands knowledge and experience, you have to have a good grasp of the lie of the land, have the sounds and effects of the different shells in your ear, you have to be able to work out in advance where they are going to land, what the scatter will be like, how to take cover.

These young recruits, of course, know as good as nothing about all that. They are decimated because they can't tell shrapnel from high explosive, and they are mown down because they are listening in terror to the howl of the great coal-box shells, which aren't dangerous because they are coming down way behind us, but don't hear the whistling noise, the quiet whirring of the little bastards with the low lateral spread. They huddle together like sheep instead of fanning out, and even the wounded are picked off like rabbits by the fighter planes.

The pale, turnip faces, the pitifully clenched hands, the wretched bravery of these poor devils, who advance and attack regardless, these poor plucky devils, who have been so browbeaten that they don't even dare to scream out, and just whimper softly for their mothers as they lie there with their chests and guts and arms and legs torn to pieces, and shut up when someone comes along.

Their dead, downy, thin-featured faces have that awful absence of any expression that you see in dead children.

You get a lump in your throat when you see them, the way they go over, and run, and drop. You want to thrash them for being so stupid, and pick them up and take them away from here, away from this place where they don't belong. They are wearing battledress, trousers and army boots, but for most of them the uniform is too big and flaps about, their shoulders are too narrow, their bodies too slight; there weren't any uniforms available in these children's sizes.

To every one old soldier, between five and ten of the recruits are killed.

A surprise gas attack carries off a lot of them. They didn't even begin to expect what was waiting for them. We find a whole dugout full of them, their faces blue and their lips black. In one of the shell holes some of them have taken their gas-masks off too soon; they didn't realize that the gas lies longest down at the bottom, and when they saw others without their masks they tore theirs off, and swallowed enough to burn their lungs to pieces. There is no hope for them; they are choking to death, coughing up blood and suffocating.

★

In one section of the trench I suddenly find myself face to face with Himmelstoss. We have taken cover in the same dugout. Everyone is lying down out of breath, waiting for the advance.

Although I am pretty agitated, when I rush out one thought still comes into my head: I can't see Himmelstoss. I dive back quickly into the dugout and find him in the corner, pretending to be wounded, even though he only has a slight scratch. His face looks as if he has been beaten up. It's shell shock – after all, he is new here. But it makes me mad that the young recruits are outside and he is down here.

'Out!' I shout.

He doesn't move. His lips quiver, his moustache twitches.

'Out!' I shout again.

He pulls his legs in, presses himself against the wall and bares his teeth like a mad dog.

I grab him by the arm and try to pull him up. He makes a

strangled noise. Then something in me snaps. I grab him by the shoulders and shake him like a sack, so that his head swings backwards and forwards, and scream into his face, 'You shit, get out of here – you little shit, you bastard, trying to hide, are you?' His eyes glaze over, and I bang his head against the wall – 'You sod' – I hit him in the ribs – 'You swine' – I shove him forwards, headfirst out of the dugout.

Just at that moment a new wave of troops comes over. They have a lieutenant with them. He sees us and shouts, 'Move on, move on, close up, close up –' and his command does what my blows couldn't manage. Himmelstoss hears the superior officer, looks around as if he has just woken up, and runs to catch up.

I follow on, and see him bounding along, the old, smart, parade-ground Himmelstoss again, who has even overtaken the lieutenant and is away out in front . . .

*

Continuous fire, defensive fire, curtain fire, trench mortars, gas, tanks, machine-guns, hand-grenades – words, words, but they embrace all the horrors of the world.

Our faces are crusted with dirt, our thoughts are a shambles, we are dead tired; when the attack comes, a lot of our men have to be punched hard so that they wake up and go along; our eyes are red and swollen, our hands are ripped, our knees are bleeding and our elbows raw.

Is it weeks that pass – or months – or years? It is only days. We watch how time disappears before our eyes in the ashen faces of the dying, we shovel food into ourselves, we run, we throw, we shoot, we kill, we hurl ourselves down, we are weak and dulled, and the only thing that keeps us going is that there are even weaker, even more dulled, even more helpless men than us who look at us wide-eyed, and take us for gods who can sometimes outrun death himself.

In the few rest periods we try to teach them. 'Look, see that one like a toffee-apple? That's a mortar coming across. Keep down, it'll go over us. But if it comes your way, get the hell out! You can run away from those.'

We make sure that they can hear the malicious buzz of the little ones that you barely notice – they have to learn to recognize a sound like the buzzing of flies amongst all the noise. We teach them that these are much more dangerous than the big ones that you can hear long before. We show them how to hide from airmen, how to play dead when they are overtaken by an attack, how to prime a hand-grenade so that it explodes half a second before impact. We teach them to dive for cover as fast as they can into a shell hole when they see a shell with an instantaneous fuse, and we demonstrate for them how to clean out a whole trench with a handful of grenades. We teach them the difference in the detonation time between enemy hand-grenades and ours, make sure they know what a gas shell sounds like, and show them all the tricks that might just save them from being killed.

They listen obediently – but when it all starts they are usually so worked up that they get it wrong again after all.

Haie Westhus is carried off with his back torn open; you can see the lung throbbing through the wound with every breath he takes. I manage to take his hand – 'That's me done for, Paul,' he groans, and bites his arm because of the pain.

We see men go on living with the top of their skulls missing; we see soldiers go on running when both their feet have been shot away – they stumble on their splintering stumps to the next shell hole. One lance-corporal crawls for a full half-mile on his hands, dragging his legs behind him, with both knees shattered. Another man makes it to a dressing station with his guts spilling out over his hands as he holds them in. We see soldiers with their mouths missing, with their lower jaws missing, with their faces missing; we find someone who has gripped the main artery in his arm between his teeth for two hours so that he doesn't bleed to death. The sun goes down, night falls, the shells whistle, life comes to an end.

The scrap of churned-up earth where we are has been held against superior forces, and we have only had to give up a few hundred yards. But for every one of those yards there is a dead man.

*

Relief troops take over from us. The truck wheels roll along beneath us, we stand numbed, and when they shout, 'Mind the wire!' we bob down. It was summer when we came past here, the trees were still green, but now they have begun to look autumnal, and the night is grey and damp. The trucks stop. We climb down, a ragged bunch, all that there is left of a whole list of names. In the dark to either side of us there are people calling out the numbers of regiments and companies. And with every shout a little handful moves away from the rest, a sparse, tiny handful of dirty, pallid soldiers, a terribly small handful, a terribly small remainder.

Then someone shouts out the number of our company – we can hear that it is our company commander, so he must have made it; his arm is in a sling. We move towards him and I pick out Kat and Albert, we join together, prop each other up and look at each other.

And we hear our number called again, and then again. He can go on calling, but they won't hear him in the clearing stations or out in no man's land.

Again: 'B company over here!'

And then more quietly: 'Nobody else from B Company?'

He is silent, and then his voice sounds hoarse when he asks, 'Is that all?' Then he gives the command: 'Number off!'

It is a grey morning. It was still summer when we went up the line and there were a hundred and fifty of us. Now we are shivering. It is autumn, the leaves rustle, the voices are tired as they call out: 'One – two – three – four –' and they are silent after thirty-two. And there is a long silence before the voice asks, 'Any more?' – and waits a bit and then says quietly, 'By squads . . .' but then breaks down, and can only finish the command with, 'B Company –' painfully, – 'B Company – march at ease.'

A line, a short line, stumbles off into the morning.

Thirty-two men.

7

They take us back further behind the line than usual, back to an infantry base depot, so that they can get our company up to strength. We need more than a hundred men.

For the moment we just idle around when we are off duty. After a couple of days Himmelstoss comes over to talk to us. He has changed his high and mighty attitude since being in the trenches. He suggests a truce with us, and I am willing, because I saw how he carried Haie Westhus out of the fighting when his back had been ripped apart. Besides, now that he talks to us sensibly, we have no objections to him standing us a drink in the canteen. Only Tjaden is suspicious and keeps his distance.

But even he is won over when Himmelstoss tells us that he's going to be standing in for the ginger-headed cook, who's off on leave. To prove it he comes up with two pounds of sugar for us and half a pound of butter just for Tjaden. He even arranges for us to be detailed to the kitchens for the next three days to peel potatoes and turnips. The food he gives us there is one hundred per cent officers' mess quality.

So at the moment we've got the two things any soldier needs to keep him happy: good food and rest. It isn't much, when you think about it. A few years ago we would really have despised ourselves. Now we are pretty well content. You can get used to anything – even being in the trenches.

This habit of getting used to things is the reason that we seem to forget so quickly. The day before yesterday we were still under fire, today we are fooling about, seeing what we can scrounge around here, tomorrow we'll be back in the trenches. In fact we don't really forget anything. All the time we are out here the days at the front sink into us like stones the moment they are over, because they are too much for us to think about right away. If we even tried, they would kill us. Because one thing has become clear to me: you can cope with all the horror as long as you simply duck thinking about it – but it will kill you if you try to come to terms with it.

In the same way that we turn into animals when we go up the line, because it is the only way we can survive, when we are back behind the lines we become superficial jokers and idlers. We can't do anything about it – it's compulsive. We want to go on living at any price, and therefore we can't burden ourselves with emotions that might be all very nice to have in peacetime, but are out of place here. Kemmerich is dead, Haie Westhus is dying, there'll be a few problems with Hans Kramer's body on Judgement Day when they try to resurrect what was left after the shell hit him, Martens lost both legs, Meyer is dead, Marks is dead, Beyer is dead, Hammerling is dead, a hundred and twenty men are lying out there somewhere with a bullet in them. It's all a bloody business, but what's that got to do with us – we're alive. If it were possible to save them – well, then you should just watch us, we wouldn't care if we got it ourselves, we'd just go at it, because we've got plenty of guts when we need them; we don't have much in the way of ordinary fear – we're afraid of death, of course, but that's different, that's physical.

But our mates *are* dead, and we can't help them. They are at peace – who knows what we might still have to face? We want to chuck ourselves down and sleep, or stuff as much food into our bellies as we can, and booze and smoke, so that the passing hours aren't so empty. Life is short.

★

The horror of the front fades away when you turn your back on it, so we can attack it with coarse or black humour. When someone is dead we say he's 'pushing up the daisies', and we talk about everything the same way, to save ourselves from going mad; as long as we can take things like that we are actually fighting back.

But we do not forget. All that stuff in the war issues of the papers about the wonderful cheeriness of the troops, who start arranging little tea-dances the minute they get back from being under heavy fire in the line, is complete rubbish. It isn't because we are naturally cheerful that we make jokes, it's just that we keep cheerful because if we didn't, we'd be done for. All the same, it can't hold all that much longer – the jokes get more bitter with every month that passes.

One thing I do know: everything that is sinking into us like a stone now, while we are in the war, will rise up again when the war is over, and that's when the real life-and-death struggle will start.

The days, the weeks, the years spent out here will come back to us again, and our dead comrades in arms will rise again and march with us, our heads will be clear and we will have an aim in life, and with our dead comrades beside us and the years we spent in the line behind us we shall march forward – but against whom, against whom?

★

A while ago there was a concert party for the troops near here. Coloured posters advertising the performance are still stuck up on a hoarding. Kropp and I stand and gaze wide-eyed at one of them. We can't imagine that such things still exist. The picture is of a girl in a light summer frock with a shiny red belt around her waist. She is standing with one hand resting on a low balustrade, and she is holding a straw hat in the other. She is wearing white stockings and white shoes, elegant shoes with buckles and high heels. Behind her is the sea, bright blue and shining, dotted with white-crested waves, and over to one side of her you can make out the curve of a sunlit bay. The girl is beautiful, with a little nose, red lips and long legs, unbelievably clean and tidy – she must take two baths a day, and her fingernails surely never have any dirt under them – at the worst a bit of sand from the beach.

Next to her stands a man in white slacks with a blue jacket and a yachting cap, but he doesn't interest us nearly as much.

For us, the girl on the poster is a miracle. We have forgotten completely that such things exist, and even now we can scarcely believe our eyes. At any rate, we haven't seen anything like this for years, nothing remotely approaching this for light-heartedness, beauty and happiness. We get the churned-up feeling that this is it, this is what peace must be like.

'Just look at those flimsy shoes – she wouldn't be able to march for many miles in them!' I say, and then at once I feel stupid, because it is ridiculous to think about marching when you are looking at a picture like that.

'How old do you reckon she is?' asks Kropp.

I have a guess: 'Twenty-two at the most, Albert.'

'She'd be older than us, then, wouldn't she? I bet she's no more than seventeen.'

Our flesh tingles. 'Albert, that would be a bit of all right, wouldn't it?'

He nods. 'I've got a pair of white slacks at home, too.'

'White slacks are one thing,' I say, 'but a girl like that . . .'

We look each other up and down. Not much of a picture there, two faded, darned and dirty uniforms. It is hopeless comparing ourselves with her.

The first thing we do is to tear the picture of the young man off the hoarding, taking great care not to damage the girl. At least that's a start. Then Kropp suggests, 'Why don't we go and get deloused?'

I am a bit dubious about it, because it damages your stuff and the lice are back within a couple of hours anyway. But after we have gazed at the picture again, I agree. I even go a step further: 'We might see if we could get our hands on a clean shirt from somewhere –'

For some reason Albert reckons, 'Socks would be even better.'

'Maybe socks as well. We could scrounge around a bit.'

At that point Leer and Tjaden wander over; they see the poster and within seconds the conversation gets pretty lewd. Leer was the first one in our class at school to have a girlfriend and he used to tell us interesting details. His enthusiastic comments about the picture are quite specific and Tjaden joins in vigorously.

It doesn't really bother us. You can't have soldiers without a bit of dirty talk; it's just that we aren't really in the mood for it at the moment, so we clear off, and quick-march ourselves across to the delousing station, feeling as if we're heading for some high-class and fashionable gents' outfitters.

★

Our billets are in houses close to the canal. On the far side of the canal there are ponds with poplar trees around them – and on the far side of the canal there are women as well.

The houses on our side have been emptied. Sometimes you still see local people in the houses on the other side.

In the evenings we go for a swim. Three women come walking along the canal bank. They walk slowly and they don't look away, even though we aren't wearing any trunks.

Leer shouts across to them. They laugh, and stop to have a look at us. We shout across any broken French that comes into our heads, all mixed-up and hurried, just so that they don't go away. The things we shout are not exactly drawing-room pleasantries, but where would we have picked up that sort of vocabulary anyway?

One of the women is slim and dark. You can see her teeth gleaming when she laughs. Her movements are quick, and her skirt blows loosely against her legs. Even though it is cold in the water we are very excited and do our best to keep them interested, so that they don't go away. We try jokes on them, and they answer us, even though we don't understand. We laugh and wave. Tjaden has more sense. He runs back to our quarters, grabs an army-ration loaf and holds it up.

This has a great effect. They nod and beckon us to come across the canal. But we are not allowed to do that. The far side of the canal is strictly out of bounds. There are sentries on all the bridges. You can't do anything without a pass. We make them understand that they should come over to us; but they shake their heads and point to the bridges. The sentries won't let them through either.

They turn round and start to walk slowly along the canal, still keeping to the towpath. We swim along with them. After a couple of hundred yards they turn off and point to a house that is a bit apart, with trees and bushes round it. Leer asks if that is where they live.

They laugh – yes, that is their house.

We shout across that we'll come when the sentries can't see us. At night. Tonight.

They put their hands together, rest them against their cheeks and shut their eyes. They understood. The slim dark one does a few dance steps. A blonde girl trills, 'Bread. . . good . . .'

We reassure them hurriedly that we will bring some with us. And other nice things as well – we roll our eyes and try to show them in sign language. Leer nearly drowns trying to indicate 'some sausage'. If we had to, we would promise them an entire supply depot. Then they go, although they turn back and look at us several times. We climb on to the bank on our side of the canal and make sure that they go into the house, just in case they were tricking us. Then we swim back up the canal.

No one is allowed across the bridge without a permit, so we shall just have to swim over after dark. We are in a state of great excitement and it doesn't subside. We can't sit still and wait in one place, so we go to the canteen. They have beer in, and there is also some kind of punch.

We drink the punch and tell each other fantastic lies about our experiences. Everyone is happy to believe everyone else, and we all wait impatiently for our chance to trump the last story with an even taller one. We can't keep our hands still, we smoke cigarette after cigarette until Kropp says, 'I suppose we could take them a few cigarettes as well.' Then we put them into our caps to save them.

The sky turns pale green, like an unripe apple. There are four of us, but only three can go – we have to get rid of Tjaden, so we buy him so much of the punch and so much rum that he is staggering. When it gets dark we go back to our quarters, Tjaden in the middle. We are hot and more than ready for the adventure. I'm having the slim, dark girl – we've already sorted that out.

Tjaden collapses on to his palliasse and starts to snore. At one point he wakes up and grins at us so wickedly that we get quite a fright in case he was just shamming, and we bought him all that punch for nothing. Then he falls back and goes to sleep again.

The three of us take a whole loaf each, and we wrap them in newspaper. We put the cigarettes in as well, and three good portions of the sausage we were given this evening. It's a very respectable present.

For the moment we put all the stuff into our boots; we have to take boots with us so that we don't step on barbed-wire or glass over on the other side. Since we have to swim first, we can't take any other clothes. Anyway, it is dark, and we aren't going far.

We set off, boots in hand. We slip quickly into the water, turn on to our backs and swim that way, holding the boots and their contents up over our heads.

We climb out carefully when we get to the other side, take out the packages, and put on our boots. We stick the things we've brought under our arms. And off we trot, wet, naked, wearing nothing but our boots. We find the house at once. It stands dark in the bushes. Leer trips over a tree root and takes the skin off his elbow. 'Doesn't matter,' he says cheerfully.

There are shutters on the windows. We creep around the house and try to look through the gaps. Then we get a bit impatient. Kropp is suddenly hesitant, 'What if some major is in there with them?'

'Then we'll just have to bugger off,' says Leer with a grin. 'He can always read off our rank and number down here,' and he smacks himself on the bottom.

The main door of the house is open. Our boots make a bit of a noise. A door opens and there is light, a woman gives a frightened scream. 'Sssh, sssh,' we say, '*camarade, bon ami . . .*' and we lift up the packages in supplication.

By now we can see the other two as well, the door opens wide and we have the light on us. They recognize us, and all three of them collapse into fits of laughter at our get-up. They double up and hold their sides for laughing there in the doorway. How supple their movements are.

'*Un moment* –' They disappear and then throw us various bits and pieces of clothing and we wrap them round ourselves as best we can. Then they let us in. There is a small lamp burning in the room, it is warm, and smells a little of perfume. We unpack our parcels and hand them over to the girls. Their eyes shine, and you can see that they are hungry.

Then we all become a bit embarrassed. Leer mimes eating and things liven up again – they fetch plates and knives and fall upon the food. They hold every single slice of the sausage up to admire it before they eat it, and we sit there proudly watching them.

They babble away at us in their own language – we don't understand a great deal, but we can hear that the words are friendly ones. Perhaps we look very young to them. The slim dark one strokes my hair and says what all French women always say – '*La guerre – grand malheur – pauvres garçons . . .*'

I catch her arm and press my mouth to her palm. Her fingers hold my face. Her fascinating eyes are above me, the pale brown of her skin, her red lips. From her mouth come words that I can't understand. I can't fully understand her eyes, either – they are saying more than we expected when we came here.

There are rooms nearby. As we go out, I catch sight of Leer, who is having a fine old time with the blonde. He knows what he is about, of course. But me – I am lost in feelings of remoteness and quiet turmoil, and I give way to them. My wishes are a curious mixture of desire and abandonment. I become dizzy – there is nothing here that I can hold on to. We left our boots at the door, and they gave us slippers, so that there is nothing there any more that could give me back the soldier's confidence and boldness; no rifle, no belt, no battledress, no cap. I let myself sink into the unknown, let whatever will happen, happen – because in spite of everything, I am afraid.

The slim dark girl moves her eyebrows when she is thinking, but they are still when she talks. Even then, the sounds are sometimes not quite words and they die away or pass half-formed over me in an arc, a path, a comet. What have I ever known about all this – what do I know now? The words of this foreign tongue which I can barely understand lull me to sleep, down into a quietness in which the room dissolves, brown and dimly lit, and only her face above me is alive and clear.

There are so many different things you can see in a face, when only an hour ago it was still that of a stranger, but it now has taken on a tenderness that comes not from inside it, but from the night, the world and the blood – they seem to come together and shine out from it. The objects in the room are touched and transformed by it, they become special, and I can almost respect my own pale skin when the lamp shines on it and it is caressed by that cool, brown hand.

How different all this is from the business in the other-ranks' brothels, the ones we have permission to visit and where you have to stand in long queues. I don't want to think about them; but they come into my head anyway, and it gives me a jolt, because it's possible that you can never get that sort of thing out of your mind.

But then I feel the lips of the slim, dark girl, and push myself against them, close my eyes and try as I do so to wipe it all out, the war and the horror and the pettiness, so that I can wake up young and happy. I think of the girl on the poster and I believe for a moment that my life depends on getting her – and so I press myself deeper into the arms that close around me, hoping that a miracle will happen.

★

Somehow or other we find ourselves all together again. Leer is very lively. We say our passionate goodbyes and slip on our boots. The night air cools our heated bodies. The poplars loom up huge in the darkness and make a rustling noise. The moon is in the sky and in the waters of the canal. We don't run, we stride along side by side.

'That was worth a loaf of bread,' says Leer.

I can't bring myself to speak. I don't even feel happy.

Then we hear footsteps, and duck down behind a bush.

The steps come closer, right past us. We see a naked soldier wearing boots, just like us, galloping along with a parcel under his arm. It is Tjaden, going full steam ahead. He is already out of sight.

We laugh. He'll curse us tomorrow.

We make it unnoticed back to our straw mattresses.

★

I'm called to the orderly room. The company commander gives me a leave pass and a travel pass and tells me to have a good journey. I have a look to see how much leave I've been given. Seventeen days – fourteen days' leave and three for travelling. It isn't enough, and I ask whether I can have five days' travel time. Bertinck points to the leave pass and only then do I notice that I don't have to come straight back to the front. When my leave period is up I have to report to a camp on the moors for a training course.

The others are envious. Kat gives me the sound advice that I ought to try and get a cushy job. 'Play your cards right and you could stay there for the duration.'

As far as I'm concerned it would have been better to get leave in a week's time, because that's how long we are staying here, and it is good here –

Of course I have to stand drinks all round in the canteen. We are all a bit drunk and I get melancholy; I'll be away for six weeks, and of course it is a great stroke of luck for me, but what will it be like when I come back? Will they all still be here? Haie and Kemmerich have gone already – who's going to be next?

We have our drinks and I look at them all one after the other. Albert is sitting next to me and smoking, he is cheerful, we have always been together; Kat is perched opposite him, Kat with his rounded shoulders, broad fingers and calm voice; Müller with his buck teeth and braying laugh; Tjaden with his mousey eyes; Leer, who has grown a beard and looks as if he's forty.

Thick smoke hovers over our heads. Where would the soldier be without tobacco? The canteen is a place of refuge, and beer is more than a drink, it is a sign that here you can stretch your limbs out without danger. And we do – our legs are stretched out before us, and we spit, companionably and vigorously. What an impression all this makes on you when you know you are going on leave the next day!

That night we go over to the other side of the canal again. I am almost afraid to tell the slim dark girl that I am going on leave and that, when I come back, we shall certainly be somewhere further on – so that we shan't see each other again. But she just nods and doesn't seem to react too much. I don't understand properly at first, but then I get it. Leer is right. If I'd been sent to the front, then it would have been *pauvre garçon* again, but going on leave – they don't want to know about that, it isn't as interesting. Well, she can go to hell with her whispering and her words. You believe in a miracle, but really it just comes down to loaves of bread.

After I've been deloused the following morning I march off to the field rail-head. Albert and Kat come with me. When we get to the train stop we hear that it will be a few hours before I can leave. The other two have to go back because they are on duty. We say goodbye.

'Look after yourself, Kat; look after yourself, Albert.'

They leave, waving a couple of times. Their figures get smaller. I know every step, every move they make, I would be able to recognize them miles away. Then they have gone.

I sit down on my pack and wait.

Suddenly I am full of a raging impatience to get away from here.

*

I bed down on any number of stations; I queue up at any number of canteens; I squat on any number of wooden train seats – but then the scenery outside becomes disturbing, mysterious and familiar. It slips past the window as evening falls, with villages in which thatched roofs have been pulled down like caps over white-washed, half-timbered buildings, with wheatfields shimmering like mother-of-pearl in the slanting rays of the sun, with orchards and barns and old lime trees.

The names of the stations take on a familiarity which makes my heart beat faster. The train puffs and puffs, I stand by the window and hold on to the wooden frame. These names mark out the boundaries of my youth.

Level meadows, fields, farmyards; a lonely team of horses moves against the sky along a path parallel to the horizon. A level-crossing barrier with farm labourers waiting in front of it, girls waving, children playing on the embankment, tracks that lead off into the countryside, smooth pathways and no guns.

It is evening now, and if the train were not still puffing onwards, I should scream. The plain spreads out broadly, and in the distance the pale blue silhouette of the hills comes into sight. I can make out the lines of Dolbenberg Hill, it's easy to recognize the jagged hilltop, which breaks off abruptly behind the crest of the trees. Behind that we'll get to the town.

But now the red-gold sunlight floods across the world and blurs it all, the train rattles round one bend and then another; and in that light stands the long row of poplars, unreal, distorted and dark, one behind the other and far away, made out of shadow, light and longing.

Slowly the field rolls away past us, and the poplars with it. The train swings round them, narrowing the spaces between them until they become a block, and for a moment I can only see one single tree. Then the others emerge again from behind the first one, and they stay there for a long time, silhouetted and lonely against the sky, until they are hidden from sight by the first houses.

A level-crossing. I am standing at the window, unable to tear myself away. The others are already gathering their things together, ready to get off. I say the name of the street to myself as we cross it – Bremen Street – Bremen Street –

There are cyclists, cars, people down there, a grey street and a grey underpass – it embraces me as if it were my mother.

Then the train stops and we are in the station, with all its noise, shouts and signboards. I heave my pack on to my shoulders and do up the strap, get hold of my rifle and stumble down the steps of the train.

On the platform I glance around, but I don't recognize any of the people as they hurry about. A Red Cross nurse offers me something to drink. I turn away, because she smiles at me so inanely, so full of her own importance: Look at me, everybody, I'm giving a soldier a cup of coffee. She even addresses me as her 'comrade' – and that really is the limit.

Outside the station the river is rushing along beside the street, hissing white over the weir by the mill bridge. The old square watch-tower is just there, with the huge, richly coloured lime tree in front of it, and the evening behind it.

We often used to sit here – how long ago that was – and we would walk across the bridge and breathe in the cool, stagnant smell of the water as it backed up; we leaned out over the calm water of the river on this side of the weir, where green weeds and algae clung to the buttresses; and on hot days we enjoyed the spray on the far side of the weir as we chatted about our teachers.

I cross the bridge, and look to the left and to the right; the water is still full of algae, and it still arches over the weir in bright spurts. In the tower itself, the laundry-women are still standing as they always did, with bare arms over the white washing, and the heat from their irons streams out through the open windows. Dogs trot along the narrow street, people are standing by their front doors, and they look at me as I go past, dirty and weighed down with my pack.

In that cafe we ate ice-creams and smoked our first cigarettes. I recognize every building in this street as I put them behind me – the grocer's, the chemist's, the baker's. And then I am standing in front of the brown door with the worn-down handle, and my hand feels heavy. I open the door; the amazing coolness greets me, and my eyes can't see clearly any more.

The stairs creak under my boots. Above me a door clicks open, someone looks over the banisters. It was the kitchen door that opened, they are in the middle of cooking potato pancakes, and you can smell them all through the house – of course, it's Saturday evening, and that must be my sister bending over the stair-well. For a moment I feel ashamed and hang my head; then I take off my helmet and look up. Yes, it is my eldest sister.

'Paul –' she shouts, 'Paul –'

I nod, my pack bangs against the banisters, my rifle is so heavy.

She throws the door open and shouts, 'Mother, Mother, it's Paul –'

I can't go on. Mother, Mother, it's Paul.

I lean against the wall and grip my helmet and my rifle. I grip them as hard as I can, but I can't move another step, the staircase blurs before my eyes, I thump my rifle-butt against my foot and grit my teeth in anger, but I am powerless against that one word that my sister has just spoken, nothing has any power against it. I try with all my might to force myself to laugh and to speak, but I can't manage a single word, and so I stand there on the stairs, wretched and helpless, horribly paralysed and I can't help it, and tears and more tears are running down my face.

My sister comes back and asks, 'What's the matter?'

This makes me pull myself together, and I stumble up to our landing. I lean my rifle in a corner, put my pack down against the wall and prop my steel helmet on top of it. The webbing and the bits and pieces have to go, too. Then I say furiously, 'Well give me a handkerchief then, can't you?'

She gets one from the cupboard for me and I wipe my face. On the wall above me hangs the glass case with the butterflies I used to collect.

Now I hear my mother's voice coming from the bedroom.

'Isn't she up?' I ask my sister.

'She's ill –' she answers.

I go in to see her, give her my hand and say as calmly as I can, 'Here I am, Mother.'

She is lying still in the semi-darkness. Then she asks me anxiously – and I can feel how her eyes are searching over me – 'Have you been wounded?'

'No, I'm on leave.'

My mother is very pale. I don't dare put on the light. 'And there I am lying here crying,' she says, 'instead of being pleased.'

'Are you ill, Mother?' I ask.

'I shall get up for a little while today,' she says, and turns to my sister, who is constantly ready to pop into the kitchen so that the food doesn't burn. 'Open the jar of cranberry sauce – you like that, don't you?' she asks me.

'Yes, Mother. I haven't had that for a long time.'

'It's as if we guessed you would be coming,' laughs my sister, 'just when it's your favourite food, potato pancakes, and now we'll even have cranberries with them.'

'Well, it is Saturday,' I answer.

'Sit down by me,' says my mother.

She looks at me. Her hands are white and sickly looking, and thin, compared to mine. We speak little, and I am grateful that she doesn't enquire about anything. What would I be able to say, anyway? That everything that could happen has happened? I am out of it, I'm in one piece and I'm sitting beside her. And in the kitchen my sister is getting supper ready and singing while she does so.

'My dear son,' says my mother softly.

We have never been a very demonstrative family – poor people who have to work hard and cope with problems very rarely are. They can't really understand that sort of thing either, and they don't like constantly going on about things that are perfectly obvious. If my mother says 'my dear son' to me, that is just as valid as somebody else making heaven knows what kind of flowery speech. I know for sure that the jar of cranberries is the only one they have been able to find for months, and that they have kept it specially for me, just like the slightly stale biscuits that she gives me now. I'm sure that she will have got hold of them by chance at some time, and put them aside for me straightaway.

I sit beside her bed and through the window the chestnut trees in the garden of the inn opposite flash gold and brown. I breathe slowly in and out and say to myself, 'You are home, you are home.' But there is an awkwardness that will not leave me, I can't get used to everything yet. There is my mother, there is my sister, there is the glass case with my butterflies, there is the mahogany piano – but I am not quite there myself yet. There is a veil and a few steps between me and them.

And so I go out and fetch my pack, bring it to the bed and get out the things I have brought back for them: a whole Edam cheese that Kat conjured up for me, two army-issue loaves, three-quarters of a pound of butter, two cans of liver sausage, a pound of lard and a bag of rice.

'I'm sure you can do with these –'

They nod.

'Things are pretty bad here?' I ask.

'Yes, there isn't much to be had. Do you get enough out there?'

I smile and point to the things I've brought. 'It isn't always as much as that, but we still manage.'

Erna takes the food away. Suddenly my mother grips my hand and asks hesitantly, 'Was it very bad out there, Paul?'

Mother, what kind of an answer can I give you? You won't understand and never will. And I don't want you to. Was it bad, you ask – you, Mother. I shake my head and say, 'No, Mother, not really. After all, there are lots of us together, and that means that it isn't so bad.'

'Yes, but a little while ago Heinrich Bredemeyer was here, and he told us stories of how terrible it is out there now, with the gas and all the rest of it.'

It is my mother saying these things. She says 'with the gas and all the rest of it'. She doesn't know what she is saying, she is just afraid for me. Should I tell her how we once found three enemy trenches, where everyone was fixed and rigid as they stood, as if they'd been struck like it? On the parapets, in the dugouts, wherever they happened to be, they were standing or lying with their faces blue, dead.

'Oh, Mother, they say all sorts of things,' I reply, 'Bredemeyer was just spinning a yarn. You can see, I'm in one piece and I've put on weight.'

Faced with my mother's anxious concern for me, I manage to get a grip on my own emotions. I'm able to walk about again, and talk, and answer questions without being afraid of suddenly having to support myself against the wall because the whole world has turned as soft as rubber and my veins as fragile as tinder.

My mother wants to get up, so while she does so I go out into the kitchen to talk to my sister. 'What's wrong with her?'

She shrugs. 'She's already been in bed for a couple of months now, but we weren't to write and tell you. She's seen a few doctors. One of them told us that it's probably cancer.'

*

I go along to district HQ to report. I wander slowly through the streets. Occasionally people stop and have a word with me. I don't stay for long, because I don't feel like talking too much.

When I come out of the barracks a loud voice shouts at me. Still lost in thought I turn round and find myself face to face with a major. He bawls me out: 'Forgotten how to salute?'

'I'm sorry, Major,' I say, still confused, 'I didn't see you.'

His voice gets even louder. 'Can't you even address an officer properly?'

What I'd really like to do is hit him in the face, but I control myself or else my leave will be done for, put my heels together and say, 'My apologies, sir, I am afraid I did not see you, sir.'

'Then be so good as to keep your eyes open,' he snaps. 'What's your name?'

I tell him.

His fat red face still has outrage written all over it. 'Regiment?'

I respond in the prescribed military manner. He still isn't satisfied. 'Where are you stationed?'

But now I've had enough, and say, 'Somewhere between Langemarck and Bixschoote.'

'What do you mean?' he asks, bewildered.

I explain to him that I have just arrived on leave an hour ago, and I imagine that now he will push off, but I am mistaken. He gets even angrier. 'I suppose you think that's acceptable, bringing your front-line manners back here! Never! Good discipline is still the order of the day here, thank God!'

Then he gives me the order: 'Twenty paces back, at the double!'

A dull rage is seething inside me. But I can't do anything against him – he could have me arrested on the spot if he wanted. So I double back, march forward and half a dozen yards from him I give him a parade-ground salute, and don't take my hand away until I am another six yards past him.

He calls me back and informs me generously that on this occasion he has decided to temper justice with mercy. Still standing at attention, I indicate gratitude. 'Dismiss,' he orders. I do a smart about face and leave.

This spoils the evening for me. I get off home and throw my uniform into a corner – I was going to do that anyway. Then I get my civilian suit out of the wardrobe and put it on.

I've got out of the habit of wearing it. The suit is a bit short and a bit tight – I've put on some weight in the army. I have trouble fixing the collar and tying the tie. In the end my sister knots it for me. And how lightweight this suit feels. You think you are only wearing your shirt and underpants.

I look at myself in the mirror. It's a strange sight. Looking back in bewilderment at me is a tanned and overgrown sixteen-year-old on his way to church for his confirmation.

My mother is pleased that I am wearing civvies; it makes me look more like my old self to her. My father would have preferred me to wear my uniform, though, because he would like to take me to see his friends dressed like that.

But I refuse.

★

It is good to be able to sit somewhere quietly, as we can in the garden of the inn opposite, under the chestnut trees, next to the skittle alley. The leaves are falling, on to the table and on to the ground, but only a few, the first. I've a glass of beer in front of me – we learned to drink in the army. The glass is half empty, so that I have a few good, cool pulls yet, and besides, I can order a second or a third if I like. There's no roll call and no heavy fire, the owner's children are playing in the skittle alley and the dog comes and rests its head on my lap. The sky is blue and the green spire of St Margaret's church rises up between the leaves of the chestnut trees.

All this is good, and I love it. But I can't get on with the people. The only one who doesn't ask me questions is my mother. With my father it is different. He'd like me to tell him a bit about what it is like out there: what he wants is both touching and silly, and I have no real relationship with him any more. What he would really like best is a constant flow of stories. I can see that he has no idea that these things can't be put into words, although I'd like to do something to please him. But it would be dangerous for me to try and put it all into words, and I'm worried that it might get out of hand and I couldn't control it any more. Where would we be if everybody knew exactly what was going on out there at the front?

And so I limit myself to telling him a few funny bits. Then he asks me whether I've ever been in hand-to-hand fighting. I say that I haven't, and get up to leave.

That doesn't help matters, though. In the street, after I've had a couple of shocks because the screeching of the trams sounds like a shell coming towards me, someone taps me on the shoulder. It is my German master, who lets fire with all the usual questions: 'Now, what's it like out there? Rough, I'll be bound, rough? Yes, it's terrible, but we have to stand firm. And after all, at least you're all fed well out there, I hear. You look good, Paul, fit. Naturally, things are worse here, of course they are, goes without saying, our soldiers always come first.'

He drags me off to his local bar. I am greeted with great enthusiasm and one of the assistant headmasters shakes my hand and says, 'Well, you're just back from the front? How's morale out there? Pretty good, pretty good, eh?' I explain that everyone would like to come home. He gives a great roar of laughter. 'I bet they do! But first of all you've got to wallop those Froggies. Do you smoke? Here, have one of these, my dear fellow. Waiter, a beer for our young warrior.'

Unfortunately I have accepted the cigar, so I have to stay. Every one of them oozes goodwill, and there's nothing to be done. All the same I'm irritated, and puff away as fast as I can. Just for something to do I toss down a glass of beer in one gulp. Another is ordered for me immediately; everyone knows what they owe to the soldiers. They are arguing about what we ought to annex. The assistant headmaster, who has sacrificed his gold watch-chain to the war effort and is wearing an iron one, wants the most: all of Belgium, the French coalfields and great tracts of Russia. He gives very precise reasons why we need them, and insists on his point of view until the others eventually give way and agree with him. And then he starts to explain where the breakthrough has to be made in France; in the middle of it he turns to me and says, 'You lads out there should hurry up a bit with your eternal trench fighting. Just chuck 'em out, and the war will be over.'

I tell him that the soldiers think a breakthrough is impossible.

The other side simply has too much in the way of reserves. Besides, the war is really not like people imagine it.

He dismisses this in a superior manner and makes quite clear to me that I don't know what is going on. 'Yes, of course, the individual soldier thinks that, but you have to look at the whole thing,' he says, 'and there you just can't make a judgement. You can only see your own small sector, and therefore you have no overview. You are doing your duty, you are risking your life, and that deserves every honour – every one of you should get the Iron Cross – but first and foremost the enemy front in Flanders has to be broken through and then rolled up from the top downwards.'

He snorts and wipes his beard. 'Rolled up completely, that's what's got to happen, from the top down to the bottom. And then on to Paris.'

I'd like to know how he thinks it can be done, and I toss back the third glass of beer. He orders another one for me immediately.

But I leave. He tucks a few more cigars into my pocket and sends me off with a friendly slap on the shoulder. 'All the best! And let's hope that we soon get some proper news from you lads.'

★

I really imagined that leave would be different. A year ago it actually *was* different. I suppose I'm the one who has changed in the meantime. A great gulf has opened up between then and now. I didn't know then what the war was really like – we had only been in quiet sectors. Now I can see that I have become more brittle without realizing it. I can't come to terms with things here any more, it's another world. Some people ask questions, others don't, and you can see that they are pleased with themselves for not asking; quite often they even say with an understanding look on their faces that it's impossible to talk about it all. They make a big thing of it.

I like being alone best, with no one to disturb me. Because everyone always comes round to the same topic of conversation, how badly things are going, how well they are going, one thinks this way, the next person the other way – and they quickly get on to the things that make up their own worlds. I'm sure that I was just like them myself, before; but now I can't find any real point of contact.

They just talk too much. They have problems, goals, desires that I can't see in the same way as they do. Sometimes I sit with one of them in the little garden of the pub and try to get the point across that this *is* everything – just sitting in the quiet. Of course they understand, they agree, they think the same way, but it's only talk, only talk, that's the point – they *do* feel it, but always only with half of their being, a part of them is always thinking of something else. They are so fragmented, no one feels it with his whole life; anyway, it is impossible for me to put what I mean into proper words.

When I take a look at them, in their rooms, in their offices, in their jobs, then I find it all irresistibly attractive, and I want to be part of it too, and forget the war. But at the same time it repulses me, it is so restricted, how can that fill a whole life, it deserves to be smashed to bits, how can things *be* like that when shrapnel is whizzing over the trenches out there and the Verey lights are going up, the wounded are being dragged back on tarpaulins and the lads are taking cover in the trenches? These people here are different, a kind I can't really understand, that I envy and despise. I keep thinking of Kat and Albert and Müller and Tjaden – what are they up to? Perhaps they are sitting in the canteen, or swimming – and soon they'll have to go up the line again.

*

In my room there is a brown leather sofa behind the table. That is where I sit.

There are lots of pictures pinned to the walls, pictures I once cut out of magazines. Postcards and drawings that took my fancy, too. In the corner there is a small iron stove. On the wall facing me are the shelves with my books.

I lived in this room before I became a soldier. I bought the books one at a time with money I earned by tutoring, lots of them second-hand, all the classics, for example, and each volume cost me a decent amount, hardbacks, in stiff blue cloth. I bought complete works, because I was thorough, and I didn't trust the editors of selections to have chosen the best. So I only bought 'Complete Works'. I read them with zeal and honesty, but most of them did not really appeal to me. I got so much more from the other books, from modern literature, and those books were much dearer, too. I came by a few of them in a less than honourable fashion – I borrowed them and never returned them because I couldn't bear to part with them.

One shelf is full of school books. I didn't take care of them and they are very dog-eared. Pages have also been torn out – for various reasons. And below them are stacked exercise books, paper and letters, drawings and essays.

I try to think myself back into that time. It is still there in the room, I can feel it at once, the walls have preserved it. My hands are lying on the back of the sofa; now I make myself comfortable, tuck my legs in and sit easily, cradled in the sofa's arms. The little window is open, and shows me the familiar view of the street with the church spire looming up at the end. There are a few flowers on the table. Pens, pencils, a shell for a paperweight, the inkwell – nothing here has changed.

It will be just like this, if I am lucky, when the war is over and I come home for good. I shall sit here, the same as before, and look at my room, and wait.

I feel agitated; but I don't want to be, because it isn't right. I want to get that quiet rapture back, feel again, just as before, that fierce and unnamed passion I used to feel when I looked at my books. Please let the wind of desire that rose from the multi-coloured spines of those books catch me up again, let it melt the heavy, lifeless lead weight that is there somewhere inside me, and awaken in me once again the impatience of the future, the soaring delight in the world of the intellect – let it carry me back into the ready-for-anything lost world of my youth.

I sit and I wait.

I remember that I have to go and see Kemmerich's mother; I could visit Mittelstaedt as well, he must be at the barracks. I look out of the window. Behind the sunny street scene you can see the line of the hills, indistinct and pale, and it merges into a bright autumn day and I'm sitting with Kat and Albert by a fire eating baked potatoes in their jackets.

But I don't want to think about that, and I push the thought away. Let the room speak, let it take me up and carry me along, I want to feel that I belong here and I want to listen, so that when I have to go back to the front I shall know this: the war will sink and drown when the wave of our homecoming sweeps across it, the war will be over, it will not devour us, it has no real power over us, its hold on us is only a superficial one.

The spines of the books stand side by side. I know them all, and I remember putting them in order. With my eyes I implore them: speak to me – take me up – take me up again, you old life – you carefree, wonderful life – take me up again –

I wait, wait.

Pictures flash past, they don't fix themselves, they are just shadows and memories.

Nothing – nothing.

My impatience grows.

Suddenly a terrible feeling of isolation wells up inside me. I can't get back, I'm locked out; however much I might plead, however much I try, nothing moves, and I sit there as wretched as a condemned man and the past turns away from me. At the same time I am frightened of conjuring it up too much because I don't know what would happen then. I am a soldier. I have to cling to that.

I get up wearily and look out of the window. Then I take one of the books and flick through it to try and read. I put it aside and take up another one. There are passages in it that I have marked. I look through it, flick through the pages, take out more books. There is already a pile beside me. Others join it, more quickly now – single sheets of paper, exercise books, letters.

I stand silent in front of them, as if I were on trial.

Dispirited.

Words, words, words – they can't reach me.

Slowly I put the books back in their places on the shelves.

It's over.

I leave the room quietly.

★

But I don't give up yet. Although I don't go and sit in my room again I tell myself by way of comfort that a couple of days aren't the be-all and the end-all. I'll have time afterwards – later on, years of it – for all this. Meanwhile I go and visit Mittelstaedt at the barracks and we sit in his room, which has an atmosphere I don't like, but which I am used to.

Mittelstaedt has a bit of news for me which galvanizes me at once. He tells me that Kantorek has been called up for the Home Guard. 'Just think of it,' he says, and fetches a couple of good cigars, 'I come straight out of the military hospital and walk right into him. He sticks out his hand and squeaks, "Well, if it isn't Mittelstaedt, how's it going, my boy?" I give him a stare and I tell him, "Home Guardsman Kantorek, duty is duty and pleasure is pleasure, you of all people should know that, guardsman! Stand up straight when you speak to a superior." You should have seen his face! A cross between a pickled gherkin and a dud shell! He had another little go at being familiar. This time I bawled him out even harder. Then he brought up his big guns and asked me confidentially, "Would you like me to arrange for you to take the school-leaving exam under the special regulations?" He wanted to remind me, see? Then I got really angry and thought I'd do a bit of reminding too. "Home Guardsman Kantorek," I said, "two years ago your sermonizing drove us all to enlist; Josef Behm as well, and he didn't really want to go. He was killed three months before he would have been conscripted. Without you, he would have waited until then. Now: dismiss! I shall be speaking to you again." It was no problem getting myself assigned to his company, and the first thing I did was take him down to the stores and make sure his kit is really special. You'll soon see.'

We go out on to the parade-ground. The company has fallen in. Mittelstaedt has them stand at ease, and inspects them.

Then I spot Kantorek and have to bite my lip to stop myself laughing. He is wearing a kind of faded blue battle-dress tunic. There are great dark patches sewn on to the back and the sleeves. That battledress must have belonged to a giant. The frayed black trousers make up for it, though; they only reach halfway down his calf. Then again, his boots are more than big enough, ancient beetle-crushers with turned-up toecaps, still laced at the side. By way of compensation his cap is too small, a dreadful, grubby, miserable little scrap of cloth. The whole picture is pitiful.

Mittelstaedt stops in front of him. 'Home Guardsman Kantorek, do you call those buttons polished? You never seem to learn. Far from satisfactory, Kantorek, far from satisfactory –'

Inwardly I am roaring with delight. At school Kantorek used to criticize Mittelstaedt in exactly the same tone of voice: 'Far from satisfactory, Mittelstaedt –'

Mittelstaedt continues his disapproving comments. 'You ought to take a lesson from Boettcher, his turn-out is an example, you might learn something from him.'

I can scarcely believe my eyes. Yes, Boettcher is there as well, Boettcher, the school janitor. And he really *is* exemplary. Kantorek shoots me a look as if he would like to eat me alive. But I just grin harmlessly right at him, as if I haven't recognized him at all.

How stupid he looks with his little cap and his uniform. And once upon a time we used to be terrified of a creature like that, when he was perched on the teacher's chair and prodding us with his pencil while we were learning the French irregular verbs that were not of the slightest use to us later on in France. It's still barely two years ago – and now here is Home Guardsman Kantorek, with all the mystique rudely stripped away, bow-legged, with arms like pot-handles, his buttons badly polished and looking ridiculous, a quite impossible soldier. I can't reconcile him with that threatening figure at the front of the class, and I would really like to know how I would react if this miserable scarecrow were ever allowed suddenly to ask me, an old soldier, 'Bäumer, give me the imperfect of *aller* . . .'

For the moment, Mittelstaedt has them practise skirmishing. For this he graciously appoints Kantorek platoon leader.

Thereby hangs a tale. In skirmishing, you see, the platoon leader always has to be twenty paces ahead of his men; so if the order comes 'At the double, about turn!' the skirmishing line just has to about face, but the platoon leader, who is now suddenly twenty paces behind the line has to rush forward so that he gets twenty paces in front of the men. That makes forty paces altogether at the double. But hardly has he got there when the order comes 'At the double, about turn!' and he has to belt forty paces across to the other side as quickly as he can. In all this the group merely carries out a few steps and a leisurely about face, while the platoon leader is rushing about like a fart in a colander. The whole manoeuvre is one of Himmelstoss's tried and tested recipes.

Kantorek can't expect anything else from Mittelstaedt, because he once made sure that he failed the end-of-year exams and was kept back a year, and Mittelstaedt would be daft not to make the most of this opportunity before he is sent back to the front. Perhaps you really do die a bit more easily if the army gives you a chance like that just once in a while.

Meanwhile Kantorek is scurrying backwards and forwards like a stuck pig. After a while Mittelstaedt tells them to stop, and he begins the terribly important exercise of crawling. Holding his rifle in the regulation manner, Kantorek drags his incredible shape on his elbows and knees through the sand right in front of us. He is panting heavily, and that panting is music to our ears.

Mittelstaedt encourages him by offering Kantorek-the-Home-

Guardsman comforting quotations from Kantorek-the-Schoolmaster. 'Home Guardsman Kantorek, we are fortunate to be living in a time of greatness, and so we need to pull ourselves together and learn to overcome misfortunes.'

Kantorek spits out a dirty scrap of wood that has managed to get in between his teeth and sweats.

Mittelstaedt leans down to him and assures him with great fervour, 'And in the face of trivialities we must never lose sight of the greater experience, Home Guardsman Kantorek!'

I'm only surprised that Kantorek doesn't explode with a great bang, especially since they now move on to PE, during which Mittelstaedt does a wonderful Kantorek imitation by grabbing hold of the seat of his trousers during an exercise on the horizontal bar, so that he can lift his chin up straight over the bar itself, all accompanied by a constant flow of pearls of wisdom. That's exactly what Kantorek used to do to him in the old days.

After this they are detailed for further duties. 'Kantorek and Boettcher – fetching the bread supply! Take the handcart!'

A couple of minutes later the pair of them set off with the handcart. Kantorek, who is furious, keeps his head well down. The janitor is quite happy, because he's only got light duty.

The bakery is at the other end of town. They have to cross the whole town twice.

'They've been doing it for a few days now,' grins Mittelstaedt. 'People are already starting to wait specially, so that they can see them.'

'Fantastic,' I say, 'but hasn't he put in a complaint?'

'He tried. Our commanding officer laughed like a drain when he heard the story. He can't stand schoolmasters. Besides, I'm going out with his daughter.'

'He'll mess up the exam for you.'

'Who cares?' says Mittelstaedt calmly. 'And in any case the complaint he made couldn't be upheld because I was able to show that he mostly had light duties.'

'Couldn't you really hammer him for once?' I ask.

'No, he's too much of a weed for that,' replies Mittelstaedt in a spirit of chivalry and generosity.

★

What is leave? Just a deviation that makes everything afterwards that much harder to take. Already the idea of saying goodbye is creeping in. My mother looks at me without saying anything. I know she is counting the days – every morning she is unhappy. It's already a day less. She has tidied my pack away somewhere because she doesn't want to be reminded by it.

The hours pass quickly when you are brooding. I try to shake it off and go out with my sister. She's going to the slaughterhouse to get a few pounds of bones. These are highly prized, and early in the morning people are already queueing to get some. A good few of them faint.

We are out of luck. After we have taken it in turns to stand there for three hours, the queue disperses. The supply of bones has run out.

It's a good job that I can draw my rations. I take some of my stuff to my mother, and that way we all get food that is a bit more nourishing.

The days get harder and harder, my mother's eyes get sadder and sadder. Four days left. I have to go and see Kemmerich's mother.

★

It would be impossible to put it down on paper. That trembling, sobbing woman shaking me and screaming, 'Why are you still alive when he's dead?' and then weeping all over me and shouting, 'Why are you out there at all – you're just children –' until she sinks down into a chair, still crying, and asks, 'Did you see him? Did you see him then? How did he die?'

I tell her that he was shot through the heart and killed instantaneously. She looks at me doubtfully: 'You're lying. I know better. I know what a hard death he had. I heard his voice, I felt his terror in the night – tell me the truth, I want to know, I have to know.'

'No,' I say, 'I was right next to him. He was killed outright.'

She begs me, softly now, 'Tell me. You must. I know you just want to make me feel better, but can't you see that you are hurting me more than if you told the truth? I can't stand the uncertainty, tell me how it was, no matter how horrible. It will still be better than what I shall have to think otherwise.'

I shall never tell her, she'd have to make mincemeat out of me first. I'm sorry for her, but it also strikes me that she's being a bit stupid. Why can't she just accept it, Kemmerich is still dead whether she knows or not. When you have seen so many dead men you can't really see the point of so much grief about a single one of them any more. So I tell her rather impatiently, 'He died instantly. He didn't feel a thing. His face was quite calm.'

She doesn't say anything. Then she says, slowly, 'Do you swear to that?'

'Yes.'

'By everything you hold sacred?'

God, is there *anything* I hold sacred? You soon change your views on that sort of thing where we are.

'Yes, he died instantly.'

'And may you not come back yourself if you haven't told the truth?'

'May I not come back myself if he didn't die instantly.'

I would swear by anything in the world. But she seems to believe me. She sighs heavily, and cries for a long time. She wants me to tell her how it was, so I invent a story that by now I almost believe myself.

When I leave, she kisses me and gives me a photograph of him. He's in his recruit's uniform, leaning against a round table, the legs of which are rustic birch branches, and there is a painted forest as a background. The table has a beer tankard on it.

*

It's the last evening at home. Nobody is much inclined to talk. I go to bed early, get hold of my pillow, hold tight to it and put my head into it. Who knows when I shall be lying in a feather bed again?

My mother comes into my room, very late. She thinks I am asleep and I pretend that I am. It would be just too hard to talk, to be awake together.

She sits there until it is nearly morning, although she is in pain and is often bent double with it. In the end I can't take it any longer and pretend to wake up.

'Go to bed, Mother, you'll catch cold sitting here.'

'I'll have plenty of time to sleep later,' she replies.

I sit up. 'I don't have to go straight back to the front, Mother. I've got four weeks in camp first. When I'm there I might be able to come over one Sunday.'

She says nothing. Then she asks softly, 'Are you very frightened?'

'No, Mother.'

'I wanted to say something else to you. Be careful of those French women. They're no good, those women out there.'

Oh Mother, Mother, to you I'm still a child – why can't I just put my head in your lap and cry? Why do I always have to be the stronger and calmer one? I'd like to be able to weep for once and be comforted, and anyway I'm really not much more than a child – the short trousers I wore as a boy are still hanging in the wardrobe. It was such a little while ago, why did it pass?

I say, as calmly as I can, 'There aren't any women where we are stationed, Mother.'

'And make sure you take good care when you are at the front, Paul.'

Oh Mother, Mother! Why don't I take you in my arms and die with you? What wretched creatures we are!

'Yes, Mother, I'll take care.'

'I shall pray for you every day, Paul.'

Oh Mother, Mother! Why can't we get up and go away from here, back through the years, until all this misery has vanished from us, back to when it was just you and me, Mother?

'Maybe you can get a posting that won't be so dangerous.'

'Yes, Mother. It's quite possible they will put me in the kitchens.'

'You take a job like that, whatever the others say –'

'I'm not worried about what people say, Mother –'

She sighs. Her face is a pale glow in the darkness.

'You really must go to bed now, Mother.'

She doesn't answer. I get up and put my bedspread around her shoulders. She holds on to my arm and she is in pain. I take her across and stay with her for a little while. 'You have to get better by the time I come back, Mother.'

'Yes, son, yes.'

'You really mustn't send me your rations, Mother. We get enough to eat out there. You need it more here.'

How wretched she looks, lying there in bed, this woman who loves me more than anything in the world. When I'm just about to go she says quickly, 'I got hold of two pairs of underpants for you. They are good quality wool. They'll keep you warm. You mustn't forget to pack them.'

Oh Mother, I know what these two pairs of underpants have cost you in queueing and running around and begging! Oh Mother, Mother, it is quite incomprehensible that I have to leave you! Who has more right to have me here than you? I'm still sitting here and you are still lying there, and there are so many things we should say to each other, but we shall never be able to.

'Goodnight, Mother.'

'Goodnight, Son.'

The room is dark. My mother's breathing is uneven. Meanwhile the clock ticks. There is a breeze outside the windows. The chestnut trees are rustling.

In the vestibule I stumble over my pack, which they have got ready for me, because I have to leave very early in the morning.

I bury my head in my pillow, I clench my fists round the iron uprights on my bedstead. I should never have come home. Out there I was indifferent, and a lot of the time I was completely without hope – I can never be like that again. I was a soldier, and now it is all suffering, for myself, for my mother, for everything, because it is all so hopeless and never-ending.

I should never have come home on leave.

8

I know the barracks at the training camp out on the moors. This was where Himmelstoss decided to educate Tjaden. But I recognize hardly any of the people; as usual, there have been lots of changes. I remember seeing one or two when I was here before, but only in passing.

I carry out my duties mechanically. I spend most evenings at the Soldiers' Club. There are newspapers there, but I don't read them. There is a piano, though, and I like to play it. Two girls serve us, one of them quite young.

The camp is surrounded by a high barbed-wire fence. If you get back late from the Soldiers' Club you're supposed to have a pass. Mind you, if you get on to decent terms with the sentries you can slip through anyway.

Every day we practise company manoeuvres on the moors, amongst the juniper bushes and the silver birches. It's all perfectly bearable, as long as you are not too demanding. You run forwards and throw yourself down, with your breath blowing the flowers and stalks of the heathland plants this way and that. Seen from that close to the ground, the sand is as pure as if it were in a laboratory, made up out of many tiny little grains. You get a strange urge to dig your fingers into it.

But best of all are the woodlands, with the birch trees at the edges. They are constantly changing colour. The trunks may be shining and dazzlingly white, with the pastel green of their leaves waving between them, silky and airy; and then in the next moment it all changes to an opalescent blue, with silver coming in from the edges and dabbing the green away; but then all at once it can deepen almost to black at one point, when a cloud crosses the sun. And this shadow flits along like a phantom between the trunks, and suddenly they are pale again, as it passes further across the moors to the horizon – and now the birch trees are like ceremonial banners, their white trunks standing out against the red-gold flame of their changing leaves.

I often become completely absorbed in this interplay of the most gentle lights and translucent shadow, so much so that I nearly miss some of the commands – when you are on your own you start to look at nature, and to love it. And I haven't many contacts here, nor do I want any, beyond normal day-to-day living. You don't get to know other people well enough for anything more than a chat and a game of cards in the evenings.

Next to our barracks is the big POW camp for Russian soldiers. It is separated from us by wire fencing, it is true, but the prisoners still manage to get over to us. They behave in a very shy and nervous manner, even though they are mostly big and bearded; because of this, they seem to us like meek and mistreated St Bernard dogs.

They creep around our barracks and raid the rubbish bins. Heaven knows what they find there. Our own rations are short and, more to the point, not very good, with things like turnips cut into six pieces and boiled, or carrot-tops that are still dirty. Brown-flecked potatoes are a great luxury, and the best we get is a watery rice soup which is supposed to have strips of beef in it. But they are cut so thinly that you can't even find them.

In spite of this it all gets eaten, of course. On those occasions where someone is really so well off that he doesn't need to wolf down everything he's got, there are other men right beside him who are happy to take it off him. Only the absolute dregs that can't be reached with a spoon are washed out and dumped into the garbage vats. Sometimes they are accompanied by a few turnip peelings, mouldy crusts of bread and all sorts of other refuse.

This cloudy murky water is what the POWs are after. They

scoop it greedily out of the stinking vats and carry it away in tins under their tunics.

It is odd seeing these men – our enemies – at such close quarters. Their faces make you stop and think, good peasant faces, broad foreheads, broad noses, broad lips, broad hands, shaggy hair. They really ought to be ploughing or harvesting or apple-picking. They look even more good-natured than our own farmers from over in Frisia.

It is sad to watch their movements, to see them begging for food. They are all pretty weak, because they get just enough to keep them from starving. We have nowhere near enough to fill our own bellies – they have dysentery, and many of them show us their blood-stained shirt-tails, covertly and with nervous glances. Their backs and their heads are bowed, their knees bent, they look up at you with their heads on one side when they stick their hands out and beg, beg in those gentle, soft bass voices redolent of warm stoves in comfortable rooms back in their homeland.

Some of the men kick them so that they fall over – but only a few do that. Most don't hurt them, they just walk past them. Occasionally, when they are especially persistent, it is true, you do lose your temper and give them a kick. If only they wouldn't look at you the way they do – how much misery there can be in two little spots that you could cover with your thumbs, their eyes.

In the evenings they come across to the barracks to trade things. They will exchange anything they have for bread. Sometimes they are successful, because they have good boots, whereas ours are poor. The leather of their high boots is wonderfully soft, like suede. The farmers' sons among us, who get butter and so on sent to them from home, can afford them. The price of a pair of boots is between two and three loaves of army-issue bread, or one loaf and a small salami.

But nearly all of the Russians have already handed over the things they had long ago. Now they only have shoddy stuff to wear and they try to barter little ornaments and carvings that they have made from bits of shrapnel or from the copper driving bands of shells. These things don't bring much in, of course, even though they have taken a great amount of effort to make – they'll go for nothing more than a couple of slices of bread. Our country people are hard and crafty when they are bargaining. They hold the piece of bread or the sausage right under the Russian's nose until he goes pale with greed, he rolls his eyes, and he'll agree to anything. Our men pack up their booty with all the ceremony they can muster, then slowly and carefully they cut themselves a hunk of bread from their own supplies, take a piece of the good, hard sausage with every mouthful, and get stuck into it, as a reward to themselves. It is annoying watching them having their evening meal, what you'd really like to do is clout their thick heads. They seldom share anything. To be fair, people just don't get to know each other well enough.

★

I'm often on guard duty over the Russians. In the darkness you can make out their figures as they move about like sick storks, like huge birds. They come right up to the wire-netting and put their faces against it, with their fingers in the mesh. Often many of them will stand together. And they breathe in the winds that blow across from the moors and the woods.

Only rarely do they speak, and then only a word or two. They behave more humanely, I could almost think in a more brotherly manner towards one another, than we do here. But perhaps that is because they are unhappier than we are. And yet the war is over as far as they are concerned. Still, just waiting for the next bout of dysentery is no kind of life either.

The home guardsmen who are in charge of them say that they were more lively at the beginning. There were the kinds of dealings and conflicts between them that you always get, and apparently fists were raised and knives used to come out. Now they are dulled and indifferent, and most of them don't even masturbate any more because they are too weak, although usually it is so bad that you get whole barracks at it at the same time.

They stand by the wire; often one staggers away, and then another one quickly takes his place in the line. Most of them are silent; only a few beg for dog-ends.

I watch their dark figures. Their beards blow in the wind. I know nothing about them except that they are prisoners-of-war, and that is precisely what shakes me. Their lives are anonymous and blameless; if I knew more about them, what they are called, how they live, what their hopes and fears are, then my feelings might have a focus and could turn into sympathy. But at the moment all I sense in them is the pain of the dumb animal, the fearful melancholy of life and the pitilessness of men.

An order has turned these silent figures into our enemies; an order could turn them into friends again. On some table, a document is signed by some people that none of us knows, and for years our main aim in life is the one thing that usually draws the condemnation of the whole world and incurs its severest punishment in law. How can anyone make distinctions like that looking at these silent men, with their faces like children and their beards like apostles? Any drill-corporal is a worse enemy to the recruits, any schoolmaster a worse enemy to his pupils than they are to us. And yet we would shoot at them again if they were free, and so would they at us.

Suddenly I'm frightened: I mustn't think along those lines any more. That path leads to the abyss. It isn't the right time yet – but I don't want to lose those thoughts altogether, I'll preserve them, keep them locked away until the war is over. My heart is pounding; could this be the goal, the greatness, the unique experience that I thought about in the trenches, that I was seeking as a reason for going on living after this universal catastrophe is over? Is this the task we must dedicate our lives to after the war, so that all the years of horror will have been worthwhile?

I take out my cigarettes, break each one in half and give them to the Russians. They bow, and then light them. Now little points of red are glowing in some of their faces. I find this comforting; they look like little windows in the houses of some village at night, revealing that behind them there are rooms which are havens of safety.

The days pass. One misty morning another Russian is buried; a few of them die every day now. I happen to be on sentry duty when he is laid to rest. The POWs sing a chorale; they sing in harmony and it sounds as if they were hardly voices at all, but as if an organ were playing, far away on the moor.

The funeral is soon over.

In the evening they are standing by the wire again, and the wind blows across to them from the birch woods. The stars are cold.

By now I've got to know a few of them who can speak German pretty well. One of them is a musician, and he tells me that he had been a violinist in Berlin. When he hears that I play the piano a little, he fetches his violin and plays. The others sit down and lean their backs against the wire-netting. He stands and plays, and often he has that far-away look that violinists get when they close their eyes, and then he strikes up a new rhythm on the instrument and smiles at me.

Presumably he is playing folk songs; the others hum the tunes with him. They are like dark hills, and the humming is deep, subterranean. The voice of the violin stands out like a slim girl above them, and it is bright and alone. The voices stop and the violin remains – it sounds thin in the night, as if it were freezing; you have to stand close by – it would probably be better in a room – out here it makes you sad to hear it wandering about, all alone.

*

I don't get any Sunday passes because, after all, I've just had a long leave. So on the last Sunday before I go, my father and my oldest sister come to visit me. We spend the whole day sitting in the Soldiers' Club. Where else could we go? We don't want to go to the barracks. In the afternoon we go for a walk on the moor.

The hours drag by; we don't know what to talk about. And so we talk about my mother's illness. It's now definite that it's cancer, she's already in hospital and waiting for an operation. The doctors hope that she will get better, but we've never heard of cancer being cured.

'Which hospital is she in?' I ask.

'In the Queen Louisa,' says my father.

'What kind of a ward?'

'Public. We'll have to wait and see what the operation will cost. She wanted to go into the public ward herself. She said she'd have someone to talk to then. Besides, it's cheaper.'

'But then she'll be with all those other people. I only hope she can get some sleep at night.'

My father nods. His face is drawn and full of lines. My mother has been ill a lot; it's true that she has only ever gone into hospital when she was forced to, but for all that it has cost us a great deal of money, and my father's life has really been taken up by it.

'If only we knew what the operation will cost –' he says.

'Haven't you asked?'

'Not in so many words, you can't really – you don't want the doctor to turn against you, because he still has to operate on Mother.'

Yes, I think bitterly, that's the way we are, the way poor people are. They don't dare ask the price, and worry themselves half to death about it instead; but the others, the ones who can afford it, it's perfectly natural to them to settle the price beforehand. The doctor isn't going to turn against them in any case.

'The dressings afterwards are so expensive, too,' says my father.

'Doesn't the sickness fund pay anything towards it?' I ask.

'Your mother has already been ill for too long.'

'Have you got any money, then?'

He shakes his head. 'No, but I can do some more overtime.'

I know what he means: he'll stand at his work-table until midnight and fold and glue and trim. At eight in the evening he'll eat some of that far from nourishing stuff they get on their ration cards. After that he'll take a powder for his headache and carry on working.

To cheer him up a bit, I tell him a few stories that come into my mind, army jokes and so on, where a general or a sergeant gets dropped in it.

Afterwards I see them both to the station. They give me a pot of jam and a parcel of potato pancakes that my mother managed to cook for me.

Then their train leaves and I walk back.

In the evening I spread some of the jam on a pancake, and eat a few. I don't enjoy them. So I go out to give the pancakes to the Russians. Then it occurs to me that my mother cooked these herself, and that she was probably in pain when she was standing over the hot stove. I put the parcel back into my pack and only take two pancakes over to the Russians.

9

We've been travelling for a number of days. Then the first aircraft appear in the sky. We roll along past transport convoys. Guns, guns. We change to the field railway. I try to find my regiment. Nobody knows exactly where it is at the moment. I stay overnight somewhere, draw my rations somewhere in the morning, and get a few vague instructions. And so I set off on my way again, with my rifle and pack.

When I get to where the regiment is supposed to be, the place has been shot to pieces and there isn't anybody there. I find out that we have been turned into a so-called flying division, one they can send wherever things are hottest. I don't like the sound of that. People tell me about the large-scale losses that we are supposed to have suffered. I ask about Kat and Albert. Nobody knows anything about them.

I carry on searching, wandering about all over the place. For one night, and then for another, I have to camp out like a Red Indian. Then I get definite news, and I am able to report to the guard room by the afternoon.

The sergeant keeps me there. The company will be back in two days and there's no point in sending me out. 'How was leave?' he asks. 'Good, eh?'

'Yes and no,' I reply.

'Right, right,' he sighs, 'if only you didn't have to go away again. That always mucks up the last half good and proper.'

I hang about until the next morning when the company gets in, grey, dirty, ill-tempered and gloomy. Then I jump up and push in amongst them, looking around – there's Tjaden, Müller blowing his nose, and there are Kat and Kropp. We put our palliasses together. I'm feeling guilty, though there isn't any reason why I should. Before we turn in I bring out the rest of the potato pancakes and jam, so that they can have some too.

The two outside pancakes are a bit mouldy, but they are still edible. I take these myself and give the less stale ones to Kat and Kropp.

Kat chews and asks me, 'I bet these are from your mother?'

I nod.

'They're good,' he says, 'you can taste where they're from.'

I could almost weep. I don't know myself any more. But things will get better again here with Kat and Albert and the others. This is where I belong.

'You're in luck,' whispers Kropp just before we go to sleep at last, 'there's word that we are being sent to Russia.'

To Russia. There's no war there any more.

In the distance there is the thundering of the front. The hut walls rattle.

★

Suddenly it is all spit-and-polish. Every five minutes we have to parade. We are inspected from all sides. Anything torn is replaced with something decent. I get hold of a spotless new tunic. Kat, of course, manages a whole new uniform. The rumour starts up that peace is coming, but the alternative rumour seems more likely, that we're being transported to Russia. But why would we need better gear for Russia? Then at last it filters through to us: the Kaiser is coming to review the troops. That's why there have been so many inspection parades.

For a week you might have thought that we were in training camp, because there is so much work and drill going on. Everyone is bad tempered and edgy, because we are not keen on all this spit-and-polish, and even less so on parade-ground marching. Things like that annoy soldiers even more than being in the trenches.

At last the moment arrives. We stand to attention and the Kaiser appears. We are curious to see what he looks like. He paces along the parade line and I'm a bit disappointed; from his pictures I had imagined him to be bigger and more powerful, but mainly to have a great booming voice.

He gives out a few medals and chats to one or two of the soldiers. Then we are marched off.

Afterwards we talk about it. 'So that was the supreme commander, the head of them all,' says Tjaden in amazement. 'Absolutely everyone has to stand to attention in front of him, whoever they are.' He thinks about it. 'Even Hindenburg has to stand to attention in front of him, right?'

'He certainly does,' confirms Kat.

Tjaden isn't finished yet. He ponders for a while, and then asks, 'Does a king have to stand to attention in front of an emperor?'

Nobody is quite sure, but we don't think so. They are both so high up that proper standing to attention doesn't apply.

'You don't half talk some nonsense,' says Kat. 'The main thing is that *you* know when to stand to attention.'

But Tjaden is completely fascinated by it. His imagination, which is not usually very fertile, starts to work overtime. 'Now just a minute,' he announces, 'I really can't believe that an emperor has to go to the lavatory just like I do.'

'You can bet your life he does,' laughs Kropp.

'And if you take away the number you first thought of, then Bob's your uncle,' adds Kat by way of explanation. 'Tjaden, the lice have got to your brain – the best thing you can do is get to the latrines yourself and come back when you're thinking straight and not talking like a kid.'

Tjaden clears off.

'There is one thing I'd like to know, though,' says Albert, 'and that's whether there would still have been a war if the Kaiser had said no.'

'I'm sure there would,' I put in. 'After all, they say that he didn't want to fight at all at the beginning.'

'Well, if not just him, then perhaps if, let's say twenty or thirty people in the world had said no?'

'Maybe not then,' I admit. 'But they all *did* want a war.'

'It's funny when you think about it,' continues Kropp. 'We're out here defending our homeland. And yet the French are there defending their homeland as well. Which of us is right?'

'Maybe both,' I say, though I don't believe it.

'Well then,' says Albert, and I can see that he is trying to drive me into a corner, 'our teachers and preachers and newspapers all tell us that we are the only ones with right on our side, and let's hope it's true – but the French teachers and preachers and newspapers all insist that they are the only ones in the right. How does that figure?'

'I don't know,' I reply, 'but at any rate there *is* a war and every month more countries want to take part.'

Tjaden comes back. He is still worked up and joins in the debate again straight away by asking how a war starts in the first place.

'Usually when one country insults another one badly,' answers Kropp, a little patronizingly.

But Tjaden isn't going to be put off. 'A country? I don't get it. A German mountain can't insult a French mountain, or a river, or a forest, or a cornfield.'

'Are you really that daft or are you just pretending?' grumbles Kropp. 'That isn't what I mean. One nation insults another . . .'

'Then I shouldn't be here at all,' answers Tjaden, 'because I don't feel insulted.'

'It's hopeless trying to explain anything to you,' says Kropp with some irritation, 'it's got nothing to do with a yokel like you.'

'In that case I can certainly go home, then,' insists Tjaden, and everybody laughs.

'Come on, it means the nation as a whole, that is, the state –' calls out Müller.

'The state, the state –' Tjaden snaps his fingers dismissively – 'military police, ordinary police, taxes – that's your state. If you want anything to do with that lot, thanks very much, but leave me out of it.'

'That's true,' says Kat, 'you've got something right for once, Tjaden; there's a big difference between a homeland and a state.'

'But they do go together,' says Kropp after a moment's thought. 'You can't have a homeland without the state.'

'Right, but just think for a minute – we are almost all ordinary people, aren't we? And in France the majority are workers, too, or tradesmen or clerks. Why on earth should a French locksmith or a French shoemaker want to attack us? No, it's just the governments. I'd never seen a Frenchman before I came here, and most of the Frenchmen won't have seen one of us. Nobody asked them any more than they did us.'

'So why is there a war at all?' asks Tjaden.

Kat shrugs. 'There must be some people who find the war worthwhile.'

'Well I'm not one of them,' grins Tjaden.

'No, and nor is anybody else here.'

'So who, then?' persists Tjaden. 'It's no use to the Kaiser. He's got everything he needs anyway.'

'No, you can't say that,' counters Kat, 'up to now he hadn't had a war. And all top-grade emperors need at least one war, otherwise they don't get famous. Have a look in your school history books.'

'Generals get famous because of wars, too,' says Detering.

'More famous than emperors,' agrees Kat.

'And I bet there are other people behind it all who are making a profit out of the war,' grumbles Detering.

'I think it's more a kind of fever,' says Albert. 'Nobody really wants it, but all of a sudden, there it is. We didn't want the war, they say the same thing on the other side – and in spite of that, half the world is at it hammer and tongs.'

'They tell more lies on the other side than our lot do, though,' I put in. 'What about those leaflets the POWs had on them, where they said that we eat Belgian babies? People who write things like that ought to be strung up. They're the real villains.'

Müller gets up. 'Anyway, it's better that war is here than in Germany. Just have a look at no man's land.'

Tjaden voices his full agreement. 'That's true. But it would be better if there were no war at all.'

He walks off, proud to have got the last word over us high-school recruits for once. And in fact his views are typical enough out here, you meet them time and again, and there is no real argument that you can put up against them, because they override any understanding of wider issues. The feelings of nationalism that the ordinary soldier has are expressed in the fact that he is out here. But it doesn't go any further; all his other judgements are practical ones and made from his own point of view.

Albert lies down on the grass in annoyance. 'It's better not to talk about the whole damn thing.'

'Doesn't change anything, anyway,' agrees Kat.

On top of it all, we have to hand in nearly all the new things that we were issued, and we get our old gear back. The good quality stuff was only for the troop inspection.

★

Instead of going to Russia we go up the line again. On the way we pass through what is left of a wood, with half-blasted tree-trunks and the ground looking as if it had been ploughed up. There are some massive craters. 'Christ, this place took a pounding,' I say to Kat.

'Mortar fire,' he replies, and then points upwards.

Dead men are hanging in the trees. In one of them a naked soldier is squatting in the branches; his helmet is still on his head, but otherwise he has nothing on. There is only the top half of him up there, a head and body with the legs missing.

'What happened there?' I ask.

'Blown out of his uniform,' grunts Tjaden.

'It's funny,' says Kat, 'but we've seen that a few times. When a trench mortar goes off you actually do get blown out of your clothes. It's the blast that does it.'

I look around. It really is true. In some trees there are just bits of uniform, others have a bit of bloody pulp that was once a human limb sticking to them. There is one body which only has a scrap of underpants on one leg and the tunic collar around the neck. Otherwise it is naked. The uniform is hanging in the nearby trees. Both arms are missing from the body, as if they have been wrenched out of their sockets. I come across one of them in the undergrowth twenty paces away.

The dead man is lying on his face. The earth is black from the blood underneath the arm sockets. The ground is scuffed by his feet, as though he went on kicking for a while.

'It's no joke, Kat,' I say.

'Nor is a bit of shrapnel in the guts,' he says with a shrug.

'The main thing is not to let it all get to you,' adds Tjaden.

All this can't have happened too long ago, because the blood is still fresh. Since all the soldiers we find are dead we don't hang about there, but just report the business at the next dressing station. After all, there's no reason why we should do the donkey work for the stretcher-bearers.

★

A patrol has to be sent out to establish how many of the enemy positions are still manned. Because I've had leave, I still feel a bit awkward as far as the others are concerned, and for that reason I volunteer to join it. We agree on a plan of action; crawl through the wire, and then separate, so that we can move forward independently. After a while I find a shallow crater and slip into it. I take a look at things from there.

The area is being covered by moderate machine-gun fire. They are sweeping it from all sides, and the fire is not very heavy, but still enough for you to make sure you keep your head well down.

A Verey light goes up. The terrain looks barren in the pale glow. By contrast, it seems so much darker when the night closes in again. They told us back in the trenches that there are supposed to be black soldiers in the opposite trenches. That's bad, because they are hard to see, and besides, they are very good at reconnaissance patrols. Curiously enough, they can often be just plain careless. Both Kat and Kropp have been on patrols where they have shot black soldiers out on counter-reconnaissance who were so keen on cigarettes that they were smoking as they moved along. All Kat and Albert had to do was to get a glowing tip in their sights and aim at that.

A small shell whistles down and strikes close to where I am. I hadn't heard it coming and it gives me a real fright. At that moment I'm overcome by mindless panic. I'm out here on my own in the dark and wellnigh helpless – for all I know two eyes have already been watching me for ages from another shell hole and there is a hand-grenade just waiting to blow me to bits. I try to pull myself together. This isn't my first patrol and it isn't even a particularly dangerous one. But it is the first one I've been on since I was on leave, and on top of that the terrain is still pretty unfamiliar to me.

I tell myself firmly that I am getting worked up for nothing, that there is probably no one watching for me in the dark because if there were they wouldn't be firing so low.

It's no use. Thoughts buzz round in my head in complete confusion – I hear my mother's warning voice, I see the Russians leaning against the wire-netting, with their beards blowing in the wind, I get a bright and wonderful picture of a canteen with comfortable chairs, then of a cinema in Valenciennes, and then, horrible in my tortured imagination, of a gun barrel, grey and unfeeling, following me around silently wherever I try to turn my head: sweat is breaking out from every pore.

I am still lying in the hollow I found. I look at my watch; only a few minutes have passed. My forehead is wet, there is dampness all round my eyes, my hands are shaking and I'm coughing quietly. It's nothing more than a bad attack of fear, of common-or-garden cold terror at the prospect of sticking my head out and crawling on.

All my tense readiness melts into the desire to stay lying down. My limbs are glued to the ground, I try to move, but I can't – they just won't come away from it. I press myself into the earth, I cannot move forwards, and I decide to stay where I am.

But right away a new wave comes over me, a wave of shame, of regret, and yet still one of self-preservation. I lift myself up slightly to have a look around. My eyes are stinging and I stare into the darkness. Then a Verey light goes up and I duck down again.

I am fighting a crazy, confused battle. I want to get out of my hollow in the ground and I keep on slipping back in; I say to myself, 'You've got to, it's to do with your mates, not some stupid order,' and straight after that: 'So what? I've only got the one life to lose.'

It's all because of that leave, I tell myself bitterly by way of an excuse. But I don't believe it myself, I just feel horribly drained. I raise myself up slowly and stretch out my arms, then raise my back and prop myself half on the edge of the shell hole.

Then I hear sounds and get down again. In spite of the thunder of the guns you can pick out suspicious noises completely clearly. I listen – the sound is coming from behind me. It is our soldiers moving through the trench. Now I can even hear muted voices. From the sound of it it might even be Kat speaking.

Suddenly a surprising warmth comes over me. Those voices, those few soft words, those footsteps in the trench behind me tear me with a jolt away from the terrible feeling of isolation that goes with the fear of death, to which I nearly succumbed. Those voices mean more than my life, more than mothering and fear, they are the strongest and most protective thing that there is: they are the voices of my pals.

I'm no longer a shivering scrap of humanity alone in the dark – I belong to them and they to me, we all share the same fear and the same life, and we are bound to each other in a strong and simple way. I want to press my face into them, those voices, those few words that saved me, and which will be my support.

★

I slip warily over the edge, and snake forwards. I creep along on all fours; things are going well, I fix the direction, look about me and take note of the pattern of artillery fire so that I can find my way back. Then I try to make contact with the others.

I am still afraid, but now it is a rational fear, which is just an extraordinarily enhanced cautiousness. It is a windy night, and the shadows move back and forth in the sudden flashes from the gunfire. By this light you can see too much and too little. Often I freeze suddenly, but there is never anything there. In this way I get quite a long distance forward, and then turn back in a curve. I haven't made contact. Every few feet closer to our trench makes me more confident, but I still move as fast as I can. It wouldn't be too good to stop one just at this moment.

And then I get another shock. I'm no longer able to make out the exact direction. Silently I crouch in a shell hole and try and get my bearings. It has happened more than once that a man has jumped cheerfully into a trench, and only then found out that it was the wrong side.

After a while I listen again. I still haven't sorted out where I am. The wilderness of shell holes seems so confusing that in my agitated state I no longer have any idea which way to go. Maybe I am crawling parallel with the trenches, and I could go on for ever doing that. So I make another turn.

These damned Verey lights! It feels as if they last for an hour, and you can't make a move, or things soon start whistling round you.

It's no use, I've got to get out. By fits and starts I work my way along. I crawl crabwise across the ground and tear my hands to pieces on ragged bits of shrapnel as sharp as razor-blades. Often I get the impression that the sky is becoming lighter on the horizon, but that could just be my imagination. Gradually I realize that I am crawling for my life.

A shell hits. Then straight away two more. And then it really starts. A barrage. Machine-guns chatter. Now there is nothing in the world that I can do except lie low. It seems to be an offensive. Light-rockets go up everywhere. Incessantly.

I'm lying bent double in a big shell hole in water up to my waist. When the offensive starts I'll drop into the water as far as I can without drowning and put my face in the mud. I'll have to play dead.

Suddenly I hear their shellfire give way. Straight away I slip down into the water at the bottom of the shell hole, my helmet right on the back of my neck and my mouth only sufficiently above water to let me breathe.

Then I remain motionless – because somewhere there is a clinking noise, something is coming closer, moving along and stamping; every nerve in my body tenses up and freezes. The clinking noise moves on over me, the first wave of soldiers is past. All that I had in my head was the one explosive thought: what will you do if someone jumps into your shell hole? Now I quickly pull out my small dagger, grip it tight and hide it by keeping my hand downwards in the mud. The idea keeps pounding in my brain that if anyone jumps in I'll stab him immediately, stick the knife into his throat at once, so that he can't shout out, there's no other way, he'll be as frightened as I am, and we'll attack each other purely out of fear, so I have to get there first.

Now our gun batteries are firing. There is an impact near me. That makes me furiously angry, that's all I need, to be hit by our own gunfire; I curse into the mud and grind my teeth, it's an outburst of rage, and in the end all I can do is groan and plead.

The crash of shells pounds against my ears. If our men launch a counter-offensive, I'm free. I press my head against the earth and I can hear the dull thunder like distant explosions in a mine – then I lift my head to listen to the noises above me.

The machine-guns are rattling away. I know that our barbed-wire entanglements are firm and pretty well undamaged; sections of them are electrified. The gunfire increases. They aren't getting through. They'll have to turn back.

I collapse into the shell hole again, tense almost to breaking point. Clattering, crawling, clinking – it all becomes audible, a single scream ringing out in the midst of it all. They're coming under fire, the attack has been held off.

★

It's got a little bit lighter. Footsteps hurry by me. The first few. Past me. Then some more. The rattle of the machine-guns becomes continuous. I am just about to turn round a bit when suddenly there is a noise and a body falls on to me in the shell hole, heavily and with a splash, then slips and lands on top of me –

I don't think at all, I make no decision – I just stab wildly and feel only how the body jerks, then goes limp and collapses. When I come to myself again, my hand is sticky and wet.

The other man makes a gurgling noise. To me it sounds as if he is roaring, every breath is like a scream, like thunder – but it is only the blood in my own veins that is pounding so hard. I'd like to stop his mouth, to stuff earth into it, to stab again – he has to be quiet or he'll give me away; but I am so much myself again and suddenly feel so weak that I can't raise my hand against him any more.

So I crawl away into the furthest corner and stay there, my eyes fixed on him, gripping my knife, ready to go for him again if he moves – but he won't do anything again. I can hear that just from his gurgling.

I can only see him indistinctly. I have the one single desire – to get away. If I don't do so quickly it will be too light; it's already difficult. But the moment I try to raise my head I become aware that it is impossible. The machine-gun fire is so dense that I would be full of holes before I had gone a step.

I have another go, lifting up my helmet and pushing it forwards to gauge the height of fire. A moment later a bullet knocks it out of my hand. The gunfire is sweeping the ground at a very low level. I am not far enough away from the enemy trenches to escape being hit by one of the snipers the moment I tried to make a break for it.

It gets lighter and lighter. I wait desperately for an attack by our men. My knuckles are white because I am tensing my hands, praying for the firing to die down and for my mates to come.

The minutes trickle past one by one. I daren't look at the dark figure in the shell hole any more. With great effort I look past him, and wait, just wait. The bullets hiss, they are a mesh of steel, it won't stop, it won't stop.

Then I see my bloodied hand and suddenly I feel sick. I take some earth and rub it on to the skin, now at least my hand is dirty and you can't see the blood any more.

The gunfire still doesn't die down. It's just as strong now from both sides. Our lot have probably long since given me up for lost.

★

It is a light, grey, early morning. The gurgling still continues. I block my ears, but I quickly have to take my hands away from them because otherwise I won't be able to hear anything else.

The figure opposite me moves. That startles me, and I look across at him, although I don't want to. Now my eyes are riveted on him. A man with a little moustache is lying there, his head hanging lopsidedly, one arm half crooked and the head against it. The other hand is clasped to his chest. It has blood on it.

He's dead, I tell myself, he must be dead, he can't feel anything any more; that gurgling, it can only be the body. But the head tries to lift itself and for a moment the groaning gets louder, the forehead sinks back on to the arm. The man is not dead. He is dying, but he is not dead. I push myself forward, pause, prop myself on my hands, slip a bit further along, wait – further, a terrible journey of three yards, a long and fearsome journey. At last I am by his side.

Then he opens his eyes. He must have been able to hear me and he looks at me with an expression of absolute terror. His body doesn't move, but in his eyes there is such an incredible desire to get away that I can imagine for a moment that they might summon up enough strength to drag his body with them, carrying him hundreds of miles away, far, far away, at a single leap. The body is still, completely quiet, there is not a single sound, and even the gurgling has stopped, but the eyes are screaming, roaring, all his life has gathered in them and formed itself into an incredible urge to escape, into a terrible fear of death, a fear of me.

My legs give way and I fall down on to my elbows. 'No, no,' I whisper.

The eyes follow me. I am quite incapable of making any movement as long as they are watching me.

Then his hand falls slowly away from his chest, just a little way, dropping only an inch or two. But that movement breaks the spell of the eyes. I lean forward, shake my head and whisper, 'No, no, no' and lift up my hand – I have to show him that I want to help him, and I wipe his forehead.

The eyes flinched when my hand came close, but now they lose their fixed gaze, the eyelids sink deeper, the tension eases. I open his collar for him and prop his head a bit more comfortably.

His mouth is half open and he makes an attempt to form some words. His lips are dry. I haven't got my water bottle, I didn't bring it with me. But there is water in the mud at the bottom of the shell hole. I scramble down, take out my handkerchief, spread it out, press it down, then cup my hand and scoop up the yellow water that seeps through it.

He swallows it. I fetch more. Then I unbutton his tunic so that I can bandage his wounds, if I can. I have to do that anyway, so that if I get caught the other lot can see that I tried to help him, and won't shoot me outright. He tries to push me away, but his hand is too weak. The shirt is stuck fast and I can't move it aside, and since it is buttoned at the back there is nothing for it but to slit it open.

I look for my knife and find it again. But as soon as I start to cut the shirt open his eyes open wide again and that scream is in them once more, and the look of panic, so that I have to close them, press them shut and whisper, 'I'm trying to help you, comrade, *camarade, camarade, camarade* –' and I stress the word so that he understands me.

There are three stab wounds. My pack of field dressings covers them but the blood flows out underneath, so I press them down more firmly, and he groans.

It's all I can do. Now we must just wait, wait.

★

Hours. The gurgling starts up again – how long it takes for a man to die! What I do know is that he is beyond saving. To be sure, I have tried to convince myself otherwise, but by midday this self-delusion has melted away, has been shot to pieces by his groans. If I hadn't lost my revolver when I was crawling along I would shoot him. I can't stab him.

By midday I am in that twilight area where reason evaporates. I am ravenously hungry, almost weeping for want of food, but I can't help it. I fetch water several times for the dying man and I drink some of it myself.

This is the first man I have ever killed with my own hands, the first one I've seen at close quarters whose death I've caused. Kat and Kropp and Müller have all seen people they have hit as well, it happens often, it's quite common in hand-to-hand fighting –

But every gasp strips my heart bare. The dying man is the master of these hours, he has an invisible dagger to stab me with: the dagger of time and my own thoughts.

I would give a lot for him to live. It is hard to lie here and have to watch and listen to him.

By three in the afternoon he is dead.

I breathe again. But only for a short time. Soon the silence seems harder for me to bear than the groans. I would even like to hear the gurgling again; in fits and starts, hoarse, sometimes a soft whistling noise and then hoarse and loud again.

What I am doing is crazy. But I have to have something to do. So I move the dead man again so that he is lying more comfortably, even though he can't feel anything any more. I close his eyes. They are brown. His hair is black and slightly curly at the sides. His mouth is full and soft underneath his moustache; his nose is a little angular and his skin is tanned – it doesn't seem as pale as before, when he was still alive. For a moment his face even manages to look almost healthy, and then it gives way quickly to become the face of a dead stranger, one of the many I have seen, and every one of them looks alike.

His wife is bound to be thinking of him just now: she doesn't know what has happened. He looks as if he used to write to her a lot; she will go on getting his letters, too – tomorrow, next week – maybe a stray one in a month's time. She'll read it, and he'll be speaking to her in it.

My state of mind is getting worse all the time, and I can't control my thoughts. What does his wife look like? Like the slim dark girl in the house by the canal? Doesn't she belong to me? Perhaps she belongs to me now because of all this! If only Kantorek were sitting here by me! What if my mother saw me in this state – The dead man would surely have been able to live for another thirty years if I'd taken more care about how I was going to get back. If only he had been running a couple of yards further to the left he'd be back in his trench over there writing another letter to his wife.

But this will get me nowhere, it's the fate we all share. If Kemmerich's leg had been a few inches further to the right, if Haie had leaned an inch or two further forward –

★

The silence spreads. I talk, I have to talk. So I talk to him and tell him directly, 'I didn't mean to kill you, mate. If you were to jump in here again, I wouldn't do it, not so long as you were sensible too. But earlier on you were just an idea to me, a concept in my mind that called up an automatic response – it was that concept that I stabbed. It is only now that I can see that you are a human being like me. I just thought about your hand-grenades, your bayonet and your weapons – now I can see your wife, and your face, and what we have in common. Forgive me, *camarade*! We always realize too late. Why don't they keep on reminding us that you are all miserable wretches just like us, that your mothers worry themselves just as much as ours and that we're all just as scared of death, and that we die the same way and feel the same pain. Forgive me, *camarade,* how could you be my enemy? If we threw these uniforms and weapons away you could be just as much my brother as Kat and Albert. Take twenty years from my life, *camarade,* and get up again – take more, because I don't know what I am going to do with the years I've got.'

He is silent, the front is quiet apart from the chatter of machine-guns. The bullets are close together and this is not just random firing – there is careful aiming from both sides. I can't get out.

'I'll write to your wife,' I tell the dead man breathlessly, 'I'll write to her, she ought to hear about it from me, I'll tell her everything that I'm telling you. I don't want her to suffer, I want to help her, and your parents too and your child –'

His uniform is still half open. It is easy to find his wallet. But I am reluctant to open it. Inside it will be his paybook with his name. As long as I don't know his name it's still possible that I might forget him, that time will wipe out the image of all this. But his name is a nail that will be hammered into me and that can never be drawn out again. It will always have the power to bring everything back, it will return constantly and will rise up in front of me.

I hold the wallet, unable to make up my mind. It slips out of my hand and falls open. A few pictures and letters drop out. I collect them up and go to put them back in, but the pressure that I am under, the complete uncertainty of it all, the hunger, the danger, the hours spent with the dead man, these things have all made me desperate, and I want to find out as quickly as possible, to intensify the pain so as to end it, just as you might smash an unbearably painful hand against a tree, regardless of the result.

There are photographs of a woman and of a little girl, small amateur snapshots, taken in front of an ivy-covered wall. There are letters with them. I take them out and try to read them. I can't understand most of them, since they are difficult to decipher and I don't know much French. But every word I translate hits me like a bullet in the chest – or like a dagger in the chest –

My head is nearly bursting, but I am still able to grasp the fact that I can never write to these people, as I thought I would earlier on. Impossible. I look at the photos again; these are not rich people. I could send them money anonymously, if I start earning later. I cling to this idea, it is at least a straw to grasp at. This dead man is bound up with my life, and therefore I have to do everything for him and promise him everything so that I can be rescued. I swear wildly that I will devote my whole existence to him and to his family. I assure him of this with wet lips, and deep within me, while I am doing so, there is the hope that I can buy my own salvation that way, and maybe get out of this alive – it's a little trick of the mind, because what you promise are always things that you could only see to *afterwards*. And so I open the paybook and read slowly: Gerard Duval, compositor.

I write down the address on an envelope with the dead man's pencil, and then in a great hurry I shove everything back into his tunic again.

I have killed Gerard Duval, the printer. I think wildly that I shall have to become a printer, become a printer, a printer –

★

By the afternoon I am calmer. All my fears were groundless. The name no longer bothers me. The attack has passed. 'Well, pal,' I call across to the dead man, but now I say it calmly, 'Your turn today, mine tomorrow. But if I get out of all this, pal, I'll fight against the things that wrecked it for both of us: your life, and my –? Yes, my life too. I promise you, pal. It must never happen again.'

The sun's rays are slanting. I am numb with exhaustion and hunger. Yesterday seems nebulous to me. I no longer have any hopes of getting out of here. So I doze fitfully, and don't even realize that it is evening again. Twilight. It seems to come quickly now. Another hour. If it were summer, another three hours. Another hour.

Now I suddenly start to tremble in case anything goes wrong. I am not thinking about the dead man any more, he's of no importance to me. All at once my desire for life comes back and everything that I promised before gives way in the face of that desire. But just so as not to attract bad luck at this stage I babble mechanically, 'I'll do everything, everything that I promised you' – but I know already that I won't.

It suddenly occurs to me that my own mates might shoot at me if I crawl their way: they don't know it's me. I'll shout out at the first possible point where they might understand me. Then I'll wait there, I'll lie in front of the trench until they answer.

The first star. The front is still quiet. I breathe out and talk to myself in my excitement: 'Don't do anything stupid now, Paul – keep calm, Paul, calm – then you'll be OK, Paul.' It's a good move for me to say my own name, because it sounds as if someone else were doing it, and is that much more effective.

The darkness deepens. My agitation subsides and to be on the safe side I wait until the first light-rockets go up. Then I crawl out of the shell hole. I have forgotten the dead man. In front of me is the young night and the battlefield bathed in pale light. I pick out a shell hole; the moment the light dies away I rush across, feel my way onwards, get to the next one, take cover, hurry on.

I get nearer. Then by the light of one of the rockets I see something in the barbed-wire that moves for a moment before it stops, so I lie still. The next time, I spot it again, it must be men from our trench. But I'm still cautious until I recognize our helmets. Then I shout.

My own name echoes back to me straight away as an answer: 'Paul – Paul.'

I shout again. It is Kat and Albert, who have come out with a tarpaulin to look for me.

'Are you wounded?'

'No, no –'

We tumble into the trench. I ask for something to eat and gobble it down. Müller gives me a cigarette. I give a brief account of what happened. After all, it is nothing new; that sort of thing has happened plenty of times. The only difference in the whole thing was the night attack. But once in Russia Kat had to lie up for two days behind the Russian lines before he could break through.

I don't say anything about the dead printer.

It's not until the following morning that I find I can't hold out any longer. I have to tell Kat and Albert. They both calm me down. 'You can't do anything about it. What else could you do? That's why you're out here.'

I listen to them, comforted, feeling better because of their presence. What sort of rubbish did I dream up in that shell hole?

'Have a look at that,' says Kat, and points.

There are some snipers standing on the parapet. Their rifles have telescopic sights and they are keeping an eye on the sector facing our trench. Every so often a shot rings out.

Then we hear shouts – 'That was a hit!' 'Did you see how high he jumped?' Sergeant Oellrich turns around proudly and notes his score. He is in the lead in today's shooting list with three direct hits confirmed as certain.

'What do you think of that?' asks Kat.

I nod.

'If he goes on that way he'll have another sharpshooter's badge by this evening,' reckons Kropp.

'Or he'll soon be promoted to staff sergeant,' adds Kat.

We look at each other.

'I wouldn't do it,' I say.

'All the same,' says Kat, 'it's a good idea for you to watch him just now.'

Sergeant Oellrich goes back to the fire-step. The end of his rifle moves this way and that.

'You don't need to waste another thought on that business of yours,' nods Albert.

I can't even understand it myself any more.

'It was just because I had to stay there with him for such a long time,' I say. 'After all, war is war.'

There is a short, dry crack from Oellrich's rifle.

10

We've landed a good job. Eight of us have been detailed to guard a village that has been evacuated because it had been under such heavy shelling.

Our main task is to keep an eye on the supply dump, which hasn't been emptied yet. We have to draw our own supplies from what's left there. And we are just the men for the job – Kat, Albert, Müller, Tjaden, Leer, Detering – the whole group of us is there. Mind you, Haie is dead. But even so we've been amazingly lucky, because all the other squads have had far more losses than we have.

We pick a concrete cellar to use as a dugout, with a stairway leading down to it from outside. In addition, the entrance is protected by a separate concrete wall.

Now we really get busy. This is a chance not only to stretch our legs but also to give our souls a bit of breathing space. And we make the most of chances like this, because our situation is too desperate for us to waste much time on sentiment. Sentimental thoughts are only possible as long as things are not absolutely awful. But we don't have any choice except to be pragmatic. So pragmatic, in fact, that I sometimes shudder when, just for a moment, an idea strays into my head from the old days before the war. But thoughts like that never stay with me for long.

We have to take our situation as lightly as we can. That's why we seize every opportunity, and why terror finishes up cheek by jowl with tomfoolery, in stark juxtaposition and without any midway stage. We can't help it, we just throw ourselves into it.

Here, too, we work like mad to create a paradise, a paradise, needless to say, of guzzling and sleeping.

First of all we fit the place out with mattresses that we drag over from the houses. Even a soldier's bottom enjoys something soft to sit on for a change. The floor in the middle of the room is the only place we leave empty. Then we go and find ourselves bedcovers and quilts, wonderfully soft affairs. There's plenty of everything in the village. Albert and I find a mahogany four-poster that can be taken apart – it has a blue silk canopy and a lace coverlet. We sweat like pigs shifting it, but you just can't pass up a thing like that, when it is sure to be shot to bits in a day or so anyway.

Kat and I go for a little patrol through the houses. In a very short time we have found a dozen eggs and a couple of pounds of fairly fresh butter. In one of the rooms there is a sudden loud noise and an iron stove comes hurtling past us through the wall and then out through the opposite wall a few feet from where we are. Two holes. It's from the house opposite, which a shell has just hit.

'Lucky again,' grins Kat, and we carry on foraging. All of a sudden we prick up our ears and then dash off. And within minutes we are standing in wide-eyed enchantment; there, running about in a little pigsty are two live piglets. We rub our eyes and then risk another cautious look: they are really and truly still there. We grab hold of them – there's no doubt about it, they are two genuine little pigs.

They will make a magnificent meal. No more than a few dozen yards from our dugout there is a small house that used to serve as officers' quarters. In the kitchen is a massive cooking range with two gridirons, pots, pans and kettles. It is all there, there is even a shed full of ready-chopped firewood – a regular Aladdin's cave.

Two men have been out since morning in the fields looking for potatoes, carrots and peas. We are very particular, and will have nothing to do with the canned stuff from the supply depot – we want fresh vegetables. There are already two cauliflowers in the pantry.

The piglets have been slaughtered. Kat saw to that. We decide to have potato pancakes with the roast. But we can't find anything to grate the potatoes with. However, we soon find a way round it. With some nails we punch a good number of holes into tin lids – and hey presto they are graters! Three men put on heavy-duty gloves to protect their fingers when they are grating, two more peel the potatoes and we're well on our way.

Kat takes charge of the piglets, the carrots, the peas and the cauliflower. He even makes a white sauce for the cauliflower. I cook the potato pancakes, four at a time. Within ten minutes I've got the knack of tossing them so that when the pancakes have been cooked on one side they will fly up into the air and turn over, so I can catch them again in the pan. The pigs are being roasted whole. Everything is arranged around them as if they were on an altar.

Meanwhile some visitors have arrived, a couple of W/T operators, whom generously we invite to the meal. They sit in the living room, where there is a piano. One plays and the other one sings a folk song from Saxony. He sings it with great feeling, but with quite a strong regional accent. For all that, we are caught up by the mood as we stand there by the stove preparing all the good things.

Gradually we notice that we are coming in for a bit of a pasting. The observation balloons have spotted the smoke from our chimney and we're coming under fire. It's those bloody daisy-cutters, the little shells that make a small hole and scatter fragments low and wide. The whistling gets closer and closer around us, but we can't possibly abandon the food. The bastards are getting our range. A few bits of shrapnel whizz through the kitchen window. The roasts are nearly ready, but cooking the potato pancakes is more of a problem. The impacts are so close together now that shrapnel is hitting the wall of the house more and more often, and coming in through the windows. Every time I hear the whistle of one of the things coming over, I duck down by the window wall with my frying pan and the pancakes. Then I straighten up again and carry on cooking.

The soldiers from Saxony stop playing – a bit of shrapnel has hit the piano. We are pretty well ready too, and we arrange our withdrawal. After the next impact two men sprint the fifty-odd yards to the dugout with the saucepans full of vegetables. We watch them disappear.

Another shot. Everyone ducks, and then two men trot off, each with a pot of excellent coffee, and reach the dugout before the next shell lands.

Kat and Albert grab the *piece de resistance:* the big dish with the piglets, now roasted and golden-brown. There is a howling noise, they bob down briefly, and then tear across the fifty yards of open ground.

I cook four last potato pancakes – I have to take cover twice while I'm doing so – but it does mean another four pancakes for us, after all, and it's my favourite food.

Then I grab the plate with the great pile of pancakes and press myself against the door of the house. There is a hiss, a crash, and I dash out, clutching the plate to my chest with both hands. I am nearly there when there is a whistling noise and it is getting louder, so I leap up like a deer, skid around the concrete wall while shrapnel pounds against it, and fall down the steps into the cellar; my elbows are skinned, but I haven't lost a single pancake and I didn't even upset the plate.

We start the meal at two. It lasts until six. Until half past we drink coffee – officers-only coffee from the supply dump – and as we do so, we smoke officers-only cigars and cigarettes, also from the supply dump. On the dot of half past six we begin supper. At ten we throw the pork bones out of the door. Then we have rum and brandy, once again from the thrice-blessed supply dump, and once again long, fat cigars with bands. Tjaden insists that only one thing is missing: a few girls from one of the officers-only knocking shops.

Later still that evening we hear a miaowing. A little grey cat is sitting in the doorway. We coax it in and give it something to eat. While we are doing that we get peckish again ourselves. We go to bed still chewing.

But we have a terrible night. The food was too rich and too greasy. Fresh sucking-pig has a lively effect on the guts. There is a continuous to-ing and fro-ing in the dugout. There are always two, three men at a time sitting around outside with their trousers down, cursing. I'm up nine times myself. At about four in the morning we set a new record: all ten men, the guard detail and the visitors, are squatting outside.

Burning houses stand like torches in the night. Shells thunder down and make their impact. Columns of munitions trucks roar down the road. The supply dump has been ripped open on one side. In spite of the shrapnel, the drivers move in like a swarm of bees and steal loaves of bread. We don't bother to stop them. If we were to say anything, the most that would happen is that we would get a good thumping. So we take a different line. We explain to them that we have been detailed to guard the supplies, and since we know where everything is, we offer them the tinned stuff and swap it for things we haven't got. What difference does it make? Everything will be shot to pieces in a day or so anyway.

We fetch bars of chocolate for ourselves from the supplies and eat them whole. Kat says chocolate is good when you've got the runs.

Nearly two weeks pass with eating, drinking and taking it easy. Nobody bothers us. The village gradually disappears under the shelling, and we have a good time. As long as just a small part of the supply dump is still there, we don't care what happens, and what we would really like to do is to end the war here.

Tjaden has become so genteel that he only smokes his cigars half-way down. He explains in a superior fashion that this is the style appropriate to his breeding. Even Kat is cheerful. His first words in the morning are 'My man, fetch the caviare and the coffee!' We have all become amazingly upper-crust, everyone takes everyone else to be his valet, addresses him in an aristocratic manner and issues orders. 'Kropp, the sole of my foot is a little itchy; kindly be so good as to remove that louse.' And with that Leer stretches his leg out to him like a prima donna, and Albert grabs it and pulls him up the stairs. 'Tjaden!' – 'What?' – 'You may stand at ease, Tjaden, my good man, and kindly note that the response is not "What?" but "Yessir, right away, sir." So we'll try again. Tjaden!' Tjaden makes what is by now his automatic response, and once more quotes the famous line from German literature indicating which part of his anatomy he would like kissed.

At the end of a further week we get orders to withdraw. The good times are over. Two large trucks come to fetch us. They are already piled high with planks of wood, but Albert and I stack our four-poster with the blue silk canopy up on top, together with the mattresses and a couple of lace coverlets. Inside the bed, at the head end, we both have a sack full of best quality provisions. We keep running our hands over them; the salamis, the tins of liver pâté, the canned food and the boxes of cigars gladden our hearts. All the men have similar sacks with them.

In addition to this, Kropp and I have salvaged two red plush armchairs. They are on the bed, and we lounge in them as if we were in a box at the theatre. The silk cover of the canopy billows out above us. Each of us has a long cigar in his mouth. And so we survey the landscape from on high.

In between us is a parrot cage that we found to keep the cat in. We have brought the cat with us, and it is inside the cage, lying in front of its dish and purring.

The trucks roll slowly along the road. We sing as we go. Behind us the shells are sending up great spurts of earth from the village, which has now been abandoned completely.

*

A few days later we are sent out to evacuate a district. On the way we meet the escaping locals, who have been ordered to leave. They are carting their bits and pieces away with them on barrows, in prams and on their backs. Their figures are bowed, their faces full of misery, despair, haste and resignation. The children hold on to their mothers' hands, and sometimes an older girl will be looking after the smaller ones as they stumble forwards, forever turning to look behind them. A few of them are carrying pitiful little dolls. They all pass us by in silence.

We are still in marching order, because the French are not likely to shell a village when their people are still there. But a few minutes later there is a screeching in the air, the earth shudders, men scream out – a shell has smashed into our rear-guard. We dive apart and throw ourselves on to the ground, but at that very moment I feel how that tenseness slips away from me, the tenseness that usually makes me do the right thing instinctively when I'm under fire, and the thought 'You're done for' jerks into my head with a choking, terrible fear – and the next minute a blow like a whiplash cuts across my left leg. I hear Albert scream – he was right by my side.

'Get up, Albert, run!' I shout, because we are lying without any cover in the open.

He stumbles to his feet and runs. I stay at his side. We have to get over a hedge. It's taller than we are. Kropp grabs hold of the branches, and I get him by the leg, he screams, but I give him enough leverage and he hurtles over. In one movement I get over after him, and land in a pond behind the hedge.

Our faces are covered with pondweed and slime, but it is good cover, and we wade out until we are up to our necks. When a shell comes howling across we duck our heads under the water.

After we have done that about a dozen times I've had enough. And Albert groans, 'Let's move, otherwise I'll fall over and drown.'

'Where did you get it?' I ask.

'In the knee, I think.'

'Can you walk?'

'I think so –'

'Right. Let's go.'

We make it to the ditch by the side of the road and run along, bent double. The gunfire follows us. The road leads to the ammunition dump. If that goes up, nobody will even find one of our buttons afterwards. So we change our plans and set off at an angle across country.

Albert slows down. 'Run on, I'll catch you up,' he says, and throws himself on to the ground.

I pull him up by the arm and give him a shake. 'Get up, Albert, if you lie down now you'll never be able to move on again. Come on, I'll prop you up.'

At last we reach a small dugout. Kropp throws himself down and I bandage him. The wound is just above the knee. Then I look at myself. My trousers have blood on them, and so does my arm. Albert ties his field dressings around the wounds. He is already unable to move his leg, and we are both amazed at how we have managed to get this far at all. It's only fear that did it: we would still have run for it if our feet had been shot away – we'd have run on the stumps.

I can still crawl a little, and I shout out when an open cart comes past, and we're picked up. It is full of wounded men. A medical orderly is there and he shoves a tetanus jab into each of us.

At the dressing station we arrange things so that we are put side by side. They give us some thin beef broth, which we treat with contempt, but finish off greedily – we've been used to better things recently, but we are hungry all the same.

'We'll be heading for home now, Albert,' I say.

'With any luck,' he replies. 'But I wish I knew exactly what I've got.'

The pain gets worse. The bandages are burning like fire. We drink and drink, one mug of water after another.

'How far above the knee was I hit?' asks Kropp.

'A good four inches, Albert,' I say, though in reality it isn't much more than an inch.

'One thing I've decided,' he says after a little while, 'if they take my leg off, I'll do myself in. I don't want to go through life as a cripple.'

And so we lie there with our thoughts, and wait.

*

That same evening they take us to the chopping-block. I'm frightened, and try to think quickly what I should do; because everyone knows that the surgeons in these clearing stations are quick to amputate. With the numbers they have to deal with it is simpler than a complicated patch-up job. I remember what happened to Kemmerich. On no account am I going to let them chloroform me, even if I have to crack a couple of skulls to stop them.

Things go well. The doctor prods around in the wound until I am on the point of passing out. 'Don't make such a fuss,' he snaps, and carries on digging about. His instruments gleam under the bright light like malevolent animals. The pain is unbearable. Two orderlies hold my arms tight, but I get one free and am just about to swing out and get the surgeon in the face when he notices and jumps away. 'Chloroform him,' he shouts furiously.

That makes me calm down. 'I beg your pardon, doctor, I'll keep quiet, but please don't chloroform me.'

'Well, well,' he mutters, and picks up his instruments again. He's blond, thirty at the most, with fraternity duelling scars on his face and repulsive gold-rimmed glasses. I can see that he's messing about with me now, because he is just poking around in the wound and peering at me over his glasses from time to time. I squeeze the hand-grips as tightly as I can but I'd rather die than let him hear another peep out of me.

He has fished out a sliver of metal and chucks it across to me. He seems to be satisfied with my behaviour, because he now puts my leg carefully in splints and tells me, 'It's off home tomorrow for you.' Then they put the leg in plaster. When I am back with Kropp I tell him that it looks as if there will be a hospital train tomorrow.

'We'll have to have a word with the medical duty sergeant so that we can stay together, Albert.'

With a few well chosen words I manage to slip the sergeant a couple of my high quality cigars. He sniffs one and asks, 'Got any more of these?'

'A good handful of them,' I tell him, 'and my pal over there –'

pointing at Kropp – 'has some as well. We would be very pleased to pass them over to you tomorrow – out of the window of the hospital train.'

He cottons on, of course, has another sniff, and says, 'Done.'

We don't get a moment's sleep during the night. Seven men die in our room. One of them sings snatches of hymns in a high, strained tenor for an hour until it gives way to the death rattle. Another gets out of bed and crawls to the window. He is found lying in front of it, as if he wanted to look out for the last time.

★

We are lying on our stretchers at the station. We are waiting for the train. It's raining and the station hasn't any roof. Our blankets are thin. We've already been waiting for two hours.

The sergeant looks after us like a mother. Although I'm feeling very ill I don't stop concentrating on our plan. I let him see the packet of cigars as if by accident, and give him one as an advance payment; for that the sergeant gets a tarpaulin and puts it over us.

'Bloody hell, Albert,' I remind him, 'that four-poster, and the cat . . .'

'And the armchairs,' he adds.

Yes, the red plush armchairs. We sat on those chairs in the evenings like kings, and we had the bright idea of renting them out afterwards by the hour. One hour, one cigarette. We'd have had a good life and a good business.

'Albert –' something else occurs to me – 'what about those sacks of food?'

We become melancholy. We could have done with those things. If the train were to go a day later, I'm sure Kat would have found us and brought us our gear.

It's a bloody nuisance. We've got gruel in our bellies, thin clearing-station grub, and in those sacks of ours there are tins of ham. But we are so weak that we can't get worked up about it.

The stretchers are soaking wet when the train arrives later that morning. The sergeant arranges for us to be in the same carriage. There are lots of Red Cross nurses. Kropp is put into a lower berth. They lift me out to get into the bed above him.

'For Christ's sake!' I blurt out, suddenly.

'What's the matter?' asks the nurse.

I have another look at the bed. It has been made up with snowy white linen, unimaginably clean linen with the creases where it has been ironed. But my shirt hasn't been washed for six weeks and it's filthy.

'Can't you manage to get in by yourself?' asks the nurse anxiously.

'I can manage that,' I say, sweating, 'but please can't you take those bedclothes away first.'

'Whatever for?'

I feel as filthy as a pig. And I'm supposed to get in to a bed like that? 'It'll get –' I pause.

'– a bit dirty?' she asks, encouragingly. 'That won't hurt, we'll just wash it again afterwards.'

'No, it's not just that –' I say in confusion. This sudden confrontation with the civilized world is too much for me.

'If you can be out there in the trenches, surely we can wash a bedsheet or two?' she goes on.

I look at her. She looks crisply turned out and young, well scrubbed and genteel, like everything else on this train; it's hard to believe that it isn't intended for officers only, and it makes you feel uncomfortable, and even a bit threatened.

But the wretched woman behaves like a member of the Inquisition and forces me to say it out loud. 'It's just –' and I stop again; surely she must know what I mean?

'What else is wrong?'

And in the end I positively shout out, 'It's because of the lice!'

She laughs. 'Well, they have to have a good time occasionally, too.'

So then I don't care any more. I scramble into bed and get under the covers.

I feel a hand on the bed-cover. The sergeant. He clears off with the cigars.

An hour later we notice that the train is moving.

*

I wake up in the night. Kropp is restless, too. The train is rolling quietly over the rails. It is still all too much to take in: a bed, a train, going home.

I whisper, 'Albert?'

'Yes –'

'Any idea where the lavatory is?'

'I think it's the door over there on the right.'

'I'll have a look.'

It's dark, I grope for the edge of the bed so that I can slide down carefully. But I miss my footing and slip, the plaster-cast doesn't give me any support and with a crash I'm lying on the floor.

'Damn!' I say.

'Did you hit anything?' asks Kropp.

'I should think you could have heard that,' I grumble, 'my head . . .'

At the back of the carriage a door opens. The nurse comes in with a lamp and sees me.

'He fell out of bed –'

She takes my pulse and feels my forehead. 'But you don't seem to be feverish . . .'

'No –' I admit.

'Were you dreaming?'

'Something like that,' I reply, avoiding the issue. Here we go again with the questions. She looks at me with her clear eyes and she is so clean and delightful that it is even more difficult for me to tell her what I need.

I'm helped back up into bed. That's good. When she has gone I shall have to have another try at getting down. If she were an old woman it would be easier to say what the matter is, but she is so young, twenty-five at the most, and it's no good – I can't tell her.

Then Albert comes to the rescue; he's not embarrassed and anyway, he isn't the one with the problem. He calls out to the nurse. 'Nurse, he wanted . . .' but even Albert doesn't know how to put it properly and decently. Out at the front you can express it with a single verb, but here, to a lady like this . . . And then suddenly he remembers his schooldays, and he continues smoothly, 'He wanted to leave the room, nurse.'

'Oh, I see,' says the nurse, 'but he doesn't have to get out of bed for that, with a leg in plaster.' And she turns to me and asks, 'What is it that you need, then?'

I am absolutely mortified by this new twist, because I haven't the slightest idea what the technical terms are for these functions. The nurse helps me out.

'A big job or a little one?'

Oh my God! I'm sweating like a pig and answer in embarrassment, 'Well, just a little one . . .'

Anyway, it does the trick.

I get a bottle. A few hours later I'm no longer the only one, and by morning we're all used to it and ask for what we want without a second thought.

The train goes slowly. From time to time it stops, so that the dead can be taken off. It stops a lot.

*

Albert is feverish. I'm feeling wretched because of the pain, but what is worse is the fact that there are probably lice underneath the plaster cast. It itches horribly and I can't scratch it.

We doze through the days. The countryside rolls quietly past the windows. On the third night we reach Herbesthal, on the German border. The nurse tells me that Albert is going to be taken off at the next stop because of his fever. 'How far is the train going?' I ask.

'To Cologne.'

'Albert,' I say, 'we'll stay together, you wait.'

The next time the nurse does her rounds I hold my breath so that my face swells and goes red. She stops. 'Are you in pain?'

'Yes,' I groan, 'it came on suddenly.'

She gives me a thermometer and moves on. I wouldn't be one of Kat's apprentices if I didn't know what to do. Army-issue thermometers are no match for old soldiers. All you have to do is get the mercury to go up, and then it will stay where it is in the thin tubing and not go down again.

I stick the thermometer under my arm, pointing downwards, and keep pressing against the bulb with my forefinger. Then I shake it up. That way I get it to over 100° Fahrenheit. That isn't enough, though. A match held judiciously near the bulb brings it up to 102°.

When the nurse comes back I gasp out, then make my breathing shallow and irregular, goggle at her with eyes that are a bit staring, fidget restlessly and whisper, 'I can't stand it any more . . .'

She jots my name down on a card. I'm quite sure that they won't open up my plaster-cast unnecessarily.

Albert and I are taken off the train together.

*

We are in bed in a Catholic infirmary, in the same ward. This is a piece of luck, because the Catholic hospitals are known for good treatment and good food. This military hospital is full up with men from our train-load, and there are plenty of serious cases amongst them. We are not taken in for examination today, because there aren't enough doctors. Flat hospital trolleys with rubber wheels are constantly being moved along the corridor, and there is always somebody stretched out on them. A bloody awful position to be – stretched out like that – it's only bearable when you're asleep.

We have a very disturbed night. Nobody can sleep. We doze off a bit towards morning. I wake up again when it gets light. The doors are open and I can hear voices coming from the corridor. The others wake up. One of them, who has already been in for a few days, tells us what is going on. 'Up here the sisters say prayers in the corridor every morning. They call it their morning devotions. They open the doors so that you can get your share of benefit from it.'

I'm sure they mean well, but our bones and our heads are aching.

'It's ridiculous,' I say, 'when we've only just got to sleep.'

'The less serious cases are up here, that's why they do it,' he replies.

Albert groans.

I get angry and shout, 'Be quiet out there!'

A minute later a nurse appears. In her black-and-white habit she looks like a pretty tea-cosy. Someone says, 'Please shut the door, Sister.'

'We're having prayers, that's why the door is open,' she replies.

'But we want to sleep –'

'Prayers are better than sleep.' She stands there and smiles in all innocence. 'And besides, it is already seven o'clock.'

Albert groans again.

'Shut the door,' I snap.

She is quite at a loss, apparently unable to understand such an attitude. 'But we are praying for you as well.'

'Makes no difference. Shut the door!'

She disappears, leaving the door open. The litany starts up again. I'm now furious, and shout, 'I'm going to count to three. If it's not quiet by then, I'll let fly.'

'Me too,' adds someone else.

I count to five. Then I take a bottle, aim, and throw it through the door into the corridor. It smashes into a thousand pieces. The prayers stop. A whole swarm of nurses come in and make reproachful noises.

'Shut that door!' we scream.

They withdraw. The little one who came in before is the last to leave. 'Heathens,' she twitters. But she *does* close the door.

We have won.

*

The hospital inspector turns up at midday and bawls us out. He threatens us with the clink, and worse. Now military hospital inspectors, just like commissariat officers, are, it is true, entitled to a sword and pips on their shoulders, but really they are just administrators, so not even recruits take them for proper officers. And so we let him talk away. What can they do to us –?

'Who threw the bottle?' he asks.

Before I have time to wonder whether I should own up, someone says, 'I did.'

A man with a stubble of beard sits up in bed. Everyone wonders why he has taken the blame.

'It was you?'

'Correct. I became over-excited because we were wakened unnecessarily, and I lost control, so that I was not responsible for my actions.' He talks like a book.

'Name?'

'Josef Hamacher, Supplementary Reserve.'

The inspector leaves.

We are all curious. 'What on earth did you own up for? It wasn't you at all!'

He grins. 'It doesn't matter. I've got a Special Permit.'

Everyone knows what he means, of course. If you have a Special Permit, you can do anything.

'Yes,' he explains. 'I got a head wound, and when that happened they made out a document saying that I might not be responsible for my actions from time to time. Ever since then I've had a good time. No one is allowed to get me worked up. So nothing will happen to me. He'll get pretty angry down there when he finds out. And I owned up because I enjoyed the bottle-throwing. If they leave the door open tomorrow, we'll chuck another one.'

We couldn't be happier. As long as we've got Josef Hamacher, we can try anything on.

Then the silent, flat hospital trolleys come to fetch us.

Our bandages are stuck. We bellow like cattle.

★

There are eight men in our room. Peter, who has black curly hair, is the one with the most serious wound, a lung injury with complications. Franz Waechter, next to him, has a bullet wound in his arm which did not look too bad at first. But during the third night he calls out to us to ring for help, because he thinks he has begun to haemorrhage.

I ring violently. The night sister doesn't come. Earlier in the evening we were all pretty demanding of her, because our dressings had all been changed, and so we were suffering. One of us wanted his leg put this way, another of us wanted it that way, a third wanted some water, the fourth needed his pillow plumped up. Eventually the fat old nurse had grumbled crossly and closed the doors on us. Now she probably suspects that it will be the same sort of thing, because she doesn't come.

We wait. Then Franz says, 'Ring again.'

I do it. There is still no sign of her. There is only the one ward sister on our wing at night, and perhaps she is busy in one of the other rooms. 'Are you sure you are bleeding, Franz?' I ask. 'If not, they'll be down on us like a ton of bricks again.'

'It's wet. Can't anyone put the light on?'

We can't manage that, either. The switch is by the door and nobody can get out of bed. I press the bell until I can't feel my thumb any more. Maybe the nurse has nodded off. They really have a lot to do and they are all overworked, even during the day. And they have all those prayers to say.

'Should we chuck a few bottles?' asks Josef Hamacher, the one with the Special Permit.

'She's even less likely to hear that than the bell.'

At last the door opens. The old girl appears, looking sulky.

When she sees what is up with Franz she gets a move on, and shouts at us, 'Why didn't any of you call me?'

'We did ring. None of us can walk.'

He has lost a lot of blood and is bandaged up. In the morning we notice how his face has become sharper and more yellow, while last night he still looked almost healthy. A nurse comes round more often now.

★

We often get volunteer auxiliary nurses from the Red Cross. They are well meaning, but they can be a bit on the clumsy side. When they re-make our beds they often hurt us, and then they are so shaken that they hurt us even more.

The nuns are more reliable. They know how to get hold of us, but we would really prefer them to be more cheerful. Some of them do have a good sense of humour, it's true, and those are great. There is no one who wouldn't do anything in the world for Sister Tina, a wonderful nurse, who cheers up the whole wing, even when we can only see her from a distance. And there are a few more like her. We'd go through hell and high water for them. We really can't complain – you get treated like a civilian by the nuns here. On the other hand, when you think of the garrison hospitals, then you really start to worry.

Franz Waechter doesn't regain his strength. One day he is taken out and doesn't come back. Josef Hamacher knows what has happened. 'We won't see him again. He's been taken to the Dead Man's Room.'

'What Dead Man's Room?'

'You know, the Dying Room –'

'What's that?'

'The small room at the corner of this wing. Anybody who is about to snuff it gets taken there. There are two beds. It's called the Dying Room all over the hospital.'

'But why do they do that?'

'So they don't have so much work afterwards. It's easier, too, because it's right by the entrance to the mortuary. Maybe they want to make sure that nobody dies on the wards, and do it so as not to upset the others. They can keep an eye on a man better, too, if he is in there on his own.'

'What about the man himself?'

Josef shrugs. 'Usually he is past noticing much any more.'

'Does everyone know about this?'

'Anyone who has been here for a while finds out, of course.'

*

That afternoon Franz Waechter's bed is made up again. After a couple of days they come and take the new man away. Josef indicates with his hand where he is going. We watch a good few more come and go.

Relatives often come and sit by the beds crying, or talking softly and shyly. One old lady is very reluctant to leave, but she can't stay there all night, of course. She comes back very early on the following morning, but not quite early enough; because when she goes up to the bed there is already somebody new in it. She has to go to the mortuary. She gives us the apples that she had brought with her.

Little Peter is getting worse, too. His temperature chart looks bad, and one day a flat hospital trolley is put beside his bed. 'Where am I going?' he asks.

'To have your dressings done.'

They lift him on to the trolley. But the nurse makes the mistake of taking his battledress tunic from its hook and putting it on the trolley with him, so that she doesn't have to make two journeys. Peter realizes at once what is going on and tries to roll off the trolley. 'I'm staying here!'

They hold him down. He cries out weakly with his damaged lung, 'I don't want to go to the Dying Room.'

'But we're going to the dressing ward.'

'Then why do you need my tunic?' He can't speak any more. Hoarse and agitated, he whispers, 'Want to stay here.'

They don't answer, and move him out. By the door he tries to sit up. His head of black curls is bobbing, his eyes are full of tears. 'I'll be back! I'll be back!' he shouts.

The door closes. We are all rather worked up, but nobody says anything. Eventually Josef says, 'Plenty of them have said that. But once you are in there you never last.'

⋆

They operate on me and I puke for two whole days. My bones don't seem to want to knit properly, says the doctor's clerk. There's another man whose bones grow together badly and he has to have them broken again. It's all pretty wretched.

Our latest additions include two recruits who have flat feet. When he is doing his rounds the chief surgeon finds this out and stops, delighted. 'We'll get rid of that problem,' he tells them. 'We'll just do a little operation and you'll both have healthy feet. Take their names, nurse.'

Once he has left, Josef – who knows everything – gives them a warning. 'Whatever you do, don't let him operate on you. That business is the old man's medical hobby-horse. He's dead keen on anyone he can get hold of to work on. He'll operate on you for flat feet, and sure enough, when he's finished you won't have flat feet any more. Instead you'll have club feet and you'll be on crutches for the rest of your days.'

'What can we do?' asks one of them.

'Just say no. You're here to have your bullet wounds treated, not your flat feet. Think about it. Now you can still walk, but just let the old man get you under the knife and you're cripples. He's after guinea pigs for his experiments, and the war is a good time for him, just like it is for all the doctors. Have a look around the ward downstairs; there are at least a dozen men hobbling about after he's operated on them. A good few of them have been here since 1914 or 15 – for years. Not a single one of them can walk better than he could before, and for nearly all of them it's worse, most of them have to have their legs in plaster. Every six months he catches up with them and breaks the bones again, and every time that's supposed to do the trick. You be careful – he's not allowed to do it if you refuse.'

'What the hell,' says one of the two men wearily, 'better your feet than your head. Who knows what you'll get when you're back at the front. I don't care what they do to me, so long as I get sent home. Having a club foot's better than being dead.'

The other one, a young man like us, doesn't want to. The next morning the old man has them brought down and argues with them and bullies them for so long that they both agree after all. What else can they do? They are just the poor bloody infantry and he's top brass. They are brought back chloroformed and with plaster casts on.

★

Albert is in a bad way. They take him away and amputate. The whole leg from the upper thigh downwards is taken off. Now he hardly ever speaks. Once he says that he will shoot himself the minute he can lay his hands on a revolver.

A new hospital transport train arrives. Our room gets two blinded soldiers. One of them is very young, a musician. The nurses never use knives when they feed him; he's already grabbed one once out of a nurse's hand. In spite of these precautions, something still happens. The sister who is feeding him one evening is called away, and leaves the plate and the fork on the side table while she is gone. He gropes across for the fork, gets hold of it and rams it with all his force into his chest, then grabs a shoe and hammers on the shaft as hard as he can. We shout for help and it takes three men to get the fork out. The blunt prongs had gone in a long way. He swears at us all night, so that none of us can sleep. In the morning he has a screaming fit.

Again there are empty beds. One day follows another, days filled with pain and fear, with groans and with the death rattle. Even having a Dying Room is no use any more because it isn't enough; men die during the night in our room. Things just go faster than the nurses can spot.

One day, though, our door is flung open, a hospital trolley is rolled in, and there sits Peter on his stretcher, pale, thin, upright and triumphant, with his tangle of black curls. Sister Tina pushes the trolley over to his old bed with a broad smile on her face. He's come back from the Dying Room. We had assumed he was long since dead.

He looks at us. 'What about that, then?'

And even Josef has to admit that it is a new one on him.

⋆

After a while a few of us are allowed out of bed. I am given a pair of crutches, too, so that I can hobble about. But I don't use them much; I can't bear the way Albert looks at me when I walk across the ward. His eyes follow me with such a strange look in them. Because of that I often try to slip out into the corridor – I can move more freely there.

On the floor below us there are men with stomach and spinal wounds, men with head wounds and men with both legs or arms amputated. In the right-hand wing are men with wounds in the jaw, men who have been gassed and men wounded in the nose, ears or throat. In the left-hand wing are those who have been blinded and men who have been hit in the lungs or in the pelvis, in one of the joints, in the kidneys, in the testicles or in the stomach. It is only here that you realize all the different places where a man can be hit.

Two men die of tetanus. Their skin becomes pale, their limbs stiffen, and at the end only their eyes remain alive – for a long time. With many of the wounded, the damaged limb has been hoisted up into the air on a kind of gallows; underneath the wound itself there is a dish for the pus to drip into. The basins are emptied every two or three hours. Other men are in traction, with heavy weights pulling down at the end of the bed. I see wounds in the gut which are permanently full of matter. The doctor's clerk shows me X-rays of hips, knees and shoulders that have been shattered completely.

It is impossible to grasp the fact that there are human faces above these torn bodies, faces in which life goes on from day to day. And on top of it all, this is just one single military hospital, just one – there are hundreds of thousands of them in Germany, hundreds of thousands of them in France, hundreds of thousands of them in Russia. How pointless all human thoughts, words and deeds must be, if things like this are possible! Everything must have been fraudulent and pointless if thousands of years of civilization weren't even able to prevent this river of blood, couldn't stop these torture chambers existing in their hundreds of thousands. Only a military hospital can really show you what war is.

I am young, I am twenty years of age; but I know nothing of life except despair, death, fear, and the combination of completely mindless superficiality with an abyss of suffering. I see people being driven against one another, and silently, uncomprehendingly, foolishly, obediently and innocently killing one another. I see the best brains in the world inventing weapons and words to make the whole process that much more sophisticated and long-lasting. And watching this with me are all my contemporaries, here and on the other side, all over the world – my whole generation is experiencing this with me. What would our fathers do if one day we rose up and confronted them, and called them to account? What do they expect from us when a time comes in which there is no more war? For years our occupation has been killing – that was the first experience we had. Our knowledge of life is limited to death. What will happen afterwards? And what can possibly become of us?

⋆

The oldest man in our room is Lewandowski. He is forty, and has been in the hospital for ten months already with a serious stomach wound. Only in recent weeks has he made enough progress to be able to limp around a little, bent double.

For the past few days he has been very excited. His wife has written to him from the little place away in Poland where she lives, that she has managed to get enough money together to pay for the journey to come and visit him.

She is on her way and might turn up any day. Lewandowski has lost his appetite, and even gives away sausage with red cabbage when he has only eaten a couple of mouthfuls. He is forever going round the room with his letter, and all of us have read it a dozen times already, the postmark has been inspected God knows how often, and there are so many grease stains and fingermarks on it that the writing can barely be deciphered any more. The inevitable happens: Lewandowski gets a fever and has to go back into bed.

He hasn't seen his wife for two years. She had a baby after he left, and she's bringing it with her. But Lewandowski has something quite different on his mind. He had been hoping to get permission to leave the hospital when his old woman came, for obvious reasons; it's all very nice to see someone, but when you get your wife back after such a long time you want something else altogether, if at all possible.

Lewandowski has talked about all this for hours with us, because there are no secrets in the army. Nobody bothers about it, anyway. Those of us who are already allowed out have told him about a few perfect places in the town, gardens and parks where nobody would disturb him. One man even knew of a small room.

But what use is all that now? Lewandowski is confined to bed and miserable. All the joy will go out of his life if he has to miss out on this. We tell him not to worry and promise that we will sort the whole business out somehow.

His wife appears the next afternoon, a little crumpled thing with anxious, darting eyes, like a bird's, wearing a kind of mantilla with frills and bands. God alone knows where she can have inherited the thing.

She murmurs something quietly, and waits shyly by the door. She is shocked to find that there are six of us in the room.

'Come on, Marya,' says Lewandowski, swallowing his Adam's apple dangerously, 'you can come on in, nobody's going to hurt you.'

She walks round the room and shakes hands with each one of us. Then she shows us the baby, which in the meantime has dirtied its nappy. She has a large, beaded bag with her and she takes a clean nappy out of it and neatly changes the child. This gets her over any initial embarrassment, and the two start to talk to each other.

Lewandowski is extremely fidgety and keeps looking across at us miserably with his bulging round eyes.

The time is right. The doctor has done his rounds, and at most a nurse might stick her head into the room. One of us goes outside again nevertheless – to make sure. He comes back in and nods. 'No sign of man nor beast. Just tell her, Johann, and then get on with it!'

The two of them talk in their own language. The wife looks up, blushing a little and embarrassed. We grin amiably and make dismissive gestures – what is there to worry about? To hell with the proprieties, they were made for different times. Here in bed is Johann Lewandowski the carpenter, a soldier who has been crippled by a bullet, and there is his wife – who knows when he will see her again, he wants to have her and he shall have her, and that's that.

Two men stand guard at the door to intercept and occupy any nurses that might happen to come past. They reckon to keep watch for about a quarter of an hour.

Lewandowski can only lie on one side, so someone props a couple of pillows against his back. Albert gets the baby to hold, then we all turn round a bit, and the black mantilla disappears under the covers while we play a noisy and vigorous game of cards.

Everything is fine. I'm holding a damn good hand with all the high cards in clubs which has just about beaten everyone. With all this going on we have almost forgotten Lewandowski. After a time the baby begins to howl, although Albert is rocking it backwards and forwards despairingly. There is a bit of rustling and crackling and when we glance up, as if we were just doing so casually, we see that the child has the bottle in its mouth and is already back with its mother. It all worked.

We now feel like one big family, the woman is bright and cheerful, and Lewandowski lies there sweating and beaming.

He unpacks the beaded bag, and out come a couple of good sausages. Lewandowski takes the knife as if it were a bunch of flowers and saws the meat into chunks. He makes a sweeping gesture of invitation towards us all, and his little crumpled wife moves from one of us to the next, and laughs, and shares out the meat – she looks positively pretty as she does so. We call her 'mother' and she likes that, and plumps our pillows up for us.

★

After a few weeks I have to go to physiotherapy every morning. There they strap up my leg and exercise it. My arm has long since healed.

New hospital transport trains arrive from the front. The bandages are not made out of cloth any more, they are just white crêpe paper. There is too much of a shortage of proper bandage material out there.

Albert's stump heals well. The wound has practically closed. In a few weeks' time he will be sent to be fitted for an artificial leg. He still doesn't talk a lot, and he's much more serious than he was before. Often he breaks off in mid-conversation and just stares into the distance. If he hadn't been with the rest of us he'd have put an end to it long ago.

But now he is over the worst. Sometimes he even watches while we play cards.

I'm given convalescent leave.

My mother doesn't want to let me go again. She is so weak. It is all even worse than last time.

Then I'm recalled by my regiment, and go back to the front.

Leaving my friend Albert Kropp is hard. But in the army you get used to things like that.

II

We've stopped counting the weeks. It was winter when I arrived, and whenever a shell hit the ground, the frozen clumps of earth it sent up were almost as dangerous as the shrapnel. Now the trees are green again. Our lives move between base camp and front line. To an extent we have become used to it. War is another cause of death, like cancer or tuberculosis or influenza or dysentery. The fatalities are just much more numerous, and more horrible.

Our thoughts have turned to clay, they are moulded by the variation in the days – good, when we are in camp, and deadened when we are under fire. No man's land is outside us and inside us too.

Everyone feels the same, not just us out here – earlier values don't count any longer, and nobody really knows how things used to be. The differences brought about by education and upbringing have been almost completely blurred and are now barely recognizable. Sometimes those differences are an advantage in making the most of a given situation; but they have their disadvantages as well, because they give rise to inhibitions which then have to be overcome. It is as if we were once coins from various different countries; we've been melted down, and now we have all been restruck so that we are all the same. If you want to pick out differences you have to be able to examine the basic material very closely. We are soldiers, and only as an afterthought and in a strange and shamefaced way are we still individual human beings.

It is a brotherhood on a large scale, in which elements of the good fellowship you get in folk songs, of the solidarity you find among convicts, and of the desperate clinging together of those condemned to die, are all combined in some strange way to give a form of life which, in the midst of all the danger, rises above the tension and the abandonment of death, and leads to a fleeting and quite dispassionate grasping at whatever time we can gain. It is heroic and banal, if you really think about it – but who does?

It is this attitude that makes Tjaden gulp down his pea-and-ham soup as fast as he can when an enemy attack has been reported, because he doesn't know whether he will still be alive in an hour's time. We have had long discussions on whether this is the right thing to do or not. Kat thinks it isn't, because he says we have to reckon with the possibility of a stomach wound, which is much more dangerous on a full belly than on an empty one.

Things like that are problems for us, we take them seriously, and we couldn't do otherwise. Life here on the very edges of death follows a terribly clear line, it restricts itself to what is absolutely necessary, everything else is part of a dull sleep – it is our crudeness but also our salvation. If we were to make finer distinctions we would long since have gone mad, deserted or been killed. It is like a Polar expedition – every activity is geared exclusively to survival, and is automatically directed to that end. Nothing else is permissible, because it would use up energy unnecessarily. That is the only way we can save ourselves, and I often look at myself and see a stranger, when in quiet hours the puzzling reflection of earlier times places the outlines of my present existence outside me, like a dull mirror image; and then I am amazed at how that nameless active force that we call life has adapted itself to all this. Everything else is in suspended animation, and life is constantly on its guard against the threat of death. It has made us into thinking animals so that we can have instinct as a weapon. It has blunted our sensitivities, so that we don't go to pieces in the face of a terror that would demolish us if we were thinking clearly and consciously. It has awakened in us a sense of comradeship to help us escape from the abyss of isolation. It has given us the indifference of wild animals, so that in spite of everything we can draw out the positive side from every moment and store it up as a reserve against the onslaught of oblivion. And so we live out a closed, hard existence of extreme superficiality, and it is only rarely that an experience sparks something off. But when that happens, a flame of heavy and terrible longing suddenly bursts through.

Those are the dangerous moments, the ones that show us that the way we have adapted is really artificial after all, that it isn't a simple calmness, but rather a desperate struggle to *attain* calmness. In our way of life we are barely distinguishable from bushmen as far as the externals are concerned; but while bushmen can always be that way because that is the way they are, and they can at least develop their capacities by their own efforts, with us it is exactly the other way about: our inner forces are not geared to development, but to regression. The attitude of the bushmen is relaxed, as it should be; ours is completely tense and artificial.

And in the night you realize, when you wake out of a dream, overcome and captivated by the enchantment of visions that crowd in on each other, just how fragile a handhold, how tenuous a boundary separates us from the darkness – we are little flames, inadequately sheltered by thin walls from the tempest of dissolution and insensibility in which we flicker and are often all but extinguished. Then the muted roar of battle surrounds us, and we creep into ourselves and stare wide-eyed into the night. The only comfort we have comes from the breathing of our sleeping comrades, and so we wait until the morning comes.

★

Every day and every hour, every shell and every dead man wear down that thin handhold, and the years grind it down rapidly. I can see how it is already giving way around me.

Take the stupid business with Detering.

He was one of those who keep themselves very much to themselves. The unlucky thing for him was seeing a cherry tree in someone's garden. We had just come back from the front, and this cherry tree was suddenly there in front of us in the early morning light, just as we came around a bend in the road near our new quarters. It didn't have any leaves, but it was a single mass of white blossoms.

That evening Detering was nowhere to be found. Eventually he turned up, and he had a few twigs with cherry blossom in his hand. We had a laugh, and asked him if he was going courting. He didn't answer, and just lay down on his bed. That night I heard him moving about, and he seemed to be packing his things. I thought there might be trouble brewing, and went over to him. He acted as if nothing was the matter, and I said to him, 'Don't do anything daft, Detering.'

''Course not – I just can't get to sleep –'

'Why did you pick the cherry blossom?'

'I can pick cherry blossom if I want, can't I?' he said sullenly – and then he added after a while, 'I've got a big orchard with cherry trees back home. From the hayloft they look like one huge bed-sheet when they are in blossom, that's how white they are. It's at this time of the year.'

'Maybe you'll get leave. You might even be demobbed and sent home because you are a farmer.'

He nods, but his mind is elsewhere. When country people like him get into a state they have a peculiar expression on their faces, a bit bovine, but also with an almost numinous look of yearning, half idiocy and half rapture. To try and get him out of himself I ask him for a chunk of bread. He gives it to me without question. That's suspicious, because he is usually pretty stingy. So I keep an eye on him. Nothing happens, and in the morning he is his usual self.

He had probably realized that I was watching him. Two mornings later, and he is missing after all. I notice, but keep quiet about it so as to give him a bit of time – perhaps he'll make it. A few men have got through to Holland.

But at roll call his absence is spotted. A week later we hear that the military police, or rather the special battle police everyone hates, have picked him up. He was heading for Germany – that was obviously completely hopeless, and it was equally obvious that everything else he had done was simply stupid. Anyone could have worked out that he had only deserted out of homesickness and a momentary aberration. But what does a court martial miles behind the lines know about things like that? Nothing more's been heard of Detering.

★

But they break through in other ways as well, those dangerously dammed-up feelings – like steam escaping from an over-heated boiler. It's worth reporting how Berger met his end, for example.

Our trenches have long since been shot to pieces, and the front is so fluid that trench warfare is not really possible any more. Once an attack and a counter-attack have come and gone, all that remains is a ragged line and a bitter struggle from one bomb crater to the next. The front line has been broken, and little groups have dug themselves in everywhere, fighting from clusters of foxholes.

We are in one shell hole, with English troops already on one side of us – they are turning our flank and getting round behind us. We are surrounded. It is not easy to surrender. There is fog and smoke all around, and nobody would realize that we were trying to give ourselves up, and perhaps we don't even want to – no one is quite sure in times like this. We can hear the explosions of hand-grenades getting closer. Our machine-gun sweeps the sector in front of us. The water in the cooling system evaporates and we pass the container round quickly – everyone pisses into it and we have water again and can go on firing. But behind us the explosions are getting closer. In a few minutes we'll be done for.

Suddenly another machine-gun starts up from very close by. It is in a crater near us, and Berger has got hold of it; now there is a counter-attack from behind, we get out and manage to move backwards and join up with the rest.

Afterwards, by the time we have found some decent cover, one of the food carriers tells us that there is a wounded messenger dog a couple of hundred yards away.

'Where?' asks Berger.

The food carrier describes the place for him, Berger sets off to fetch the animal or to shoot it. Even six months ago he would not have bothered about it, and would have behaved sensibly. We try to stop him. But when he sets off – and he's serious about it – all we can say is 'He's crazy', and let him go. These front-line breakdowns can be dangerous if you can't wrestle the man to the ground straight away and hold him there. And Berger is over six foot and the strongest man in the company.

He really is mad, because he has to go through the barrage – but that sudden bolt from the blue that hovers over every one of us has hit him, and now he is a man possessed. The way it takes other people is to make them scream with rage, or run away, and there was one man who just kept on trying to dig himself into the earth with his hands, his feet and his mouth.

Of course there is a lot of shamming in situations like this, but even the shamming is really a symptom as well. Berger tries to put the dog out of its misery and is carried back with a shot through the pelvis, and even one of the men who fetches him gets a bullet wound in the calf.

*

Müller is dead. He got a Verey light in the stomach from close to. He lived for another half-hour, fully conscious and in terrible agony. Before he died he gave me his paybook and passed on his boots – the ones he inherited from Kemmerich that time. I wear them, because they are a good fit. Tjaden will get them after me – I've promised him.

We were actually able to bury Müller, but he probably won't rest in peace for long. Our lines are being moved back. There are too many fresh British and American regiments over there. There is too much corned beef and white flour. And too many new guns. Too many aircraft.

But we are thin and starving. Our food is so bad and full of so much ersatz stuff that it makes us ill. The factory owners in Germany have grown rich, while dysentery racks our guts. The latrine poles always have men squatting over them. The people at home ought to be shown these grey or yellow, wretched, beaten-down faces, these figures who are bent double because of the enteritis that is squeezing the blood out of their bodies so much that the best they can do is to grin through lips trembling with pain, and say 'It's hardly worth pulling your trousers up again.'

Our artillery can't really do much – they have too little ammunition, and the gun-barrels are so clapped out that they can't shoot straight, and scatter stuff over towards us. We haven't enough horses. Our new drafts are pitiful lads who really need a rest, unable to carry a pack but able to die. In their thousands. They understand nothing of the war, they just go over the top and allow themselves to be shot down. One single airman knocks off two whole companies of them just for fun, when they were just off a troop train and had no idea about taking cover.

'Germany must be nearly empty,' says Kat.

We are quite without hope that there could ever be an end to this. We can't think nearly so far ahead. You might stop a bullet and be killed; you might be wounded, and then the next stop is the military hospital. As long as they haven't amputated anything, sooner or later you'll fall into the hands of one of those staff doctors with a war service ribbon on his chest who says, 'What's this? One leg a bit on the short side? You won't need to run at the front if you've got any guts. Passed fit for service! Dismiss!'

Kat tells a story that has done the rounds all along the front, from Flanders to the Vosges, about the staff doctor who reads out the names of the men who come up for medical inspection, and, when the man appears, doesn't even look up, but says, 'Passed fit for service, we need soldiers at the front.' A man with a wooden leg comes up before him, the doctor passes him fit for service again –

'And then,' Kat raises his voice, 'the man says to him, "I've already got a wooden leg; but if I go up the line now and they shoot my head off, I'll have a wooden head made, and then I'll become a staff doctor." ' We all think that's a really good one.

There may be good doctors – many of them are; but with the hundreds of examinations he has, every soldier will at some time or other get into the clutches of one of the hero-makers, and there are lots of them, whose aim is to turn as many of those on their lists who have only been passed for work detail or garrison duty into class A-1, fit for active service.

There are plenty of stories like that, and most of them are more bitter. But for all that, they have nothing to do with mutiny or malingering; they are honest, and they call a spade a spade; because there really *is* a lot of fraud, injustice and petty nastiness in the army. But isn't it enough that regiment after regiment goes off into a fight which is becoming increasingly pointless in spite of everything, and that attack after attack is launched, even though our line is retreating and crumbling?

Tanks, which used to be objects of ridicule, have become a major weapon. They come rolling forward in a long line, heavily armoured, and they embody the horror of war for us more than anything else.

We cannot see the gun batteries that are bombarding us, and the oncoming waves of enemy attackers are human beings just like we are – but tanks are machines, and their caterpillar tracks run on as endlessly as the war itself. They spell out annihilation when they roll without feeling into the shell holes and then climb out again, inexorably, a fleet of roaring, fire-spitting ironclads, invulnerable steel beasts that crush the dead and the wounded. Before these we shrivel down into our thin skins, in the face of their colossal force our arms are like straws and our hand-grenades are like matches.

Shells, gas clouds and flotillas of tanks – crushing, devouring, death.

Dysentery, influenza, typhus – choking, scalding, death.

Trench, hospital, mass grave – there are no other possibilities.

*

In one attack Bertinck, our company commander, is killed. He was one of those fine front-line officers who are always at the forefront of every tricky situation. He had been with us for two years without being wounded, so something had to happen in the end. We are sitting in a shell hole and we have been surrounded. With the smell of cordite, the smell of oil or petrol wafts across to us. Two men with a flame-thrower are spotted, one with the cylinder on his back, the other holding the pipe where the fire shoots out. If they get close enough to reach us, we've had it, because just at the moment we can't get back.

We start to fire at them. But they work their way closer to us, and things look bad. Bertinck is with us in the hole. When he sees that we are not hitting them because the firing is so heavy and we have to concentrate too much on cover, he takes a rifle, crawls out of the hole and aims, lying there propped on his elbows. He shoots – and at the same moment a bullet smacks down by him with a crack, he has been hit. But he stays where he is and aims again – he lowers his rifle once, and then takes aim; at last the shot rings out. Bertinck drops the gun, says, 'Good' and slides back. The second man with the flame-thrower is wounded and falls, the pipe is wrenched out of the other one's hands, fire is sprayed all around and the man is burning.

Bertinck has been hit in the chest. A short while later a piece of shrapnel smashes away the lower part of his face. That same piece of shrapnel has enough force left to rip open Leer's side. Leer groans and props himself on his arms, but he bleeds to death very quickly and no one can help him. After a few minutes he sinks down like a rubber tyre when the air escapes. What use is it to him now that he was so good at mathematics at school?

*

The months drag on. This summer of 1918 is the bloodiest and the hardest. The days are like angels in blue and gold, rising up untouchable above the circle of destruction. Everyone knows that we are losing the war. Nobody talks about it much. We are retreating. We won't be able to attack again after this massive offensive. We have no more men and no more ammunition.

But the campaign goes on – the dying continues.

Summer, 1918. Never has life in its simplest outline seemed so desirable to us as it does now; the poppies in the fields near our base camp, the shiny beetles on the blades of grass, the warm evenings in the cool, half-dark rooms, black, mysterious trees at twilight, the stars and the streams, dreams and the long sleep. Oh life, life, life!

Summer, 1918. Never has more been suffered in silence as in the moment when we set off for the front. The wild and urgent rumours of an armistice and peace have surfaced again, they disturb the heart and make setting out harder than ever.

Summer, 1918. Never has life at the front been more bitter and more full of horror than when we are under fire, when the pallid faces are pressed into the mud and the fists are clenched and your whole being is saying, No! No! No, not now! Not now at the very last minute!

Summer, 1918. A wind of hope sweeping over the burnt-out fields, a raging fever of impatience, of disappointment, the most agonizing terror of death, the impossible question: why? Why don't they stop? And why are there all these rumours about it ending?

★

There are so many airmen here, and they are so skilful that they can hunt down individuals like rabbits. For every German aircraft there are five British or American ones. For every hungry, tired German soldier in the trenches there are five strong, fresh men on the enemy side. For every German army-issue loaf there are fifty cans of beef over there. We haven't been defeated, because as soldiers we are better and more experienced; we have simply been crushed and pushed back by forces many times superior to ours.

Several weeks of steady rain lie behind us – grey skies, grey, liquid earth, grey death. When we go out the damp penetrates right through our coats and uniforms – and it is like that all the time we are at the front. We can never get dry. Anyone who still has a pair of boots ties them up at the top with little bags of sand to stop the muddy water getting in so quickly. Rifles are caked in mud, uniforms are caked in mud, everything is fluid and liquefied, a dripping, damp and oily mass of earth in which there are yellow puddles with spiral pools of blood, and in which the dead, the wounded and the living are slowly swallowed up.

The storm is like a whiplash over us, the hail of shrapnel wrenches the sharp, children's cries of the wounded from the confusion of grey and yellow, and in the night shattered life groans itself painfully into silence.

Our hands are earth, our bodies mud and our eyes puddles of rain. We no longer know whether we are still alive or not.

Then heat steals into our shell holes, damp and oppressive, like a jellyfish, and on one of these late summer days, Kat topples over. I am alone with him. I bandage the wound. His shin seems to be shattered. Damage to the bone, and Kat groans in despair. 'Now of all times! Why did it have to be now . . . ?'

I comfort him. 'Who knows how much longer the whole mess will go on? At least you're out of it . . .'

The wound begins to bleed a lot. Kat cannot stay where he is while I try and find a stretcher. I don't know where the nearest casualty post is, either.

Kat is not very heavy; so I take him on my back and carry him to the rear, to the dressing station.

Twice we stop to rest. Being carried is causing him a lot of pain. We don't talk much. I've undone the neck of my tunic and I'm breathing heavily and sweating, and my face is red from the effort of carrying him. In spite of that I make us move on, because the terrain is dangerous.

'All right to move, Kat?'

'I'll have to be, Paul.'

'Let's go.'

I help him up. He stands on his good leg and steadies himself against a tree. Then I get hold of his wounded leg very carefully, he pushes upwards, and I get my arm under the knee of his good leg.

Moving becomes more difficult. Often, shells whistle past. I go as fast as I can, because the blood from his wounded leg is dripping on to the ground. We can't really protect ourselves from shell-blast, because it is over before we could have taken cover.

We get down in a small shell crater until it quietens down a bit. I give Kat some tea from my flask. We smoke a cigarette. 'Yes, Kat,' I say sadly, 'we'll get split up now after all.'

He says nothing, and just looks at me.

'Kat, do you still remember how we bagged that goose? And how you got me out of the scrap when I was still a raw recruit and I'd just been wounded for the first time? I cried, then, Kat, and it was nearly three years ago.'

Kat nods.

The fear of loneliness wells up in me. If Kat is taken out I'll have no friends here at all.

'Kat, we must get in touch again, if peace really does come before you get back.'

'With what's happened to the old leg, do you reckon I'll ever be fit for service again?' he asks bitterly.

'You'll be able to convalesce in peace and quiet. The joint is still OK. Maybe it will all be all right.'

'Give me another cigarette,' he says.

'Maybe we could do something or other together afterwards, Kat.' I am very sad, it is impossible that Kat, my friend Kat, Kat with the drooping shoulders and the thin, soft moustache, Kat, whom I know in a different way from every other person, Kat, the man I have shared these years with – it is impossible that I might never see Kat again.

'Give me your address anyway, Kat. Here's mine, I'll write it down for you.'

I tuck the piece of paper into the breast-pocket of my tunic. I feel so isolated already, even though he is still sitting there with me. Maybe I should shoot myself in the foot, just so that I can stay with him?

Suddenly Kat makes a choking noise and goes greenish-yellow. 'We'd better move,' he stammers.

I jump up, eager to help him. I hoist him up and set off with long, slow strides so as not to shake his leg too much.

My throat is parched and I have red and black spots before my eyes by the time I eventually stumble, doggedly and relentlessly, into the casualty station.

There I drop to my knees, but I have enough strength left to fall on to the side where Kat's good leg is. After a few minutes I ease myself up slowly. My legs and my hands are still shaking violently, and I have trouble finding my flask to take a drink out of it. My lips tremble as I do so. But Kat is safe.

After a time I am able to distinguish sounds from the barrage of noise battering in my ears.

'You could have saved yourself the trouble,' says an orderly.

I stare at him uncomprehending.

He points to Kat. 'He's dead.'

I can't understand what he means. 'He's got a lower leg wound,' I say.

The orderly stops. 'Yes, that as well . . .'

I turn round. My eyes are still dimmed, I have started to sweat again and it is running into my eyes. I wipe it away and look at Kat. He is lying still. 'Must have fainted,' I say quickly.

The orderly whistles softly. 'I know more about it than you do. He's dead. I'll bet you anything.'

I shake my head. 'Can't be. I was talking to him not ten minutes ago. He's fainted.'

Kat's hands are warm. I get hold of his shoulders to give him some tea to bring him round. Then I feel how my fingers are getting wet. When I take my hands out from behind his head they are bloody. The orderly whistles between his teeth. 'Told you so –'

Without my noticing it, Kat got a splinter of shrapnel in the head on the way. It's only a little hole. It must have been a tiny, stray fragment. But it was enough. Kat is dead.

I stand up slowly.

'Do you want to take his paybook and his things?' the orderly asks me.

I nod and he gives them to me.

The orderly is baffled. 'You're not related, are you?'

No, we are not related.

Am I walking? Do I still have legs? I look up, I look about me. And then I turn right round, and then I stop. Everything is just the same as usual. It's only that Private Stanislaus Katczinsky is dead.

After that I remember nothing.

12

It's autumn. There are not many of the old lot left. I am the last one of the seven from our class still here.

Everyone is talking about peace or an armistice. Everyone is waiting. If there is another disappointment, they will collapse, the hopes are too strong, they can no longer be pushed aside without exploding. If there is no peace, then there will be a revolution.

I have been given fourteen days' rest because I swallowed a bit of gas. I sit all day in a little garden in the sunshine. There will soon be an armistice, I believe in it too, now. Then we shall go home.

My thoughts stop there and I can't push them on any further. What attracts me so strongly and awaits me are raw feelings – lust for life, desire for home, the blood itself, the intoxication of escaping. But these aren't exactly goals.

If we had come back in 1916 we could have unleashed a storm out of the pain and intensity of our experiences. If we go back now we shall be weary, broken-down, burnt-out, rootless and devoid of hope. We shall no longer be able to cope.

No one will understand us – because in front of us there is a generation of men who did, it is true, share the years out here with us, but who already had a bed and a job and who are going back to their old positions, where they will forget all about the war – and behind us, a new generation is growing up, one like we used to be, and that generation will be strangers to us and will push us aside. We are superfluous even to ourselves, we shall grow older, a few will adapt, others will make adjustments, and many of us will not know what to do – the years will trickle away, and eventually we shall perish.

But perhaps all these thoughts of mine are just melancholy and confusion, which will be blown away like dust when I am standing underneath the poplars once again, and listening to the rustle of their leaves. It cannot have vanished entirely, that tenderness that troubles our blood, the uncertainty, the worry, all the things to come, the thousand faces of the future, the music of dreams and books, the rustling and the idea of women. All this cannot have collapsed in the shelling, the despair and the army brothels.

The trees here glow bright and gold, the rowan berries are red against the leaves, white country roads run on towards the horizon, and the canteens are all buzzing like beehives with rumours of peace.

I stand up.

I am very calm. Let the months come, and the years, they'll take nothing more from me, they *can* take nothing more from me. I am so alone and so devoid of any hope that I can confront them without fear. Life, which carried me through these years, is still there in my hands and in my eyes. Whether or not I have mastered it, I do not know. But as long as life is there it will make its own way, whether my conscious self likes it or not.

★

He fell in October 1918, on a day that was so still and quiet along the entire front line that the army despatches restricted themselves to the single sentence: that there was nothing new to report on the western front.

He had sunk forwards and was lying on the ground as if asleep. When they turned him over, you could see that he could not have suffered long – his face wore an expression that was so composed that it looked as if he were almost happy that it had turned out that way.

Afterword

It is now approaching seventy years since Erich Maria Remarque's first major novel, *Im Westen nichts Neues* (literally 'Nothing New on the Western Front'), appeared, first in a magazine, and then in book form, and we are eighty years from the start of the war – supposedly the war to end all wars – in which the novel is set. But just as the Great War of 1914–18 did *not* end all wars, but simply set the pattern for new and ever more mechanized killing, Remarque's novel has lost none of its impact and none of its relevance; while Remarque himself, the centenary of whose birth is now not too far away, is gradually becoming increasingly accepted as a major German writer.

Erich Maria Remarque was born in Osnabrück in Northern Germany on 22 June 1898. His original name was Erich Paul Remark, but when he published *All Quiet on the Western Front* he changed his middle name in memory of his mother, and reverted to an earlier spelling of the family name to dissociate himself from a novel that he had published in 1920, *Die Traumbude,* about art and decadence (the title of which means 'The Den of Dreams'). It has not been published in English. Remarque's name was *not* Kramer – Remark spelt backwards – even though this tale is still found in reference works from time to time.

Remarque was sixteen, then, when the First World War broke out, and he was educated – since his family was Catholic – at Catholic schools, and then at a teachers' seminary in Osnabrück, until he was called up for military service on 26 November 1916. After training in the Caprivi Barracks in Osnabrück (which he transformed into the Klosterberg barracks in his novel), he was sent on 12 June 1917 to a position behind the Arras front. During the offensive in Flanders which began on 31 July 1917, and is usually known in English as 'Third Ypres' or 'Passchendaele', Remarque was wounded by British shell-splinters, and taken eventually to the military hospital in Duisburg. During this period his mother died. He stayed on for some time as a clerk in the hospital, returned for training to Osnabrück in October 1918, and was there when the war ended. After the war he completed his teacher training and taught for a fairly short time, then worked in various different jobs, including advertising, and in 1924 began working on a magazine called *Sport im Bild (Sport in Pictures)* in Berlin. In 1925 he married a dancer, (Jutta) Ilse Zambona, from whom he was divorced in 1931. When the Nazis came to power in 1933 (and burned his books, claiming that *All Quiet on the Western Front* was a betrayal of the German front-line soldier), Remarque went to Switzerland. The Nazis deprived him of his German citizenship in 1938, and in that year (the circumstances are somewhat difficult to determine, and reports of dates and details vary) he remarried Ilse Zambona so that she, too, could get away, though they seem to have lived apart. They were divorced eventually in 1951. With the assistance of his friend, Marlene Dietrich, he was given a visa for the United States, and left France in 1939 on the last transatlantic sailing of the *Queen Mary* before the war. He settled in America, spending time in Hollywood, and then New York. Remarque was a high-profile figure, and very much part of the Hollywood and the European emigré celebrity circuit (though he was unable to make close contact with two other famous literary emigrés, Brecht and Thomas Mann). His close friendship with Marlene Dietrich continued, and his other exotic companions included Greta Garbo. In 1943, his sister Elfriede was executed by the Nazis, ostensibly for making defeatist comments, and presumably also for being the sister of the by then unreachable Remarque. The author himself said that she had been involved with the resistance against the Nazis, and was pleased when a street in Osnabrück was named after her in 1968. Remarque became an American citizen in 1947, and refused to apply for the return of his German citizenship on the grounds that it had been taken from him illegally. In 1948 he returned to Switzerland, and lived there much of the time for the rest of his life. He married the film actress Paulette Goddard in 1958. On 25 September 1970, he died of heart failure, and is buried in Switzerland.

Remarque wrote about a dozen novels in all, and several have to do with the theme of war and its aftermath, although none had quite the success of *All Quiet on the Western Front.* Many of them were filmed, sometimes with a script by Remarque himself, and occasionally with Remarque acting in them. The war novel was turned into a landmark of cinema history in 1930 by director Lewis Milestone and remains a classic; it enraged the Nazis, and Goebbels organized the disruption of showings of it in Berlin. A more recent colour version (1979) is somewhat less successful.

Remarque's other novels include a sequel to *All Quiet on the Western Front* called *The Road Back* (1931), which has a first-person narrator who is almost Paul Bäumer brought back to life. *Three Comrades* (1937), which had to be published outside Germany, is set in the years between the wars, and after the Second World War he set another vividly imagined novel, *The Spark of Life* (1952), in a concentration camp. A novel of the Second World War which has quite a lot in common with *All Quiet on the Western Front,* and which was written in America, was published in 1954 in English as *A Time to Love and a Time to Die,* although the German title actually echoes more accurately the biblical phrase, 'a time to *live* and a time to die'. Set partly on the eastern front in the early 1940s, much of the action takes place in Germany under the bombing. It is a love story as well as a picture of war, and there is, running through it, the motif of the inextinguishable spark of life in man which is present in *All Quiet on the Western Front,* and which was used as a title for the concentration camp novel. War and its results, the sufferings of ordinary people, the plight of refugees, but also the doggedness of that spark of life – these are Remarque's main themes, and it is time, perhaps, for a large-scale reconsideration of his work as a whole, something which is underway already in Germany in the setting up of a research centre in Remarque's home town of Osnabrück.

All Quiet on the Western Front is not a memoir, though of course Remarque drew on some of his own experiences in the war, and it is not a piece of historical documentation from 1918, though it is sometimes cited as if it were, but a novel. Remarque prefaces the work with a short statement declaring it to be an account of 'a generation that was destroyed by the war – even those of it who survived the shelling', and although the death of the narrator is reported objectively and briefly at the end of the book, the bulk of it portrays the war through the eyes of one soldier, albeit a sensitive one, the nineteen-year-old Paul Bäumer. There are few military historical details, no heroics, and the real enemy is death. We hardly ever see the other side, and the very word 'enemy' is rare; Bäumer refers to 'the others', or to 'those over there'. And there is no expressly political dimension. Left-wing critics often felt that Remarque had failed by not having his soldiers revolt openly. But the soldiers in the trenches did *not,* by and large, mutiny or abandon their posts, and the only one in the novel who does so, Detering, goes home to Germany rather than desert to Holland and freedom.

Much has been made of the idea of comradeship in the novel, as something positive coming out of the war. This again is deceptive – it is in fact no more than an artificial solidarity in the face of adversity, though of course real friendships do arise, as is possible anywhere. Remarque made clear in *The Road Back* how quickly the artificial comradeship of the war crumbled away as returning soldiers settled back into different (and not always justifiable) social levels in civilian life.

There are in the work some particularly memorable scenes; although they are not always remembered as accurately as they might be, and critics all too frequently attribute to Remarque in 1928 thoughts that properly belong to his narrator, Bäumer, in 1917. Thus the scene in which Bäumer and his colleagues come under fire in what is actually a recent military cemetery – fluctuations in the front line ensured that the recent dead frequently did not stay buried for long – has sometimes been presented as grotesque gothic imagery. The incident in which the soldiers cook and eat a meal under fire, on the other hand, has been thought of as an adventure, even though Remarque lets his narrator introduce the scene by telling us how the soldiers habitually seized *any* opportunity for unusual physical or mental exercise, taking things as lightly as they can, to guard themselves against thinking too deeply about the realities of their situation. Only then does the actual 'idyll' begin – Bäumer uses the word ironically because the whole proceedings are still dangerous. This is not the stuff of adventure stories.

The contrast of the realistic scenes with brief or extended speculations upon them by the narrator gives the work a narrative complexity that is not always recognized. Thus, on a superficial level, the beating up of the unpleasant drill-corporal is satisfying and memorable, but the narrator's own thoughts take the reader rather beyond this when he underlines the real lesson of the incident: that the drill-corporal ought to have no cause for complaint, since he brutalized the recruits into the assumption that, if nations can settle their problems by violence, so can the individual. In fact, the final paragraph of that chapter takes the matter even further. The soldiers leave for the front in a state of relative (but only relative) cheerfulness, while an old man who is watching them refers to them as young heroes. Remarque strips the mythology from the idea of heroism.

All Quiet on the Western Front presents the war through the eyes and mind of one schoolboy-turned-soldier, but Remarque makes it clear that Bäumer is a representative by allowing him to move frequently from the first person singular to the first person plural. Yet even this is by no means as simple as it seems, and it is well worth considering the variety and the precision with which Remarque lets his narrator use (or report other people using) the pronoun 'we'. It can refer to the Germans as a nation, to the entire

German army, to Bäumer's company, to the ordinary soldiers as a class-group, to Bäumer's squad, or to a sub-group consisting of those members of the squad with whom he was at school. In Bäumer's thoughts it can also imply all the members of his age-group – the lost generation – and this can extend very easily to all the millions of young men in all the armies. Even so, the plural gives way at the end of the novel gradually to a singular again, when Bäumer realizes that, now that most of his company and his immediate colleagues, even his close friend Katczinsky, have gone, he has to come to terms with things on his own.

Each chapter ends on a significant point or with a summarizing observation, and the brief but highly important concluding chapter of the whole book, which itself ends with Bäumer's death, is more complex than critics have sometimes assumed.

Much attention has been drawn to the statement at the end of the book made by the unidentified new external narrator that the dead Bäumer looked peaceful, and seemed almost content that things had ended like that. However, just as for most of the novel we can see into Bäumer's thoughts, at the end an outsider is speaking who *cannot* see those thoughts. Thus Bäumer only looks *almost* content, *as if* he were pleased it had ended like that. The narrator (and we) cannot know whether Bäumer really felt that way because Bäumer *is* dead. It can be no more than speculation. Indeed, Bäumer had been forced, as the war was clearly ending, to acknowledge within himself a life-force which had not been suppressed entirely, and which would make him live on, even though he could not imagine what the post-war future would be like. In that last chapter – just before his death at the end of the war – his increasing isolation has forced him away from a collective soldier-view of things, however comradely, and even away from his own personal identity, to focus on this life-force, the spark of life that is in everyone, and which *will* go on, whether the individual wants it to or not. It is tragic irony that he falls at this point, and he must then be presented by Remarque's new narrator in the third person, as an object.

For the later generations, the novel has lost none of its power. It presents within a small space a surprisingly broad picture of a modern, mechanized war, and whether or not some subsequent wars have been justified (or have been at least explicable), this war is understood by no one.

The novel shows us very clearly that war is something else: war is not about heroism, but about terror, either waiting for death, or trying desperately to avoid it, even if it means killing a complete stranger to do so, about losing all human dignity and values, about becoming an automaton; it is not about falling bravely and nobly for one's country ('he was killed instantly' was usually a lie), but about soiling oneself in terror under heavy shellfire, about losing a leg, crawling blinded in no man's land, or (in those telling hospital scenes) being wounded in every conceivable part of the body. Bäumer and his fellow soldiers discuss the nature of the war and war itself, but they do not come to any real conclusions – nor could they. They are too young, they lack the background. But their naivety, their very inability to articulate an answer is the point of the book. Bäumer dies. The reader is left to draw the conclusion.

Brian Murdoch
August 1994

Bibliography

The standard German texts are *Im Westen nichts Neues* (Berlin: Ullstein, 1929), translated into English by A. W. Wheen (London: The Bodley Head, 1929), with editions by Tilman Westphalen (Cologne: Kiepenheuer and Witsch, 1987) and with English introduction and notes by Brian Murdoch (London: Routledge, 1988).

Studies in English of Remarque and the work include: Christine R. Barker and Rex W. Last, *Erich Maria Remarque* (London: Wolff, 1979); C. R. Owen, *Erich Maria Remarque. A Critical Bio-Bibliography* (Amsterdam: Rodopi, 1984); Modris Eksteins, *Rites of Spring* (London: Bantam, 1989); Brian Murdoch, *Remarque: Im Westen nichts Neues* (Glasgow: University of Glasgow, 1991).